# BLINDING INSIGHT

KAITLYN KRUSE DETECTIVE SERIES

KAROLINE ANDERSON

PUBLISHED BY FLARE BOOKS

AN IMPRINT OF CATALYST PRESS, EL PASO, TEXAS

For further information, write info@catalystpress.org
In North America, this book is distributed by
Consortium Book Sales & Distribution, a division of Ingram.
Phone: 612/746-2600
cbsdinfo@ingramcontent.com
www.cbsd.com

In South Africa, Namibia, and Botswana,
this book is distributed by Protea Distribution.
For information, email orders@proteadistribution.co.za

9781963511727 paperback
9781963511826 ebook

Library of Congress Control Number: 2026942323

Original artwork and cover design by Jordan Anderson
http://jordanandersongraphics.com

---

# PRAISE FOR BLINDING INSIGHT

*A compelling blend of romance, mystery, and reincarnation, Anderson's third novel weaves together the past and present with striking emotional depth. There is the evolving relationship between Blake and Kaitlyn—one shaped by fate, fractured by circumstance, and rekindled through moments both tender and uncanny. Alongside this, a gripping central mystery drives the plot: the murder of a principled judge, a man of unwavering integrity. As Kaitlyn's past dream lives unfold, the narrative deepens into something richer and more layered, ultimately setting off a chain of revelations. Just when the truth feels within reach, the final twist lands with real impact, reshaping everything that came before it. The reader will be left contemplating this unexpected ending long after the final page.*

—Andrea Beck,
author of *Below the Surface*

*Karoline Anderson soars in her third novel,* Blinding Insight. *In a genre crowded with familiar formulas, this novel stands apart. Anderson creates an unforgettable cast of characters featuring Detective Kaitlyn Kruse. This captivating mystery kept me guessing until the very end. Anderson's newest novel is everything a great thriller should be. Fans of mystery and psychological suspense are in for a treat.*

—Polly Kronenberger,
author of *The Science of Understanding*

Books by Karoline Anderson

*Killer Insight*

*Finalist in the Best Thriller Book Awards*

*Dangerous Insight*

*a National Indie Excellence Award Finalist*

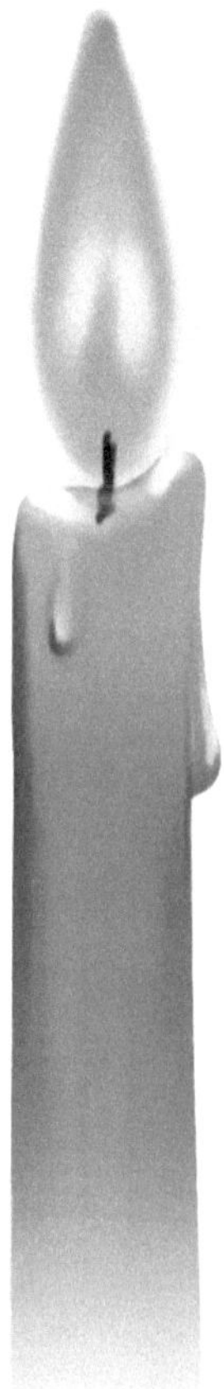

*This one's for you, Dad*

# CHAPTER ONE

The mansion is lit up like Times Square. Every interior and exterior light of the home is ablaze, keeping the darkness at bay.

*Only it's too late.* The darkness has already had its way.

Police cruisers block the ends of what, on any other summer night, would be a quiet suburban street. The mansion is visible a few houses away, as I pull up to the barricade. Emergency lights pulse from police cruisers and an ambulance parked haphazardly in front of the mansion signals recent catastrophe.

Neighbors and onlookers attracted by the disturbance line up at the crime scene tape in front of the home, unable to resist the pull of tragedy. They jostle for a glimpse of emergency personnel or a departing body, hoping for a morsel of information, a clue, as to what transpired so near them as they slept in the early hours of the night. This neighborhood has the protections of affluence—large homes outfitted with security cameras and alarm systems. But none of these defenses were adequate to prevent violence from occurring here tonight.

I roll down my window and flash my badge at the officer controlling access.

"Detective Kruse, come on through." He motions for me to pass.

I squint up at the officer, raising my hand to block out the blinding cruiser lights, until I can make out his face. It's Bob, a junior officer I've worked with in the past. His features are set in careful neutrality, giving nothing away to the onlookers.

"Bob, what's it like up there?"

He leans his hands on the edge of my open window. "It's a circus," he says, peering in at me. "Best to park back here." He points to the side of the street just past the cruiser.

"Thanks." I give him a nod and he stands aside.

Driving past the barricade, I park well back from the press vans that have set up with a view of the house. *How the hell did they find out before I did?*

The call had come at 2:03 a.m., my phone vibrating insistently on my bedside table. I groaned and imagined for a brief, sleepy moment that if I ignored it, maybe it would stop buzzing. When the vibration caused the phone to drop off the table and onto the floor, I finally gave in and grabbed it. With a mumbled, "Yeah," I held the phone to my ear, my eyes still squeezed shut against the intrusion.

The voice of my partner, Joe Riley, cut through the fuzziness in my sleep-addled head, my senses sharpening into instant focus. "Kaitlyn, we have a case. High profile. You need to get there as quickly as possible. I'm getting in my car now; I'll text you the address."

Thrust into instant motion, I hastily pulled on work

clothes, put my long dark hair in an elastic band, and grabbed my gun and badge before heading to the designated address.

*So how am I the last one here?* Glancing at my watch, I confirm I made good time. It's only 2:23 a.m.

Hurrying past the reporters and camera crews, I catch snippets of broadcasts being filmed for the morning news, airing in a few short hours.

"...outside the home of the renowned Seattle judge Harold Clifton..."

"...quiet neighborhood awoke to the sounds of emergency crews arriving..."

"...awaiting word on the judge's condition..."

News cameras turn my way and cell phone flashes shine in my face as journalists notice me making a dash for the protection on the other side of the crime scene tape. I put up a hand to block their view, but impatient questions still pelt me as I pass.

"Are you a detective?"

"Do you have any information for us?"

"Wait! We have some questions..."

Ignoring the probing microphones of the swarming news correspondents, I flash my badge at the officer standing guard in front of the crime scene tape. Without waiting for a response, I duck under the tape and head up the wide expanse of brick pavers forming the circle drive.

The mansion is impressive. Imposing. Its classic architecture features stately white fluted columns and a soaring two-story red brick facade. Grand marble stairs lead from the drive to the entry of the home. White shutters frame large picture windows, affording unobstructed views over the tree-lined street.

The blinding interior lights put the spacious rooms on full display. I catch glimpses of luxurious furnishings as I climb the stairs to the entry. The massive front doors are braced open, no longer a barrier to intrusion. Crime scene personnel come and go with single-minded intensity, absorbed in their work.

I grab shoe covers and gloves from the boxes just inside the entry, scanning the foyer while I pull them on.

I spot Joe with his dark hair, graying slightly at the temples, standing at the top of the sweeping staircase and surveying the entry. He's wearing his signature trench coat, but his typical suit and tie is replaced with a simple button-down shirt and dark pants.

Taking the stairs two at a time, I join him, breathless from hurrying.

He's picked shoes with blue laces. His shoes all have different colored laces; he selects them according to his mood. Blue seems a good omen.

"Come with me, I'll get you up to speed." He ushers me down a hallway toward the back.

"It's only been twenty minutes since you called—why do I feel like the last one to get here?" I ask in a hushed whisper.

"A neighbor noticed the first responders arriving," he sighs. "They took a video and uploaded it to TikTok. It's gone viral. Someone who saw it must've had a contact in the press. Your basic PR nightmare. The vultures probably knew before I even got the call from the responding officers."

We enter the primary bedroom, the doors flung wide open and crime scene personnel already inspecting every inch of the room. Lavish carpets and heavy curtains give the space a sense of reverent silence, all sound absorbed by the rich textiles. A huge, mahogany king bed takes center stage, a sitting area and fireplace set off to one side and the entry to the ensuite bathroom on the other. The window beside the fireplace has a breathtaking view over the Seattle harbor.

I step up beside the bed—the scene of the crime. A man in his fifties lies on the righthand side. His arms are at his sides atop the comforter, a cell phone clutched in his right hand.

Joe follows my gaze. "The 911 call originated from his cell phone, so he must've seen or heard the intruder," he says.

Judge Harold Clifton was a well-known and respected Seattle figure. "Judge Harry," as he was called by his admirers, considered himself a protector of the people, touting a responsibility to look out for the "little guy." His words. He was known for his tough rulings on big companies that attempted to take advantage of Washington citizens without the deep pockets to engage expensive legal counsel in their defense. This made him very popular with the working class. And not so popular with the owners of said big enterprises. They'll be first on our list to investigate.

The judge's head rests on a plump pillow, wavy dark hair streaked with gray pooled behind him. His dark beard is short and neatly trimmed. He's an attractive man, his features imposing, even in death. Zeus personified. He wears an expression of surprise, eyes wide, brows raised, mouth pursed in a final question. A single small hole mars the middle of his forehead. The only sign of violence.

An indent in the skin around the hole and a less-than-typical amount of powder burn indicates the killer used a silencer. My first impression is of a professional hit at contact range.

Other than the bullet wound, there's no other visible

blood. As crime scenes go, this one is pretty tidy. Without a doubt, it's a whole lot tidier than our last big case where a body was dragged down a street, a bloody path left in its wake.

"Looks like a contracted hit. A pro. Neat, quick, and quiet," Joe comments, echoing my thoughts.

Dr. Beth Mitchell, the medical examiner, is at the bedside, ready to start the next phase of her investigation. She nods at her assistant, and they pull back the overlying covers. There's no obvious blood on the bedding or his dark green silk pajamas.

Dr. Mitchell and her assistant roll the victim onto his right side and look for exit wounds. The pillow is clean. The bullet didn't exit his head so it's a small caliber round, maybe a .22. I cringe as I imagine it ricocheting around the skull, and the resulting severe damage to the brain.

"Cause of death is not going to be too complicated in this one, Detectives. Of course, we'll know more after the autopsy and tox screens, but I'm confident he died from this gunshot wound." The ME glances at us. "We know time of death occurred at 1:05 a.m., the time of the 911 call. When the operator picked up the call, she only heard what she thought was a muffled gunshot, nothing else. A two degree drop in body temperature, initial stages of lividity, and no rigor mortis is consistent with this timing as well. The phone in the judge's hand was still connected to 911 when EMS arrived." Dr. Mitchell always talks like she swallowed a science textbook.

"Thanks, Doc." Joe gives her a parting nod, and we leave her to her work.

"Do we know where the intruder entered the house?" I ask as we reach the bottom of the staircase.

"Yes." Joe points across the foyer toward the garage. "From that direction. When the responding officers arrived, they woke up the judge's wife, who was asleep in the guest room down here on the main floor." Joe points to a closed door toward the back of the house.

"She let them in, but she was confused, unaware of the emergency call placed by her husband. When they explained, she cried out and ran to check on him. The officers followed her and found the judge already dead. They immediately did a sweep of the house to search for signs of an intruder. They found the outside door that accessed the garage broken open. From there, the intruder must've gone through the garage, entering the house through the mudroom, into the foyer, and up these stairs." He points out the likely route. The intruder would've gone right past where we now stand. "There's no sign of forced entry at the door connecting the garage to the home, so it must've been unlocked."

I shake my head. "So many people leave that door unlocked."

"True, Kruse, but few people are as careful about their security as you are," Joe ribs me.

I admit, my need for security might border on obsession.

"Most people don't see the things we see," I fire back.

"For the record, I keep that door locked too," Joe allows.

Personnel carry an empty stretcher across the marble floor of the foyer, and we move out of their way. A crash beside me causes me to whirl around. Shit. I've bumped into a table with framed photos and knocked them over. All unbroken, whew! I reposition a wedding photo of the judge and his pretty young wife laughing and running through a rain of confetti, surrounded by friends and family, a photo of the judge shaking hands with the mayor, and then one of him fly fishing.

"A house this grand … wasn't it alarmed?" I ask.

"Yes. A tech crew is looking into it. The alarm didn't go off."

"Was anyone else home besides his wife?" I ask, wondering who cleans this enormous house.

"No. Sofia Clifton was the only one home. Sounds like she's pretty shaken up. She's in the kitchen now. Let's go talk to her."

# CHAPTER TWO

We find our way to the back of the home, locating the kitchen in a cozy space overlooking the backyard and view of the harbor. An adjacent breakfast nook and small sitting room are clearly the true living space, where the judge and his wife spent their time—a contrast to the more formal living room and dining area off the foyer. The kitchen shines with polished stainless-steel appliances and granite countertops, but food splatters on the stovetop suggest the kitchen is actually used.

Sofia Clifton is on a couch in the sitting room. She's wrapped in a blanket, her legs drawn up underneath her, arms clenched protectively around them. She doesn't indicate that she's heard us enter the room, not even looking over as we settle into chairs opposite the couch. Her head is turned toward the dark backyard, her eyes unfocused, her face streaked with tears. She's striking, beautiful even, despite her obvious grief.

"Mrs. Clifton?" Joe rouses her from her thoughts. She

turns toward us, looking lost and confused.

"Sofia, please," she says automatically when she registers our presence.

"I'm Detective Riley and this is Detective Kruse. We are so very sorry for your loss. Could we ask you some questions?" Joe asks gently. "Anything you could tell us might help to find out who did this."

"Of course." She visibly gathers herself and pulls the blanket tighter. She seems small and vulnerable, her brown eyes wide and her waist-length dark curls in sleep-tossed disarray.

"Could you tell us what happened tonight?" Joe asks.

Sofia nods and takes a shaky breath before she starts. "I was sleeping in the guest room down here..." She breaks off, distressed. "I can't believe I wasn't there beside him in his last moments," she says in a broken voice. Her eyes fill with tears. Wiping her face, she gets up, heading toward a box of tissues on the kitchen counter. After dabbing her eyes, she gets a glass from a cupboard and fills it from the fridge dispenser. She takes a few sips, steadying herself. "I'm sorry, detectives, but this is all very difficult to process."

"It's okay, take your time," I say.

She stands in the kitchen in her silky pink nightshirt with matching bottoms, and a pair of fuzzy socks, taking a few more fortifying sips of water. The drape of her nightshirt fabric hugs her curves and there's a telltale bump over her lower abdomen. Watching her in the kitchen, I also notice a distinctive black, wedge-shaped image pinned to the bulletin board behind her. An ultrasound. She's pregnant. Not too far along, it appears. The implications hit me: a baby that will never know its father. No wonder Sofia's so distraught. She returns to the couch with her water glass, setting it on the coffee table and wrapping the blanket back around her.

"Do you usually sleep separately?" Joe nudges her back to her admission that she wasn't sleeping in the same room as her husband.

Sofia shakes her head. "No, but Harry had a bad cough. He was worried he would pass it on to me, so he asked me to sleep in another room. I told him he was being overprotective…but he insisted. And so, I wasn't there…" She drifts off again, lost in her misery. The judge definitely wouldn't want her catching a virus from him if she's pregnant.

Sofia clearly wishes she'd been with him when he passed but it doesn't seem to have occurred to her that if she'd been in the same bed as the judge, it's more than likely she would've been killed too. Sleeping in the guest room probably saved her life. *And that of her unborn child.*

"How far along are you, Sofia?" I ask gently. The judge was in his early fifties, but his wife appears to be in her thirties. Young enough for a healthy pregnancy.

Joe glances at me. He hadn't noticed.

"Four months. A little girl. We just started picking out a crib and items for the nursery." More tears leak down her face; her lower lip trembles.

*Was her pregnancy a source of happiness or stress?* The judge was about to have a newborn at a time when many men are contemplating being a grandfather.

"Was the judge excited about becoming a father?" I ask.

"He was deliriously happy about it." Sofia's face transforms with a dreamy gaze as she reminisces. "We've been married for seven years but we didn't start trying to get pregnant until two years ago. He said he never thought he would get to be a father. The thought of having a daughter was pure magic to him. He kept bringing home little pink baby outfits. Our little family was so important to him, especially since he didn't have much in the way of other family around."

"How so?" Joe asks.

"His sister was all he had left. She lives here in Seattle, and we saw her about once a month for dinner. She's married and has two boys. Harry's parents passed away when he and Anna were in their twenties. Going through the loss together made them very close."

"What happened to their parents?"

"They were killed in an avalanche while skiing. The resort didn't post any warnings to keep skiers within the boundaries of the groomed ski runs. His parents got lost and ended up in the path of an avalanche." Sofia shakes her head sadly. "Harry felt it was a tragic, preventable accident."

"I seem to remember something about that," Joe says. "Didn't it end up in a lawsuit?"

Sofia nods. "Harry and his sister sued the resort, but they lost in court. The resort threw a huge team of lawyers up against Harry and his sister and they were overwhelmed. The lawsuit was the beginning of Harry's hatred of large companies with unlimited resources squashing the rights of victims just because they had the money to make it go away."

Her eyes get that faraway look again, exhaustion written on her face. She might not be able to continue much longer, so I bring the interview back to the case at hand. "When EMS arrived, were you still asleep?"

"I heard a noise just after one in the morning. I'm not sure what it was...maybe someone on the stairs. I woke up and listened for a while, but when I didn't hear anything more, I went back to sleep." She sips her water. "When I heard banging at the door about ten minutes later, I was confused. I let the officers in, and they said an emergency call had been placed. I knew immediately that it could only be Harry, so I ran upstairs and I…I found him…like that." She gestures to her forehead and lets out a sob. "I…I don't know what I'll do without him." She wipes at the fresh onslaught of tears.

"Do you know what time the officers arrived?" I ask.

"I checked my phone when I woke up. It was 1:14 a.m."

So, the officers and EMS arrived only nine minutes after the judge placed the call at the time of the shooting. *Pretty quick.*

"Are there any security cameras that might've caught the intruder?"

"Yes, there are some cameras and an alarm system. I'm not sure how someone got past them."

"What security company do you use?"

"Harry had a program on his computer, Ready-Set-Safe. It doesn't have a service, just personal home monitoring that activates an alarm in the house if someone breaks in."

The name prompts me to ask, "Is there a safe in the house? Have you checked to make sure no valuables are missing?"

"The officers asked me to check the safe and my jewelry. We looked in it. Nothing is missing."

"Sofia, I know this is hard, but can you think of anyone who would want to kill your husband?" I ask.

"Just the usual reasons people are angry at a judge. A ruling didn't go their way, or they suspect he'll rule against them… those kinds of things."

"So, no one specific comes to mind?"

"No, everyone loved Harry. I'm sure some of the criminals he put away held a grudge but he never told me about anyone he was worried about."

"Does anyone else have access to the house?" Joe asks.

"There's a housekeeper that comes on Tuesdays. She has a key, but she hasn't been here since last week."

So, no one had access except for the judge, his wife...and a professional killer. The assassin went right by Sofia's room on the way to shoot her husband. If the situation had been even slightly different—if she'd gone to investigate the noise she heard or had slept beside her husband—we would have two bodies tonight...Three actually...The thought gives me a chill.

"Thank you for your help," I tell Sofia. "If you will give us access to all your personal records, it will make it easier to determine who did this."

She glances up and nods briefly in acknowledgment.

We quietly exit.

I nudge Joe toward the judge's study which I passed when I entered the home. "Let's go see if there's an assassin on the security footage."

# CHAPTER THREE

The study occupies a prime location, a front corner of the home with a view out onto the street. An IT tech is settled into the sumptuous leather chair behind the judge's sizeable desk, squinting at the screen of the computer monitor.

Bookshelves stuffed with law texts and reference books, as well as an array of novels, cover every last inch of available space. The lamp on the desk casts a warm glow around the room. A bottle of scotch and a couple of glasses occupy a shelf behind the desk chair, and the faint scent of tobacco makes me wonder if cigars are stashed somewhere in the desk drawers.

The room is an oasis, an escape from daily demands. I can picture the judge sitting here, nestled into the comfortable space, enjoying a drink and relaxing.

"Simon, any luck getting in?" Joe looks over the tech's shoulder at the monitor. I swing around the desk, standing beside him to get a better view.

"Yeah. His password was his wife's name. I'm in and have

access to everything," he says.

"Anything interesting?" I ask.

"I went through his recent emails and documents. Didn't see anything concerning right off. No threats or angry messages. And I don't see any signs that he was concerned about his safety."

Simon pulls up an official-appearing website. "He had remote access to the courthouse servers. His password auto fills but the courthouse requires him to provide secondary authentication through an emailed code."

His fingers fly along the keyboard, pulling up browser bookmarks. "He didn't have much on social media except Facebook, where he mostly shared photos with someone named Anna—his sister, I think—and a few friends. His privacy settings exclude most outside access."

Simon stops typing and sits back. "I'll bring the hard drive back to the precinct so we can go through everything in more detail. The judge's phone was at his bedside. I'll look into that as well."

"How about the security system?" Joe asks.

Simon clicks on a desktop file. "The judge used a home monitoring system. There are keypads in the home, and the alarm and cameras are accessible by his phone or computer. Any alarms would be sent to him directly, but no outside monitoring was in effect." That confirms what Sofia told us.

"The alarm was turned off at 12:47 a.m. It looks like it was deactivated by someone hacking in remotely. They were careful; it's not traceable. None of the home's keypads were used."

"What about the cameras?" I ask.

"There's a camera placed outside each of the three entry

points: the front door, the sliding door by the kitchen, and the door on the other side of the garage. There aren't any cameras inside the home." He pulls up the live feeds, and all three camera views appear on the screen.

"This looks like it's above the side door that accesses the garage." Joe points to one of the feeds. "I was told that was the door where a forced entry occurred."

The tech enlarges the specified camera image and resets the time at 12:47 a.m., the time the alarm was deactivated.

We watch several minutes of footage with no movement. The audio is fuzzy. We can hear some wind and a siren off in the distance.

When the timestamp flips to 1:01 a.m., we hear footsteps approaching. Joe and I glance at each other. We're about to see the intruder for the first time. I lean forward in anticipation, holding my breath.

A figure enters the camera's view, dressed in black from head to toe, face covered with a ski mask, and hands in gloves. After trying the knob and finding the door locked, the intruder steps back a couple of paces and splinters the door with a well-placed kick, then enters the home. Quick and sure. It takes less than thirty seconds, according to the timestamp.

With the poor resolution of the footage, I can't make out any identifying features of the intruder other than a slight build and movements that are athletic and agile. Height is difficult to estimate since the camera is placed above the door, pointing downward at a steep angle.

"Looks like a pro," I comment.

"Yeah. A fast and efficient entry," Joe agrees. "And it only took four minutes from when the door camera shows the break-in to when the judge placed the 911 call. The killer must've researched the home layout ahead of time to be able to go immediately from the entry to the primary bedroom."

"The killer never looks up at the camera," I comment. "Probably knew it was there ahead of time, too."

We continue to watch the camera feed. The intruder comes back into view at 1:08 a.m., leaving the home. The killer stops briefly, spraying something on the concrete pad in front of the door, then continues spraying while backing away.

"What do you think that's for?" I ask Joe.

"Not sure but I'm guessing it's a scent to confuse a tracking dog from picking up a trail." Joe glances at his watch. "The dog team should be here already."

"Can you rewind that?" I ask the tech.

He rewinds the footage to the spot where the intruder is leaving the home.

"Shoe covers too," I point out. "The killer was definitely anticipating a tracking dog."

We continue our search of the computer files until we hear movement in the adjacent foyer, the canine search team arriving. The handler signals an excited black Labrador retriever. The dog immediately sits and stays statue still, a slight wag of the tail the only thing betraying its eagerness.

"Follow me," Joe says to the handler. He leads the way through the door to the mudroom and into the garage, heading for the side door. The handler and dog follow, and I trail along behind them. At the far side of the garage, the door to the side yard hangs open, the jamb splintered apart at the lock strike plate. A strong scent of citrus air freshener lingers.

"That scent is going to make it hard for the dog. Let's start him back here and see if he can pick up the killer's trail before the door," the handler suggests.

The dog sniffs about, picking up a scent and following it to the door. The handler follows the dog across the threshold, where it sets to sniffing and searching, pulling the handler along. After a few minutes, the dog starts circling back, confused and whining, sneezing as his sensitive nostrils inhale the overpowering citrus. After a few tries, it becomes obvious the dog is unable to follow the trail.

The handler shakes his head in frustration. "Sorry, detectives, I don't think he's going to pick up the scent again."

Joe nods. "Thanks for trying."

"Well, that's disappointing. I've almost never seen the dogs fail," Joe comments after the dog and handler depart.

"It would've been nice to at least know what direction they headed in," I agree.

We head outside to search for foot impressions, but the ground is dry and firm. The night is still cool, even though it's already June. From the footage, we know the intruder wore shoe covers, so there won't be any identifiable tracks anyway. There's a slight imprint at one spot, but no traceable tread. I'm begrudgingly impressed. This assassin was skilled, literally disappearing without a trace.

It's after 5:00 a.m. when we leave the crime scene, after doing a thorough evaluation of the rest of the home. Sofia let us into the safe, for the second time establishing that the jewelry and papers they kept inside were all accounted for. We confirmed that the guest room was slept in. We searched the entire home looking for a discarded murder weapon, a footprint, a hair, any evidence that could help in the search for the killer. In the end, we'd come to the same conclusion as the crime scene investigators that searched before we did; there wasn't a shred of evidence to be found. Other than the bullet, nothing had been left behind.

Two officers, Sally and Bob, are left to canvas the neighbors to see if anyone noticed anything that might be helpful.

Joe and I head to Barrett's Café, the coffee shop across from the precinct and our favorite place to regroup. We get some much-needed coffee and bagels to keep our tired minds on task.

Joe takes a sip of coffee. "Any thoughts?"

"A pro. Quick. Simple. Deadly. Thought of every detail," I say, putting creamer in my coffee. The first sip makes me close my eyes and sigh in gratitude.

Joe chuckles at my reaction to the coffee. "I don't think we're likely to ID the killer with forensic evidence. He was too careful."

"Agreed. We're going to have to look at motive," I say through a mouthful of bagel. "We need to find out who wanted the judge out of the way so badly they hired a contract killer. I bet we'll find a few leads if we look at his past and current cases. There must be criminals or maybe even one of these big companies the judge tended to dislike that might have a grudge against him. Once we identify those with a possible motive, we can look at their bank records for large payments or withdrawals that might've paid for a hit."

"So, where do you want to start? With the judge's cases?" Joe asks, rubbing his red-rimmed eyes.

"I think that's a good place to start. The sister might have some ideas as well."

"Sounds good." Joe agrees. "The judge's chambers are at the King County Courthouse. Let's go there now."

# CHAPTER FOUR

Joe and I settle in a courthouse conference room, waiting for the judge's clerk to meet with us. It's taking a while. I catch myself drumming my fingers on the table and looking out the glass windows overlooking the hallway, searching for someone coming our direction. So far, nothing.

I take in Joe's somewhat rumpled shirt and pants. I'm sure I look just as disheveled after the middle-of-the-night call to the crime scene. I'm purposely avoiding looking in a mirror.

My sluggish mind keeps drifting toward sleep. What are the chances I could just get in a little nap…

"Drifting off there, Kruse?" Joe chuckles, snapping me out of my sleepy thoughts. Then his face brightens, and he nods his head toward the glass door beside me.

I turn to see a tall, gangly man in an ill-fitting suit approaching. He's young, maybe late twenties. His short dark hair sticks out at various angles, an unfashionable tie doing its best to come untied. Laden with an armful of files, he attempts to open the conference room door by putting his hip into the push bar, but it doesn't budge. When a second attempt fails, I get up and open the door for him.

He stumbles into the room, trips on nothing in particular, and sends the files on the top of the pile skittering onto the table.

Giving us a sheepish look, he sets the rest of the files down and recollects the fallen ones.

Extending his arm, he announces, "Chris Tucker." His handshake is unsteady and damp, no eye contact.

We introduce ourselves. Both of us are somewhat amused by the clerk's behavior. Saying he's flustered would be like saying a tornado is a little bit windy. *What's up with this guy?* Sometimes we encounter people who are just innately uncomfortable around law enforcement. Perhaps that's all it is.

Not knowing exactly what to do with his hands, Chris runs them through his hair, causing it to stick out at new angles. He crosses his arms, then, maybe thinking this is too defensive, he puts his hands on his hips.

"Please, sit." Joe tries to put him at ease, gesturing to a chair.

Chris takes a seat and folds his hands on his lap, then changes his mind and rests his arms on the table. I want to lay a hand on his arms to stop the movement. R*elax, Chris. We're just here to find out what cases the judge has been involved in, we're not going to frisk you.* There couldn't be a bigger contrast between his behavior and the smooth actions of the killer we saw on the video.

We all look at one another, not sure who's going to take the lead.

Seeing Chris' hesitation, I start. "I'm sorry you've had some bad news this morning. From what I understand, Judge

Harry was quite well liked."

"Yeah. It came as quite a shock to everyone." He ducks his head.

"What are all these files? Do you still keep paper files for cases?" I ask.

"No, not for the more recent ones. These files are his old cases. Some of these were tried long enough ago that the offenders have already been released after serving their sentences, or they're out on probation." Chris opens a file with a stack of papers inside. "I printed out basic details of the most recent cases so we could look through them. I flagged the ones that were most controversial, where families or companies were unhappy with the judge's decisions."

"Good. We can look through those with you," I say, though my tired mind is already protesting the tedious task.

"What case was the judge presiding over before he died?" Joe asks.

"It involves a company called GuidanceLink." Chris opens the file with the stack of recent cases and pulls a couple of pages off the top. "They're being sued by their employees for breach of contract."

"I haven't heard of them. What do they do?" I ask.

"It's a tech company, about ten years old. They link high-level executives searching for a mentor with people who are interested in mentoring." Chris' demeanor transforms as his focus shifts to case details. "They've expanded from a focus on business enterprises to serve numerous industries, such as medicine, law, and even academia. The company takes a percentage of the mentoring fee. It's been very successful."

"Why are the employees suing?" Joe asks

"During 2020 and 2021, when COVID was prevalent, the

employees began working remotely. Many moved their work into their homes here in Seattle. But some even moved to other locations for various reasons: to be near family, to live in a milder climate, or to have a lower cost of living. For many, it was a chance to change their lifestyle for the better."

"Ah, and now I bet the company wants them to come back to the workplace," I surmise.

"Yes. They'd constructed an expensive modern workspace to encourage camaraderie and optimize idea exchange, and they insisted on employees returning to the site."

"What are the employees claiming?" I ask.

"They state the contracts never stipulated the location of their work, and regardless, GuidanceLink agreed that they could work from home during those years so that constituted a new verbal contract. In order to work remotely, the employees had to establish a work environment in their homes and that was an investment of their own money. They don't want this investment to be for nothing. Also, those who moved some distance away face an expensive move back to Seattle if they are required to return to the physical work environment provided by GuidanceLink."

"When are they due in court?" Joe asks.

"The case was set to start this week," Chris says.

"Has a jury already been selected?" I ask.

"No, the two parties had agreed to a bench trial…that's where only the judge presides and there's no jury," Chris responds.

"I bet GuidanceLink was pretty nervous when Judge Harry was assigned to the case, given his reputation for reprimanding large companies that use their wealth to get what they want," Joe comments.

"Indeed. They tried to have him recused due to bias but weren't successful." Chris is getting more comfortable; the practice of law is clearly his element.

We set the GuidanceLink information aside for now but it will top our list of past cases to investigate.

"Let's go through the files you pulled out. Any that stand out to you?" Joe picks up a few files and opens one randomly. I reluctantly follow his lead, delving into the tedious files, though my mind keeps drifting off task, preoccupied with fantasies of sleep.

For the next several hours, we pore over the cases with Chris. Joe has lunch delivered so we can continue the work uninterrupted. The hours seem interminably long, relieved only when Chris knocks over his drink and drowns one of the files. He's no longer shaking in his boots so he must just be clumsy. He takes the file to the men's room to dry it under the hand dryer. His quick actions indicate this may not be his first file-drowning.

After we've sorted through Judge Harry's past cases, we're left with two that stand out.

"Tell us more about these cases, Chris." I pick up the two older files we set aside.

He picks up the top one. "This one is from 2018. Apple-A-Day Orchards were sued for poor working conditions for immigrants on H-2A visas. The judge ruled for the workers. The Mason family owned the orchard, and their livelihood was severely compromised when the farm was forced to pay the settlement. From what I understand, the family sent the judge frequent post-trial motions for reconsideration. They were desperate."

Opening the other file, Chris pulls out some crime scene

photos. "In 2004, when the judge was on his criminal case rotation, he presided over the second-degree murder conviction of Barry Greenworth. He killed a man during an altercation over the value of the diamonds the man was selling." In the photos, a man with multiple stab wounds lies in a pool of blood near a dumpster in an alley.

"Greenworth was sentenced to twenty years in prison but was released last year after serving his sentence. Throughout the trial and afterward, he's always maintained his innocence. He hated the judge and sent him regular and creative death threats."

"Did the judge get a lot of death threats?"

"He got a few, but some were just on a much grander scale. Greenworth was very specific in his threats."

"Such as?"

"Such as, 'Tonight when you go home to your pretty wife, you look at her and be glad she has all her fingers. Just be glad she's safe right now—as long as I'm on the inside.'" Chris shivers involuntarily. "Pretty hard to forget. He had lots of elaborate plans for the judge. Some threatened his life."

"Wasn't he prosecuted for the threats?" I ask.

"No. They never could tie them to Greenworth. They were mailed from outside the prison and no DNA was ever recovered from one, but the Judge was certain they were from him. I asked the Judge about it once when I found one in his mail. They were signed with a dollar sign, which the judge thought stood for 'Greenworth,' but he knew that wouldn't hold up as evidence in court. He was saving the threats and hoping Greenworth would someday make a mistake he could catch him on. The threats that came in from others were so benign, the judge didn't take them seriously, but he kept them just the same."

"Could you copy these files for us, Chris? Also, we'd like to see the judge's chambers," Joe says.

Chris leads us to the secretarial pool and asks one of the secretaries to copy the two files and the details of the GuidanceLink case.

A few of the office staff, men and women alike, look teary-eyed. No doubt they've seen the early morning news reports.

Entering the judge's chambers has the feel of passing into a sacred space. The furnishings are substantial and the walls thick. It's like being in a vault. No sound enters or leaves. The space is dominated by a solid, dark cherrywood desk with a plush chair. Two smaller chairs face the desk. Behind the desk, bookcases house tidy rows of leather-bound law books. It reminds me of the judge's home study, though this government-provided space is much less grand.

The desk contains a computer and a few neatly placed personal objects, an ornate lamp, a bronze sculpture of the scales of justice, and a gavel. A worktable and chairs sit off to one side by a window. The judge's robes hang on a coat-tree in a corner behind the desk, beside a pole with a US flag.

The room exudes a sense of power.

A distinctive statue rests on a shelf behind the desk. "Is that a replica of 'The Hammering Man'?" I ask, referring to the almost fifty-foot-tall statue outside the Seattle Art Museum. That version is hammering constantly, honoring the working class. There are similar versions throughout the world.

"Yes, the judge loved that statue. Said it reminded him of how America was built. On the backs of the workers."

It seems the judge was not subtle in his views.

We search through the papers on top of the desk and

through the drawers, looking for notes or threats, finally finding a red file folder. Opening it, I scan through threats and grievances, some typed, some handwritten.

"You'll regret your decision ..."

"You made the wrong ruling ..."

These appear to be mostly benign blustering but those signed with a dollar sign are of a different quality altogether. They give me a chill. I ask Chris to copy the file for us.

A blue file under the red one has notes of appreciation and thanks. *Well, at least something positive to offset the vitriol.* We get a copy of that file also. Perhaps someone's thanks will point to an unhappy party on the other side of the case.

There are no sticky notes of personal to-do items or notes from his wife. Or photos.

"No photos of his wife?" I ask Chris.

"I asked him about that once," Chris says. "He said he didn't want any of the threats he dealt with to seep into his personal life or allow someone to think they had a way to get to him. He said he thought Greenworth found something online that linked him to his wife and started including her in the threats."

"Do you know why he kept all these notes with grievances? Seems like it's hard enough to read them the first time. I wouldn't want to relive it on a regular basis."

Chris's expression becomes grave. "I imagine it was for just such an occasion as this. To point to a killer."

*Touché, Chris.*

As we exit the building, exhaustion closes in on me.

Joe's phone rings. He answers and has a short conversation. "That was Bob. I'd asked him to look into the judge's sister, Anna Shapiro—see if we can talk to her. He says she's on a plane back from Europe. She was on vacation with her family in France. We can talk with her when she gets back."

I'm relieved by the delay. My mind is begging for some rest before we tackle the next phase of the investigation.

# CHAPTER FIVE

Arriving back at my apartment, I check the doorframe for the piece of napkin I tucked there when I left in the middle of the night. I'm in the habit of stuffing a tiny piece of something there. Sometimes it's a torn bit of napkin, sometimes a bit of paper. Something small so it's not noticeable to others. If the door opens, the paper falls out, so if the paper is still in the doorframe when I get back, I know no one has been in my apartment. A little makeshift security. My place has been broken into on past cases and this little bit of extra vigilance eases my mind.

The napkin is still in place—good.

When I let myself in, my black cat, Stalker, is at the door to greet me, squinting his green, knowing eyes at me in greeting. He rubs against my legs, and I try not to trip over him as I stumble wearily toward the couch. With a single-minded need for sleep, I lie down with my head on a throw pillow. Stalker curls up at my feet. I'll just rest for a minute...

A quick knock at my door followed by a key inserting in

the lock awakens me.

I have a momentary disoriented jolt of alarm as I hear the lock turn.

But as I awaken fully, I relax. After all, I know who it is.

Sitting up on the couch, I glance at my phone. I've slept for two hours. There are three new texts...all from Blake.

The door opens and there he is, every gorgeous inch of him. And perhaps even better than just the sight of him, he's carrying take-out food. And it smells incredible.

Stalker winds around Blake's feet to welcome him. They're friends now, but it wasn't always so.

"I never get tired of that smile." Blake grins at me, his eyes lingering on my mouth.

"What smile is that?" I ask coyly, stretching my sleep-heavy limbs.

"The one that says you're glad to see me."

"I'm very glad to see you." I slide into his arms. Resting my head against his chest feels like home. "What smells so amazing?" I ask.

"Tikka masala and naan."

Yum. He unpacks the food, laying it out on plates. I grab a cider and a beer from the fridge, and we head out to the balcony to eat. The summer sun is setting lazily over Puget Sound. The hour is getting late, but the air is just starting to cool.

"I figured you'd be exhausted since you got up in the middle of the night," he says.

I'd texted him when I got the call from Joe. He'd been working last night. As a physician in the ER, he often works overnight. Unlike me though, he'll have slept all day—at his apartment. We're still in that awkward phase where we're going back and forth between each other's places.

"Yeah, we worked right through," I acknowledge. "I slept two hours when I got home, though. I was so sound asleep, I don't think I moved a muscle."

"I heard the news about Judge Harry. Figured you caught that case."

"Yeah. It's going to be interesting." I sip the cider, enjoying the contrast of cool liquid with the warm, spicy food.

"He was pretty well liked. Did he have any enemies?"

"I suppose all judges do. For every case, there's a side that loses. Fodder for grudges. But he had a file full of gratitude to balance the file of death threats."

"It's amazing that people send death threats. What kind of person does that?"

"I suppose they do it in an attempt to influence him. Or sometimes they're seeking revenge when they feel his ruling was unfair."

"Seems ineffective. They're just putting a big red flag on themselves."

"Yep, that gives us a good place to start looking at possible suspects." I glance at Blake. "What about you? How was your shift last night?"

"Not bad. Lots of stitches. A chef cut herself trying to crack open a spaghetti squash, a teenager stepped on a piece of glass at the beach, and early this morning, a fisherman came in with a hook in his finger."

I grimace at the mental images of these wounds but at least nothing sounds life-threatening. "So, no helicopter arrivals?" Blake always says that the worst injuries come in via the helipad: car accident victims, boating accidents, drownings.

"Not last night. Did have a kid with an allergic reaction to a bee sting. Had us worried for a bit. His family was outside after dinner, and he was eating a popsicle. The bee must've been attracted by the sugar and landed on it. The kid wasn't paying attention and when he went to lick the popsicle, the bee stung the poor kid on the tongue. The swelling of his tongue was impressive. Luckily two doses of epinephrine stopped it, and we didn't have to intubate him to secure his airway."

I finish my naan and try to sneak some off Blake's plate. He playfully grabs my hand, and gives me an intent look. *Ah, there it is. That's a look I can't resist.* He pulls me in for a lingering kiss. Soon we're staggering inside, leaving a trail of clothing in our wake. *Yeah, it's still like that.*

Much later, we lie curled up cozily in bed. I rest my head on his shoulder, just enjoying drifting in and out of sleep, my exhausted mind contemplating the kind of person who sends death threats: someone with nothing to lose. I'm thinking this as I drift off into a dream...

# CHAPTER SIX

*It's early morning on what promises to be a perfect summer day; the sky is clear, and the temperature is already climbing. It's going to be a hot one—at least, as hot as it gets in Seattle. A slight breeze blows my long skirt around my legs as I walk from my car to the office building. I'm already contemplating the list of clients on my schedule for the day, thinking about what might help them, how I can guide them.*

*"Hey, Sam," Becky, the receptionist, greets me as I step off the elevator on my floor. Giving her a smile and a wave as I pass, I head straight for the break room. I pour a cup of coffee into a mug and add two creamers, taking a fortifying sip before I head for my office. As I pass the mail cubbies in the hall, I pick up a few letters and a package addressed to me. I struggle to open the door to my office with my hands full of mail, the package, and my coffee.*

*My first patient isn't for twenty minutes, so I have time to sit and enjoy a quiet moment. I slide into the chair behind my desk, looking out my window over the quiet neighborhood be-*

*yond. I love these stolen moments in the morning.*

*Sipping my coffee, I sort through my mail. It's the usual. Several pieces of junk mail, a life insurance offer, yet another survey. A thank you note from a patient that warms my heart. An interesting heavy package, about the size of a book from an encyclopedia collection. Did I order a new psychology textbook recently? I don't remember doing so, but sometimes it takes four to six weeks for them to come in the mail. Maybe I did. My name and address are neatly penned but there's no return address. Odd. I slide a letter opener into the tape holding the edges of the cardboard packaging together. Bending back the flaps, I catch a glimpse of the interior of the box and suddenly there is a ringing in my ears, a tingling surge of fear in my fingers.*

*I pull back involuntarily, then leap up out of my chair and run from the room, pulling the fire alarm as I enter the hall. As the alarm starts up, I sprint to reception and pull Becky from her chair. She looks at me, startled.*

*"A package," I manage through my panic. "It looks like a bomb."*

*Becky races after me as I scramble down the stairs and exit the building. Reaching the parking lot, I bend over, hands on my knees, catching my breath. Employees are exiting the building with confused looks, and gathering in groups in the lot. Approaching sirens can already be heard in the distance.*

*"A bomb?" Becky asks between ragged breaths, concern furrowing her brow, fear making her eyes wide.*

*"I opened a package. I should have known better. There was no return address," I pant, starting to pace.*

*"What was in it?"*

*"I saw some 9-volt batteries, some wires, and something metal like a curling iron. It scared the hell out of me, so I ran.*

*All I could think was—get everyone out!"*

*"Thank God you acted so fast. After the Unabomber targeted that Boeing plant last month, we're all on edge. Did the inside look like the bomb they talked about on the news?"*

*"It did!" I reply, noticing my hands are shaking. The Unabomber had been sending bombs in the mail for years now, and it wasn't always clear how he selected his targets. The recent Boeing plant bomb near Seattle was a little too close for my liking. The local news had been warning the public to avoid opening suspicious packages and even describing what the inside of the bombs might look like.*

*It's still early in the morning, and there aren't many people here this time of day. About twenty people are assembled in the parking lot by the time the fire trucks pull in. No one takes fire alarms very seriously, always thinking it's a drill. I hope everyone believed it this time and got out of the building.*

*The fire chief gets down from the truck in full gear and approaches the crowd. "Did anyone here pull the alarm?"*

*"It was me." I step forward.*

*"Where is the fire located?" he asks, squinting at the building, which has no signs of smoke.*

*"It wasn't a fire. I opened a package that had wires and 9-Volt batteries in it. I left it on my desk and ran out, pulling the alarm to get everyone out."*

*The chief's eyes narrow in uncertainty. This isn't his usual call. After a moment, he says, "Good thing you cleared the building, ma'am. We'll get the bomb squad in to check on the package."*

*Bringing in the bomb squad takes a while. Colleagues and other office workers continue to arrive, finding the fire engines and all the building's workers spread out in the parking lot. I repeat the story over and over in response to the questions.*

*When the bomb squad arrives, more of the neighborhood residents and passersby take notice and join us in the lot. Soon, news crews are arriving.*

*A man from the bomb squad confers with the fire chief and then looks my way. He approaches and introduces himself as Ian Doyle. I tell the story once more. He asks me specific questions about the box: what it was made from, what was on the outside, and what I saw inside.*

*Ian discusses options with his team and then they assemble and enter the building. I watch the entry anxiously, worried about Ian and his team. What if they set off the bomb?*

*After what seems like an eternity, the bomb squad re-emerges.*

*"It's safe to enter the building," Ian announces to the group at large.*

*Workers slowly meander back inside, thankful it is safe, but maybe a little disappointed to have to return to their ordinary day after all the excitement.*

*Ian motions to me and leads me into an office on the main floor. The pieces of the package are spread out on a table. There are indeed several 9-volt batteries, a metal tube, and some wires.*

*"It was wired to look like a bomb, ma'am, but it wasn't active," Ian says.*

*"Thank God."*

*"It looks like someone was trying to scare you."*

*"Well, they succeeded. I thought it might be the Unabomber."*

*"It does look like one of his packages. I've seen photos of them in our training updates, but he typically uses wooden boxes."*

*"So, it wasn't him?"*

*"No, I don't think so." He kindly doesn't say what we're both thinking—that if it had been the Unabomber, I wouldn't be talking to him right now. I'm horrified that it didn't occur to me to suspect the package before I opened it. My office wasn't the typical target, but police weren't sure yet who exactly would make the hit list. We do academic research in our office and I realize belatedly that this could make us a target. I should have been more careful.*

*Ian points to the bottom of the box. "I wanted you to look at this." I approach the box cautiously, still a little traumatized. I know it's safe...all the insides of the package are lying on the table, but all my instincts tell me not to get too close. Peering inside, I see some words on the bottom written in creepily perfect handwriting.*

*"Be careful when you eat your lunch."*

*Ice runs down my spine. I know exactly who sent this. Devin, the patient I treated and ultimately had to turn in for poisoning his colleague. This is his revenge. Devin felt justified poisoning his own lunch, knowing his colleague would take it and eat it himself. He felt the man deserved it because, after all, he was stealing the lunch. But Devin could've killed him. I have a duty to report a patient if they pose a threat to someone, so I turned him in. Ultimately, it resulted in a prison sentence that he's still serving.*

*Devin doesn't see my side, though. He can't; he's a classic narcissist, unable to see someone else's perspective. He feels I betrayed him. Devin is currently in jail, so he must've persuaded someone on the outside to send this package. What else might that person do?*

*I'll keep my lunch locked in my office from now on.*

I wake up from the dream with Sam's lingering feeling of dread…a memory of one of my past lives. When I experienced Samantha Steel's life, I was a Seattle psychologist in the 1980s. At night, I often have dreams with her memories, or those of some of my other past lives, that are brought out by events in my current life. When I'm awake, I don't remember anything about those past lives aside from the memories I've experienced as dreams.

These dreams are often disorienting when viewed from my current narrow perspective, as Kaitlyn. My first thought on waking had been—why didn't Sam call 911 with her cell phone when she got outside? It took me a minute to realize she wouldn't have owned one in the 1980s. I also hadn't realized how scared people may have been when the Unabomber first started sending bombs, before the pattern behind his targets was discerned.

I've encountered Sam's patient Devin in previous dreams. His sense of self-importance and inability to see the perspective of others make him dangerous. This is exactly the kind of person who would be sending death threats to the judge and may ultimately have killed him. I can see how it relates. It reminds me of Barry Greenworth and his threats sent to the judge from prison.

I've never told Blake about my unusual dreams and honestly, I'm afraid of what he would think. I've only ever trusted one person with my secret.

Careful not to disturb Blake, I disentangle myself from his long limbs and throw on my running clothes. Running is my therapy. It clears my head of these disconcerting dreams.

I head outside into the cool morning breeze. The present-day summer weather mirrors the summer weather in my dream. I run down the neighborhood streets, soothed by the repetitive motion, the physical exertion. I stretch my legs and enjoy just existing in the pleasant morning.

When I return, Blake is up and has breakfast cooking. He doesn't have to work until later today. I give him a quick kiss as I go by, heading for the shower.

When I emerge in my work suit, he places an omelet at the small kitchen table for me. I close my eyes in bliss at the first bite. "Mmmm. Have I told you lately that I love you?"

"Not nearly enough," he teases.

I laugh. "Well, let me count the ways…I love that you're constantly feeding me. That you love my cat..."

"By the way, speaking of your cat, I filled your automatic feeder. It was almost empty. Now that Stalker is taken care of, can I convince you to come to my place more often?"

"Stalker loves you too, you know. He wants you to stay here with us."

"I could tell by the way he hissed at me when I got up this morning."

"Old habits die hard." Stalker wasn't very friendly to Blake in the early days of our relationship but he's typically pretty accepting of him now. Stalker was lonely when I started spending more time at Blake's place. He started chewing on my throw pillows and clawing up my curtains in protest. So, we've been spending more time at my place lately. I've started to find myself wondering if we should move in together. I'm not sure if I'm ready to take that step or not, but the idea is growing more insistent.

I put the thought aside; I don't have time to contemplate it right now.

I give Blake a quick peck on the cheek as I head for the

door. He grabs me for a real kiss. I start to sink into the kiss but then remember myself and reluctantly push him away so he won't make me late for work.

# CHAPTER SEVEN

It's my turn to bring coffee, so I'm juggling two hot to-go cups from Barrett's when I meet up with Joe heading into the precinct.

"I can sure use the caffeine today," Joe says, taking a cup.

"Still tired from the early crime scene visit?"

"Sure am. I'm not in my thirties anymore, in case you hadn't noticed," he laughs, holding the door for me as we head inside.

Bob is eagerly waiting when we round the corner heading to our desks. He jumps to his feet when he spots us. Whenever I see Bob, I can't help but think of a golden retriever. If he had a tail, it would be wagging. "The case files from the courthouse arrived. I put them on your desk," he says.

"Thanks," Joe says. "How did it go with the neighbors? Did anyone see anything?"

"No one saw or heard anything until EMS arrived." He looks slightly deflated at not having better news. "The home across the street had a view of the front of the judge's house on the doorbell camera, but with the tree coverage on the side of the house and the dim lighting, we couldn't see anything at the time of the break-in."

*Darn,* I was hoping we would at least get a glimpse of the assassin. Even just the direction they approached the house from would be helpful. Or maybe an idea of height, since we couldn't tell from the angle of the security camera. *Something—anything—to go on.*

"Do you have anything else I can work on?" Bob asks.

I flip through the case files, pulling one out. "Here it is. You can track down Barry Greenworth. We need to bring him in for questioning."

"The murderer, Barry Greenworth?" Bob's eyes are wide at the mention of the famous criminal. He was probably about six when Greenworth was convicted.

"The very same." I nod, handing him the file. "And what about the judge's sister? Weren't you working on setting up an interview with her?"

"She's returning from France. She was there on vacation with her family," Bob says. He takes the Greenworth file and heads off to tackle his assignment.

Joe calls the ME to see if there is anything unexpected on the autopsy or the forensics. I can hear her loud voice answer Joe's call. We both wince at the memory it brings up. Last Thanksgiving, her loud phone voice set off a series of unfortunate events. We aren't surprised to learn that she has nothing new for us. No fingerprints, no DNA, no trace material. Nothing. The killer came and went without leaving a trace. Our only chance to identify him now is to find out who paid for his services.

We decide to start with GuidanceLink, the company being

sued in the judge's most recent case. A quick search online brings up an article reporting on the company's instant success and rapid expansion. It was started in 2015 and first year profits were in the tens of millions. The co-founders and their three original employees quickly saw the need for expansion; they outgrew the cramped office where they were sharing desks and sitting on boxes of files for lack of storage space.

The current office space was envisioned by the husband-and-wife co-founders to foster a creative and healthy work environment and to pave the way for international expansion. They spared no expense. When the Seattle IT world got wind of the project, potential employees were eager for job interviews. The company brought on dozens of employees, and word around town was that the new workers loved the unusual workspace. At least at first.

All was well until 2020 when employees began working from home. Another article documents GuidanceLink's attempt to force its employees to return to the unique, and expensive, workplace and the employees' countering lawsuit.

Now I'm interested to see the workspace at the center of the debate. I contact GuidanceLink and advise them we'll be coming for interviews and a look at the office space this morning.

As we pack up to leave, our interim captain, Deputy Chief Elizabeth Garcia, pokes her head out of her office and gestures for us to join her. As we enter, Garcia gives us a grave look. "Detectives, we're going to catch a lot of publicity on this case. The mayor is already breathing down my neck, insisting we find the judge's killer, and fast. Make sure you keep me in the loop on this one."

We fill her in on our current leads. She questions us a bit

but seems satisfied with our progress. She dismisses us with a reminder to keep checking in with her.

GuidanceLink is in a less developed area of Seattle, so we travel away from the downtown snarl of business traffic. As we approach the location on our GPS, we find ourselves in a heavily wooded area. The building comes into view, nestled into its natural environment, large evergreens standing sentinel on all sides. It's constructed almost entirely of glass so it all but disappears into the landscape. The original evergreens are still growing both outside and even within the building, the office spaces built around them. Winding wood staircases lead up to open workspaces that resemble treehouses. Ivy works its way around the structural elements, camouflaging the steel beams. Sunlight streams through the surrounding tree branches, falling on picnic benches with umbrellas cozily placed to act as outdoor workspaces. A few employees are clustered at the tables, talking and working on laptops.

Not seeing any cars, I search for an indication of where to park. Joe points out a sign that directs visitors to park in front of the building. A nearby arrow marks the employee lot, down an underground ramp.

Leaving the car in one of the five visitors' spots, we approach the front of GuidanceLink, the huge glass sliding doors opening automatically to welcome us. The pleasant smell of pine trees greets us as we enter. The workspaces are visible above us and a stream trickles over rocks on our left. The flooring is a spongy, dark material resembling compressed dirt. It's as if we're still outside.

The receptionist is a handsome man in his twenties, seated inside what appears to be a huge tree stump with the center carved out. He's wearing expensive athletic wear and has a headset on over his short blond hair. "Welcome, detectives," he says. "My name is Adam. I'll be your guide for today."

I decide not to ask the question that pops into my head as to whether or not Eve will be joining us for our tour of Eden.

"This is an unusual reception desk," I comment instead, running my hand over the smooth wood surface.

"The existing stump was modified to create a natural greeting space," Adam informs us smoothly, in his best infomercial voice.

"This is amazing, I feel as if I'm in a forest." I glance up at the sun overhead. "Doesn't it get hot in here, though?"

"The panels are electrochromic glass which can be selectively darkened to provide shade when needed. We can also open sliding panels to allow outside air in." Adam emerges from the interior of the stump. "The best view of the space is from the café. If you'll follow me." He heads toward the elevators. I can't help admiring his retreating form.

"Don't enjoy this too much," Joe whispers, noticing me watching Adam.

"Who, me?" I whisper back, giving him my best innocent look.

Joe raises an amused eyebrow.

The elevator is encased in glass, imparting a sense of vertigo as we rise rapidly to a deck overlooking the workspaces.

We exit to an open food service area currently producing today's meal. Seasoned chicken sizzles on open grills.

"We provide healthy food for our employees, without charge. Our nutritionist ensures fresh foods are available with a focus on whole foods that are as close to their natural state as possible." Adam is back in infomercial mode.

My mouth waters at the large salad bar brimming with

fresh vegetables and fruits, roasted nuts, whole grains, and grilled meats and vegetables. I silently instruct my stomach not to grumble.

From our lofty perch, we can see the workspaces spiraling off in all directions below us. Each platform has wooden flooring and glass paneling, like an upscale backyard deck. The desks have a simple wooden surface, made to blend into the lofted treehouse spaces. One larger space has a long table set out for meetings. A few employees are visible working, but the enormous space is discernibly empty.

The elevator whisks us back to the ground floor at a dizzying speed. Adam pulls up a controller on his phone and large glass panels slide apart to access the outdoor space.

"We encourage our employees to take breaks and walk on the trails surrounding the property. There is also an indoor play area." He walks us over to the far side of the space where there are hanging rings, monkey bars, and a climbing wall. And, yes, there's an adult-sized tire swing. Stationary bicycles and treadmills are placed to view the outdoor wooded space.

"Where does that stairwell on the far side of the equipment go?" Joe asks.

"We have a basement level. A quiet space without distraction. Come, I'll show you."

As we go down the spiraling stairs, it's as if we're descending into the Seattle waters. The subterranean space mimics a soothing underwater environment complete with aquatic life. A series of huge tanks are embedded in the walls, filled with fish. I spot salmon, rockfish, and flounder. The bottoms of the tanks are covered with rocks, starfish, and sea anemones. Kelp floats upward from its tethers and crabs flit among the rocks. A large cylindrical tank in the center of the room reaches from floor to ceiling, filled with undulating and glowing moon jellyfish. The ceiling is covered in an underwater photograph taken looking up to the surface of water with sunlight dappling the waves. A soundtrack plays underwater sounds. Several people are quietly working.

"This is incredible," I say. Clearly, no expense has been spared; the enormous profits from those early years were reinvested in this ground-breaking workspace. It appears the intention was for the employees to interact creatively and continue to take the company in new and innovative directions. But the workspace is going unused.

"It is." Adam nods his head agreeably. He touches his headset and listens intently, then turns to us. "GuidanceLink's co-presidents and CEO are available to meet with you now."

I recognize how clever GuidanceLink's management is. They've set this up to feel like a theme park experience, with management just the next stop on the tour. It puts them in control of the situation and makes us feel like valued guests. My estimation of their shrewdness ticks upwards. It should be interesting to meet them.

# CHAPTER EIGHT

Adam leads us back up to the ground level and from there up one of the winding wooden staircases to the platform with the large meeting table I'd seen earlier from above. Three people are seated at the desk.

Adam introduces us. "These are the co-presidents of GuidanceLink, husband and wife, Brian and Katie Lee." A surprisingly young couple stands and moves to greet us. They're dressed in casual business attire and appear to be in their early thirties. They must've founded GuidanceLink while in their twenties. Katie is thin with a curtain of long sleek black hair and a wide smile. Her husband has short black hair, and he's built like a linebacker. They greet us warmly with firm handshakes.

"This is Andre LaPointe, our CEO." Adam gestures to the other individual, who stands to greet us. He's also young. A slender, athletic type who looks like he might be more at home biking the Tour de France. He's dressed in upscale athletic wear.

"Please, take a seat." Brian gestures to chairs across from theirs. "I understand you are here to discuss our court case in light of the judge's unfortunate passing."

"Correct," Joe confirms with a nod. He settles into his chair, leaning forward on the table. "Can you tell us about the lawsuit?"

"Detectives, as you can imagine, this lawsuit has been devastating for us," Katie says, shaking her head in obvious frustration. "We dreamed of having a healthy and invigorating space for our employees to work, and it came at no small cost. We were just starting to really enjoy it when COVID hit and our employees were forced to work from home. And now... well, it's unthinkable to us that most of them don't want to return. This whole thing has left us feeling stunned and betrayed by the very people we hoped to work closely with to bring GuidanceLink to its full potential."

"You were hoping to work with these employees to explore other ventures?" I ask. It seems the founders had big plans for GuidanceLink.

"We planned to expand into many other opportunities... but that never came to be," Katie says, disappointment written on her face.

"From what I understand, when you founded the company, there were only five of you. Is that correct?" I ask.

"Yes. Katie and I had the initial idea, and we brought the others in," Brian says. He smiles and turns to look at Katie and Andre. "You should have seen us in the beginning. We were working out of a tiny little office. Five people crowded around one desk. GuidanceLink was successful so quickly that it took us all by surprise. We were overwhelmed, working crazy hours and sitting on upended boxes. When we were working on international expansion, we had a couple of couches, and we would take turns sleeping. You see, we had to be awake during the business hours of other nations. It was exhausting but truly, it was such a good time in our lives. The business was taking off; we were all excited to see it do so well and we were all friends in the trenches together. We had the time of our lives." Brian grabs his wife's hand. "Didn't we?"

"We really did." Katie grins broadly. It seems they're enjoying the moment of nostalgia. "We were working so much, it felt like we never went home. But the company was like our child. Seeing it succeed was incredible." She gives her husband's hand a squeeze and then turns to Andre. "And Andre…Andre was one of the original five. He was there in that little office all the time too. I remember you heating up those microwave burritos at all hours."

Andre smiles and nods at the memory. The smile seems a little slow to come, though. Perhaps there's something off between them.

Brian turns his attention back to us. "Our kitchen consisted of a microwave sitting on top of a mini fridge. We were so busy, we barely had time to eat."

It's interesting that they have such happy memories of their first sparse work environment, and yet when they set up the expensive dream workplace they thought they wanted, everything fell apart. "Are the other two original owners still with you?" I ask.

"No. During COVID, they sold their shares and moved on to other things. We all had different ideas of how the company should grow so we agreed to part ways while we were still on good terms. One lives in California where she started another tech company. Another is traveling the world."

"So, you three are the management of the company?"

"Yep. It's just us. We have department heads for each division. They oversee a number of employees and report back to us," Katie says.

"Do any of them have a financial stake in the company?" Joe asks.

"No, we pay them well, but they don't hold any shares. Only the three of us do."

"So, tell us about the lawsuit," Joe prompts.

Brian looks wistful. He sits back in his chair and crosses his arms. "Remote meetings were workable during COVID, but it was a compromise. We were in survival mode. The sense of camaraderie we had when everyone was together was never the same online. We held our breath and waited until it was safe to come back to the workplace. We never expected anyone to resist returning."

"Boy, were we wrong," Katie says. "Only about a third of the employees came back. The rest resisted, passively at first, and then when we threatened to withhold pay unless they returned, they formed a group to sue us." She looks nonplussed. The founders definitely saw this move as a betrayal.

"The lawsuit felt like a slap in the face," Brian says, confirming my thoughts. "We did so much for our employees. We were shocked. When we first built the space, people were competing just to get interviews. Those we hired were grateful to work here. But now, those same people—they turned on us."

"Andre, what do you think of the lawsuit?" Joe turns to the CEO, who has remained remarkably quiet.

Andre looks surprised to be included. "I expected some resistance from people to return to regular office hours.

People got used to being on their own timetable. They could walk their dog in the middle of the afternoon and then sign in again in the evening to finish projects. As long as they got the work done, they were given a lot of freedom."

"So, you were worried about insisting they return?" Joe asks.

"I saw how it might lead to some resistance." Okay, so he might be more in touch with the employees' attitudes than Katie and Brian. I wonder again if there's some contention here.

"How do you anticipate the trial going?" I ask Brian.

"Not well. Our employees found some loopholes that might allow them to continue working from home. You see, our original contracts didn't foresee this issue arising and when we allowed employees to work from home, it could be viewed as initiating a new verbal agreement." Brian runs his hands through his hair in frustration.

"How did you feel about Judge Harry?" I ask.

Brian and Katie share a quick glance. "We didn't think anything particular about him," Katie says, but the words sound forced.

"You weren't worried about his history of siding with workers in cases like these?" I persist.

"Brian and I thought he would be fair once he heard both sides." Katie looks over at Brian as she says this. It comes across like she's avoiding looking us in the eye.

"What about you, Andre?" I turn to him.

"Yeah, a judge has to be fair, right?" Andre says. It comes out like a question. He's not convinced.

"You all stand to lose a lot of money on this expensive building if your employees aren't required to return to work.

Isn't that, right?" I ask.

No one speaks. Brian gives a slight, begrudging nod.

"So, with Judge Harry out of the way, you might get a judge that is more sympathetic to your side of the lawsuit," Joe pushes. He sits forward in his chair, challenging them.

"Hey, it's not like that." Brian sits forward too, eyes flashing.

"And we wouldn't kill someone over the money," Katie says quickly, a hand on her husband's arm in warning. Andre is quiet, but he nods in agreement, following the founders' lead, as seems to be his tendency.

"Why not? Money is a powerful motive," Joe asserts, trying to get them to give something away.

"Be-because we aren't like that," Katie stammers, incensed at the line of questioning. Or at least pretending she is.

"I think we're done here," Brian stands, his posture threatening: chest thrust out, hands fisted slightly.

Joe stands, his hands wide in supplication. "Okay, okay, I just had to be sure. I apologize. Please sit." He gestures to Brian's empty chair.

Brian hesitates. Uncertainty registers on his face. Slowly he sits back in his seat, his jaw still clenched.

"I'm sorry, but I'm going to have to ask you all to account for your whereabouts on Monday at 1:00 a.m.," Joe says pleasantly, as agreeably as if he's merely asking for directions.

There's a huffy silence and for a moment I think they might refuse. I see it dawn on them that this is mandatory, not just a pleasant request. It might not be important where they were since it looks like a professional hit, but they don't know that. Unless they hired the hit.

"Brian and I were home asleep," Katie says.

"Can anyone verify that?" Joe asks.

"No."

"Andre?" Joe turns to him.

"I was home asleep too."

"Can anyone verify that?"

"No."

The fact that they didn't have a ready alibi might mean they weren't aware in advance they would need one. Unless they didn't know when the hit would be completed. Or, of course, they could be anticipating that having an alibi in the middle of the night would be suspicious itself. It's hard to be sure what it means.

"Anything else you think we should know?" I ask.

Stony silence is the response. Brian has his arms crossed defensively. Andre won't look anyone in the eye. Katie looks rattled. We're no longer on the theme park tour.

"We need to speak with your accountant next please, and we'll need to see all of your personal financial records as well." Joe says pleasantly.

Brian hesitates.

"We can get warrants," Joe says, just as pleasantly.

"That won't be necessary," Brian says. "We have nothing to hide."

Gone is the friendly atmosphere we encountered upon arriving here. We're abruptly left alone in the meeting area. It's quite a while before the accountant arrives and even longer before the company financial records we requested are brought. Thankfully, the owners' personal financial records have also been obtained, each in a separate envelope with "private" marked on the front.

We wade into the records, looking for large payments

or withdrawals and checking on the financial health of the company.

"Are you finding anything suspicious?" Joe asks sometime later, just as I begin to feel cross-eyed from going through all the mind-numbing numbers.

"No large withdrawals or payments from the company or from any of the individuals," I reply.

"Okay. I didn't find any either. Maybe we're barking up the wrong tree," Joe quips, glancing at one of the large trees left intact in the lobby, its branches reaching up to where we sit. I roll my eyes at the obvious joke.

"Is it just natural to start telling bad jokes when you become a father? You know, the horrible dad-jokes that you probably remember your own dad telling? Well, that's you now."

Joe laughs good naturedly. "Yes. That's exactly how it happens. Only gets worse when you become a grandfather." He winks.

When we exit the building, I get a look at Joe's shoes. "Ah, red shoelaces. That's why you're so fiery today."

He closes the cruiser door, so our words aren't overheard. "Could be. I also don't like liars."

"You think they're lying?" I had the same thought.

"I would bet money on it."

# CHAPTER NINE

We pick up a takeout lunch on the way back to the precinct. It's rather lacking in comparison to the lunch which we saw being prepared at GuidanceLink. Nonetheless, I down it hungrily at my desk. Joe's desk is the one across from mine and the two desks couldn't look more different. The surface of my desk is bare except for my computer and, of course, the pen holder made from a revolver cylinder that my best friend Isabella gave me as a gift when I became a detective. Joe's desk is cluttered with files and the paperwork he likes to print out, even though it's available on his computer. His keyboard is basically a paperweight.

Sofia has forwarded the personal documents we requested on the night of the murder and Simon has given us access to the judge's computer files. Joe and I sift through the data carefully. Sofia and the judge had a joint bank account. I don't find any unusual transactions: no large sums deposited or withdrawn. We look through both Sofia and Judge Harry's emails, phone records and social media, opening message after message and searching for suspicious content. I don't find anything that indicates that either Sofia or Harry was having an affair. Neither of them even had a close friend of the opposite gender. And nothing appears to be a message to a contract killer from Sofia—coded or otherwise.

After taking care of the tedious paperwork, we head over to the house to speak with the judge's wife again. Maybe she'll have some clearer ideas about who might've had a grudge against her husband now that she's had some rest and time to think.

The home looks smaller somehow without the flashing lights of the emergency vehicles and without every lightbulb glowing as it was on the night the judge died.

Sofia takes a while to answer our ring. We know she's expecting us because we called ahead, but when she appears, it looks as if she just got out of bed. Her hair is even more tangled than it was yesterday. She hasn't made any attempt at makeup, and her clothes consist of a pair of leggings and a creased t-shirt. She seems like the kind of woman who isn't used to being seen without her hair and makeup perfectly done. Now it seems she's too upset to care.

Through her thin clothing, I again note the slightly showing pregnancy. While we were investigating Sofia's records earlier, I looked up what an unborn baby looks like at four months. It's almost five inches long, as big as an avocado, the article said. Skin is translucent. Hair is starting to grow. Ears are developing and the baby can hear, which surprised me. Also, I found out that Sofia is probably just starting to feel her moving.

Letting us in, Sofia leads us to the formal living room this time. I take a seat opposite her in a stylish but stiff armchair.

After giving her a moment to gather herself, I begin. "Now that things have calmed down a bit, we wanted to ask you about the judge's current case and some of his past ones."

She nods. "Harry was strict about not discussing his current cases. Even with me. But I knew, of course, that he was overseeing the GuidanceLink case. Anyone watching the local news would know that."

"Did he have any concerns about the case that he shared with you?" I ask.

"No, he wouldn't have. I knew what the case was about from scrolling online, and that it was a bench trial. I'm sure the GuidanceLink executives would've been worried that Harry was assigned the case. He had a weak spot for the underdog. Cases where workers were taken advantage of really made him mad. It's one of the things I loved about him." She brushes briskly at a tear and smooths her tangled hair.

"Speaking of cases where employees were taken advantage of, are you aware of a case from about seven years ago where some apple orchard employees brought suit against the owner of a large orchard in Wenatchee Valley?" I ask.

"Yes. That was one of the cases that had Harry up at night pacing. I remember it was right after we got married. After the case, he told me some of the details. The Apple-A-Day Orchards barely fed those poor immigrant workers and made them climb high up in trees to pick apples even when they were sick. Some workers died because they weren't permitted to have time off to see a doctor. The whole thing sounded abusive and horrible. The orchard owner got what he deserved."

"The orchard owner lost everything. He was barely able to hang on to the land. It looks like he had to take on some outside investors just to carry on. Was the judge ever concerned they may come after him out of revenge?" Joe asks.

"If Harry was worried, he never let on. He never let that kind of thing creep into our private lives. Looking back, I think that was a real gift he gave me—at least the illusion of carrying on a normal life."

"In the past, he ruled on trials with murderers and violent offenders. Did any of them make him nervous?" Joe asks.

Sofia thinks for a moment and then shakes her head no.

"We're particularly interested in a man by the name of Barry Greenworth who was released recently after serving twenty years for second degree murder," Joe says.

"I remember the trial, though it was long before I met Harry. But it was famous in Seattle because the killing was so senseless and violent. Didn't he stab a co-conspirator something like thirty times?"

"That's right." I can't help but think of the crime scene photos. All that blood—something you can't un-see. The victim was unrecognizable. "He always maintained his innocence, and he sent the judge some pretty creative threats."

"Did he still hold a grudge after all this time?" Sofia asks.

"Based on the threats, it seemed he did," I say with a glance at Sofia's intact fingers, thinking of the threat Chris mentioned.

"I guess Harry never chose to share that with me."

*I can see why.* "Is there anything else you remember that might help us?"

Sofia thinks for a moment, pulling on her long hair. "Sorry, detectives, Harry always seemed so invincible. It never even entered my mind that someone could do this." Her eyes are glazed with unshed tears.

# CHAPTER TEN

When Joe and I part ways that night, I head over to Isabella's apartment. Somewhat reluctantly, I'll admit. Typically, I would love to spend as much time as possible with my best friend, but right now, she's fully consumed with wedding preparations. And I've discovered that all these wedding decor choices are not in my comfort zone. But when I reach her door, I put a brave smile on my face because tonight we're getting our final dress fittings done together and I love the idea of a little bonding time right now, just the two of us.

At my knock, Isabella opens her apartment door with a flourish, glitter and sequins clinging to her hair and clothing.

I pick a sequin out of her hair. "Does this stuff just start following you around after you get engaged? Because if so, I want no part of it."

She shakes her head to liberate the remaining sequins but has little success. "Yes, beware the glitter!" she says in an ominous voice, then laughs. "My mom and aunt have been putting together the centerpieces and....Come here, I need your opinion." She grabs my hand to keep me from escaping and drags me into the apartment after her.

"It's like a bridal catalog threw up in here," I comment. String lights, candles, sequins, and some sort of flouncy fabric are strewn everywhere. I dodge some large glass cylinders sitting on the floor as Isabella pulls me across the room.

"I know. The decorations have taken over my apartment. But my mom wants me to make a choice. And as the maid of honor you are required to help me. Do you like this one better, or this one?" She points to two completed centerpieces. Huge glass orbs are layered with white candles, sand, starfish, and shells. Isabella's wedding theme is nature and the ocean. If the two centerpieces she pointed out are different, I can't tell. I give her a pained face.

"Right." She laughs at the face I made. "I can't tell them apart either. I think I'll go with this one."

I nod my approval. Happy to go along with whatever she chooses. This is definitely not my area of expertise. Isabella has been gracious about letting me off the hook for certain maid of honor tasks that just aren't my thing. I've got her back for the bachelorette party, but hot glue is not my kind of gun.

"Okay, let me freshen up and then let's go." She runs a brush through her long, dark hair, removing the flotsam.

Turning, she trips over some ribbon on the floor and mutters something colorful under her breath. Mercifully, we leave, escaping the wedding decoration wreckage.

The bridal "boutique" is in fact a large store with many suites of rooms catering to the extravagant affair that wedding dress shopping has become. Fitting rooms are spacious, built for both the bride-to-be and an attendant to help her into the impossibly elaborate wedding gowns. One cannot possibly don one of these dresses without help. The fitting room opens out into a private observation area where friends and family can sit comfortably in swivel chairs and comment as the bride-to-be models each dress in front of a wall of angled mirrors.

I accompanied Isabella many months ago on the day she selected the dress. We were a seven-woman entourage composed of myself, Isabella's mom, her aunt, a cousin, and three other close friends. We sat sipping the champagne offered by the bridal attendant as Isabella modeled gown after gown.

Isabella is thirty-four and an independent woman in all respects. Her parents are from humble means and though they wish to contribute to the wedding as much as possible, Isabella and Darius know it will be a joint venture with them paying for some of it as well. With that in mind, we went looking for "the dress" with a firm budget from the outset.

The first dresses Isabella modeled were traditional; plump and frothy, encrusted with sequins and pearls. Clearly these were selected by her attendant, thinking Isabella wanted to embrace the role of princess on her wedding day. It was like putting a leopard in a tutu; incongruous, and with neither enhancing the other. She was lost in the frills, and they stole the limelight from her. We all ooohed and ahhhed on cue, but the dresses weren't right at all.

Seeing that the initial selection was falling flat, the attendant experimented with some non-traditional gowns, each of us contributing our own selections. We were getting closer. She looked gorgeous in a slim off the shoulder gown that her mother selected, but it wasn't quite special enough. After hours of dress-up, Isabella was showing signs of tiring, and she still hadn't found "the one."

Scanning the dresses for what seemed like the thousandth time, I pulled out a sleek dress in a soft, elegant material with spaghetti straps, a V-neck, scooped back and a figure skimming flared hem. "Try this one for me," I told her. She wrinkled her nose at the unfamiliar style but disappeared into the dressing room to try it anyway.

When she walked out in it, she took my breath away. As she turned to face the mirrors, I could see the moment she really saw herself. Her chin raised. She turned in front of the mirrors, taking in all the angles. We were silent, just taking it in. The simple, elegant cut showcased her beauty and didn't distract from it. She looked bold and fearless and stylish. *So—her.* I felt the tears well up, because now I could imagine her saying her vows and committing herself to Darius.

Isabella reached around, looking for the price-tag. I admit, I hadn't looked at the price, caught up in trying to find something that did her justice. It was a dress by a known designer, bound to be expensive. Now I internally winced, knowing that it would be out of our budget.

Isabella's mom also sensed the critical moment. She snatched a pair of scissors off the seamstress's desk and ran toward Isabella. The attendant cried out, seeing the scissors approaching the precious dress. Isabella's mom quickly cut the price tag off before Isabella could see it.

"It doesn't matter what it costs, this dress was meant for you. It's my wedding gift to you," she said.

Well, there wasn't a dry eye in the room.

Fast forward to tonight: we're back for the final fitting and a trial run at hair and makeup. It's just the two of us. Isabella wanted tonight to be our special moment. I endure having my hair sculpted and my face made up and then wrangle myself into the bridesmaid's dress with the help of Isabella's attendant. Then I take my place in one of the swivel chairs and await Isabella. My dress is pinching uncomfortably by the time she appears.

When Isabella walks out in front of the mirrors, I catch my breath yet again and my eyes well with tears. The dress has been expertly altered to complement her curves. The simple lines contrast her dramatic beauty, drawing attention to her rich warm skin tone, high cheek bones, and silky, dark hair. As a nod to her native heritage, she's chosen to wear her hair pulled back with two white eagle feathers tucked into an oyster-shell clasp. Pearls grace her throat and wrist. I blink back tears, trying not to let my mascara run. *She's really doing this.*

"You're gorgeous!" I tell her. "Darius is going to be a wreck when he sees you walking down the aisle toward him."

She laughs. "The man cries when we watch a sad episode of *Friends*. He's going to be a puddle no matter how I look."

"And look at *you*." She gives me an approving look. "Have you seen how you look?"

I look in the mirror and agree that, for a bridesmaid's dress, the gown is pretty flattering. A sophisticated floor-length gown in deep blue, it emphasizes all the right curves and matches the blue of my eyes. My dark hair is in loose waves, cascading down my back.

Isabella snaps a photo of me and texts it to Blake. "Catnip for later," she quips, giving me a wink.

After we're carefully extricated from our gowns, we head to Bar None for a drink. We're still wearing the flattering makeup with our perfectly done hair. We have to politely decline a couple rounds of drinks sent our way by men at the bar. After the second round, Isabella positions herself with her chin resting on her hand, displaying her rather large engagement ring.

"Subtle." I laugh.

"But effective." She grins. "So...how's Dr. McHunky?"

"Good. Still got that spark." I give her a sly grin.

"I sense a 'but.'"

"But...we're hitting that point where it's starting to seem silly for us to keep going back and forth between our apartments."

"Do you think you're ready to move in together?" she asks, one perfectly penciled eyebrow raised.

"Maybe. I'm not sure Blake is allowed to have pets in his apartment."

"So...your place?"

"No. I think if we take that step, I'd like to look for a new place. I like the idea of finding something that suits both of us."

"Sounds wise."

"How about you? Have you found that perfect house yet?" Isabella and Darius have been house hunting. I just hope they won't end up too far away for us to share a weekend run or an after-work drink.

"Not yet. I knew we had different tastes, but I didn't realize how difficult it would be to find something we both like. I want something bright and cheery, with some history. He wants something slick and new. It seems we need a house that has a split personality. Maybe we'll find an older home with character that I like, and we can renovate one side for him."

I chuckle, imagining a house split down the middle into two completely separate personalities, with paint changing in the middle and a living room with furniture with a different look on each side of the midline. "You might be on to something. But seriously, maybe you'll find an older home with the charm you're looking for but completely remodeled bathrooms and kitchen."

"Sounds perfect but does that exist?"

"In my dreams. At least you don't have a pet to consider. I never realized I would get so attached to Stalker." The cat was made an orphan when a victim lost her life. I took him in, thinking I would just take care of him until I found him a home. But now I can't imagine letting him go. He's become a part of my life.

This remaining time with unmarried Isabella is fragile and precious. It's possibly the last time we'll have a moment together, just the two of us, before she gets married in less than two weeks. I wish I could stop time and hold onto this moment. I know I'm experiencing the last of something, but it's slipping through my fingers. I'm determined to enjoy the moment enough that it lives up to its weight—the significance I'll later put on it, the anticipated nostalgia.

# CHAPTER ELEVEN

*"Abigail, we will never get you to the church on time if you don't stand still!" My mother is past having any patience with me. She spent all morning tugging my hair into an elaborate updo. With the added hair pieces and the curls, twists, and braids, it was quite an ordeal. I'm relieved that all that remains is putting on the layers that make up my wedding outfit...at least until I discovered just what that would entail.*

*Now I'm standing in my stockings and cotton chemise while my mother fusses with the laces on my corset. She can't seem to get them tight enough for her liking.*

*"Mother, these new corsets are so long and tight, I can't breathe—" I try to appeal to her, but she only pulls harder on the laces, using her foot to brace herself while she puts her strength into tying them as tightly as possible.*

*"This is a special day, you must look your best," she says in reply, as she grunts in effort.*

*I can't use any of the clever retorts on the tip of my tongue because I can barely get air into my lungs. After years of suffering with corsets, I've mastered the art of drawing tiny breaths that don't require movement of my ribcage. Resorting to this technique, I soon feel less short of breath. But the torment is far from over.*

*Next is the corset cover.*

*Then my mother attaches the bustle. I will never understand why I must place a huge horsehair pad over my caboose just to be fashionable. Oh, and the itching!*

*"Abigail, stay still!" My mother adjusts the bustle, the horsehair poking into my backside. I try to stay as still as possible. This is not the day to ruffle my mother's feathers.*

*Next are the petticoats, two placed over the bustle. Two!*

*Then the underskirt.*

*Finally, the wedding dress goes over top of it all. My mother sets to work doing up what seems like hundreds of tiny buttons on the bodice.*

*When the last button, high up on my neck, is fastened, my mother steps back to take in the effect. I'm surprised to see tears fill her eyes. "Oh, Abigail," she whispers. "You are a beautiful bride." She sighs.*

*I step in front of the full-length mirror in my mother's dressing room. I have to admit, all her ministrations have left me looking quite fetching indeed. I find myself smiling in spite of feeling like a trussed-up turkey.*

*Opening a secret compartment in her dressing table, my mother applies powder to my face and a rosy tint to my lips. I cough at the clouds of powder, waving them away. My mother shakes her head at my theatrics. She places a sixpence in one of my satin slippers and helps me put them on.*

*I must have "something old, something new, something borrowed, something blue, and a sixpence in my shoe," or so the rhyme goes. My mother feels the need to keep up with all the new traditions coming out of London. She's sewn a blue ribbon inside my dress for the "new" and the "blue."*

*Now she pulls out her precious string of pearls. "Something 'old' and something 'borrowed,'" she says as she ties them around my neck.*

*I swallow the lump in my throat. For all her prickliness, my mother truly cares.*

*She fusses over getting my veil properly placed, but I can tell it's to cover her own raw emotions. "Alright, dearest, it's time to go." I smile at the familiar endearment. She's called me "dearest" for as long as I can remember.*

*She leads me down the stairs and through the parlor. The grandfather clock strikes two o'clock as we pass. Already late!*

*As we pull up to the church, I notice the large number of carriages belonging to friends and family. My stomach clenches in knots, anticipating the large crowd inside.*

*Seeing my distress, my father grips my hand firmly. "I am so proud to walk you down the aisle and give you away," he says in a near whisper. The kind words from my austere father surprise me. He gently helps me down from the carriage and steers me toward the front entry of the church as my mother hurries to take her seat.*

*As the doors of the church open, I see William, my dear Will, standing at the front. He looks so handsome in his dark blue morning coat. And relieved ... yes, he looks relieved to see me—I'm so very late!*

*Will's face transforms as he takes in my appearance. Meeting his eyes, suddenly, my case of nerves drops away. This is where I was always meant to be...with Will. He is my true north, my kindred spirit. Being with him feels like going home.*

*The music starts and an audible gasp goes up from the guests as they stand and turn toward the church door. But I only have eyes for Will.*

*I start down the aisle, one arm supported by my father, the other clutching tight to my bouquet. When we reach the front of the church, my father passes my hand to Will.*

*The minister leads us through our vows, but I am barely listening as I recite the words. My eyes are held by Will's; everything else falls away.*

*Later, I take in the celebration at my parents' home—the large platters of venison, goose and duck, oysters, soups and vegetable side dishes, the large wedding cake in the corner, the gifts displayed on the sideboard. It's only then that I finally have a moment to take it all in: the love of friends and family.*

*I gaze at Will, across the room, catching his eye. He smiles... and I see the promise of forever written there on his face.*

I wake from the dream, as blissfully happy as Abby. Well, of course I'm dreaming of weddings after last night spent with Isabella anticipating her own union. What a contrast my past life Abby's wedding in the late eighteen hundreds was to what Isabella has planned. And that dress! The memory of the tight corset still has me short of breath.

It takes a moment for reality to set in as I remember the current murder case—the killer we must bring to justice. Another day of investigating looms ahead.

I better get a move on; we have a long drive ahead of us today.

# CHAPTER TWELVE

It's still dark when I park in the precinct lot. Joe places steaming cups of coffee in the cup holders of our cruiser as I slide into the driver's seat to take the first shift. We're headed to the "apple capital of the world," the Wenatchee Valley, and it will take a couple of hours to get there.

The drive takes us east toward the Cascades then winds through forests as it climbs toward Stevens Pass. It's a beautiful drive with the sun rising over the mountains ahead of us and glimpses of the Skykomish River running beside us. As we drive, Joe goes through the case file of Apple-A-Day Orchards.

"The orchard is owned by the Mason family. Greg Mason is married and has a son and a daughter...she died in her teens, a suicide." Joe flips through the thick file. "It sounds like the company was breaking every rule when it comes to these poor workers. Trying to cut corners and improve their profits."

I shake my head. "And all in the name of making more

money. Disgusting. I feel sorry for those workers, but why didn't they leave?"

"They were all seasonal, almost all from Mexico on H-2A visas. I suspect by the time they arrived here and discovered the working and living conditions, it was too late to change their mind."

"I see. And even though the employer was breaking the law, the workers wouldn't know the system well enough to find a lawyer to represent their rights."

"Right. Also, it says the workers were threatened with deportation if they complained. And to make matters worse, if they were sent home, they had to pay for their own transportation. According to the notes, a lawyer, Andy Rodriguez, found out about their situation and brought the case forward himself. It looks like he had a difficult time getting the workers to testify. Only a few of them agreed to be deposed."

"How did Rodriguez become aware of their situation?"

Joe flips through some notes. "A worker died of dehydration after being denied medical care. When he was finally taken to a hospital, he was too sick to recover. Rodriguez took the case on pro bono to help the workers."

"Out of the goodness of his heart?"

"Yes, but of course he would get a cut of any financial settlement."

"Why was the orchard so far out of compliance with labor laws?"

"According to the complaint, in 2018, the Safety and Access for Immigrant Victims Act was passed and visa holders were brought under the protections of the labor laws. The Apple-A-Day Orchards were slow at making these changes. The deposed workers told stories of crowded cabins with bunks jammed together to fit workers fifty to a cabin. Men and women were separated, meaning husbands and wives couldn't stay together. It says there were two outhouses for fifty workers."

"Yuck, I can't even imagine how bad the smell would be."

"Each day, they would be packed onto buses to get to the orchards, some standing in the aisles. They worked every day. No days off. Even if it was too hot or if it was raining. One worker talks about how his face would be peeling and sunburned, and his feet grew fungus from his wet and muddy boots."

"Sounds horrible. Didn't they have gloves or hats?"

"No. And he mentions how they didn't have masks to protect against the chemical sprays either. Also, you guessed it, no health care. And they couldn't take time off to go to a doctor anyway."

"Brutal."

"One woman talks about constantly lifting heavy apple boxes. She says they weren't given any breaks, but since pay was by the number of boxes of apples picked, no one wanted a break anyway. Partial boxes didn't count. She says it was hard to pick enough apples to live off the wage."

"Sounds miserable."

"A doctor went out with officers on a warrant to evaluate the conditions. He reported dehydration, heat stress, strain injuries, and chemical irritation. The report also says the food provided was barely adequate."

*What are we going to find at the Apple-A-Day Orchards today?* The company better have changed their ways. Certainly, they'll be showing us their best side. They don't want another lawsuit.

As we pass the mountains, we descend into the open valley, and the patchwork quilt of orchards comes into view. Row upon row of fruit trees stretch down to the Wenatchee River, across hillsides and eventually to the Columbia River in the east.

The weather is noticeably warmer here, and we pass fruit stands and vineyards.

"Let's stop for some breakfast," I say on a whim, pulling off at a fruit stand.

The owner is still setting up for the day, but he waves us in, happy to make a sale. We browse the boxes full of fat, plump Bing cherries and a few of the pink and yellow Rainier variety. Jars of homemade jams are stacked on shelves, and bags of dried fruit hang from rotating racks. But I don't see many apples.

Bringing a bag of fresh cherries to the register, I ask the owner about it. "I notice you don't have many apples. They not in season yet?"

"Naw, not yet. We won't get fresh apples until August. Gala first, then Honeycrisp in September, Braeburn in October. Those over there are from last year's harvest. They were in cold storage until now."

"I knew this area produced a lot of apples, but it still surprised me when I saw the number of orchards in the valley. Why do the apples grow so well here?" I ask.

"It's the hot days and cool nights in the valley. Gives the apples the deep red color and sweet flavor."

We thank the owner, and Joe takes over driving as we get back in the cruiser. Passing more apple trees, I look closer and see that the apples are still green and golf-ball sized.

We head for the address that Bob provided. His contact is the owner, Greg Mason.

At the sign for Apple-A-Day Orchards, we turn off the road, and I couldn't be more surprised by what we encounter. Instead of large trees widely spaced apart, there are many very small trees placed closely together and supported by trellises. As we pull up the long drive, the rows stretch off in every direction. The orchard appears to be a very commercial operation compared to most of the small farms we've passed. It seems the company managed a spectacular comeback after losing everything.

Even though it's not yet harvest season, there's still a bustle of activity in the fields. Several mowers are trimming grass between the rows of trees and workers are up on platforms in the orchard. The apples aren't ripe yet. *What could they be doing?*

We pass clusters of small, cheerful-looking huts, which I imagine are the workers' accommodations. They don't look like the fifty-person cabins described in the lawsuit.

There are fire pits and barbeques and picnic tables set under shady trellises in the center of each cluster of huts.

A charming stone building in the center of the orchards has signs that mark the office and gift shop and one advertising tours of the facility.

When we open the office door, a perky young woman looks up from an information desk, an automatic smile forming as she prepares to greet us. This falters as she sees our badges.

"We are here to see Mr. Mason," Joe announces.

She nods, rising from her chair. "He told me you were coming, detectives. Right this way." She leads us down a hallway and knocks on a heavy wooden door with a brass nameplate.

The door swings open briskly, and a tall man in his fifties greets us. "Detectives, I'm Greg Mason. Come on in." His voice is cordial and friendly, no hint of concern. He shakes our hands with a warm, firm grip. "Please sit."

Greg Mason is a handsome man. His posture exudes confidence. His thick blonde hair is barely starting to gray, and his figure is lean and trim. His button-up denim shirt is form-fitting enough to reveal a well-muscled torso. He wears jeans and very expensive cowboy boots.

His large desk faces out over floor-to-ceiling picture windows with a sweeping view of the orchards. It's stunning. We sit across from his large desk in small, unnaturally low chairs, our backs to the view. Seems he read the manual on how to intimidate your guests.

The receptionist brings us all bottled water, which she places on coasters.

"Now what can I do for you, detectives?" Mason asks, his brows raised, his features carefully arranged in the very picture of innocence.

"Mr. Mason, I'm not sure if you were aware of the passing of Judge Harold Clifton," Joe starts.

I watch Greg Mason's face. His features remain carefully neutral.

"I saw it on the news. So sad." He looks anything but sad. "I suspected your visit had to do with that."

"Right." Joe clears his throat, taking his time. "We know you had a strained relationship with the judge. He was pretty hard on you. Gave you a lot of reasons to hold a grudge."

"I could see how you might think that. But look around." He gestures at the striking view. "That lawsuit forced me to take in outside financing and upgrade the place. Best thing that ever happened to me. As you can see, Apple-A-Day Orchards is now a very profitable, modern farm. My workers couldn't be happier with the upgraded facilities. They're fairly compensated and have every labor protection."

It sounds just a little too good to be true.

"I'll admit I was surprised to see how much your farm is thriving," I say. "We were led to believe that the settlement imposed by the judge was financially devastating for you."

"And so it was, at first," Mason admits gravely. "But once I was forced to take on outside financing, I was able to invest in modern upgrades, which have allowed the orchard to become extremely profitable. I paid off the settlement, and my investors are pleased with the returns and continue to reinvest. So, you see, ultimately the judge's ruling changed my life for the better."

It does seem like a success story the way Mason tells it, but the tale also sounds a little rehearsed. I'm not sure what to believe.

"I can see you are skeptical, detectives. Please, allow me to take you for a tour."

Mason leads us outside to a golf cart, and we drive back down the entry road. He gestures to the trellised trees we saw coming in. "These trees are specially trained and trimmed for high-density growth and high apple yield. They are supported by trellises and wires. It's called a spindle system."

"What are the workers doing out there right now?" I ask, remembering my thought as we drove up the road that it seemed odd to have workers in the field when the apples weren't ripe yet.

"They are removing all but one apple from a cluster so

that the remaining ones have more space and grow larger. It's called 'thinning.'"

"Do you have workers all year long?"

"We rotate workers. Some return to Mexico and new ones come on the visas. There are always workers coming and going. Right now, we have trimmers and planters, maintenance workers, and thinners. The pickers and packers come August to October. Hundreds of workers will come through here in the next few months.

"And we have other workers too." He smiles. "Up on that hillside over there are the beehives to ensure good pollination of the trees." He points toward a cluster of wooden structures on a rise away from the other buildings.

"I also have a tech crew that uses computers to monitor soil moisture and deliver precise fertilizer blends. Improves the yields. It's all quite high tech now. We even have drones to monitor tree health, pests, and irrigation needs. And for security."

"If everything is so automated now, why don't you have mechanical pickers?" I ask.

"They don't beat hand-picking. Too many bruises on the apples. We do have GPS-guided tractors, though. They pull a line of large harvesting bins with picking platforms. Workers stand on the platforms to pick, putting the apples in the bins, and then full bins are brought to the packing house where they are washed and sorted. Apples are then packed and sent to market, and some are put in cold storage. Those sorting and packing buildings are up on the other side of that hill. We give tours of the orchard and buildings, and it's proved to be just as lucrative a business as the apples themselves."

Mason pulls the golf cart up to the workers' huts. They're

arranged in clusters around an outdoor area surrounded by wooden pergolas. Clusters of huts are arranged in a line leading away from the road. There are so many huts that the line disappears over the next hillside. I can see why they need hundreds of workers in harvest season.

Mason shows us the inside of one of the huts. It's clean and cozy with a kitchen area, showers, and several bedrooms. A lone worker is eating his lunch at one of the outdoor picnic tables. It feels a little staged.

"José, could you join us?" Mason gestures to the man who comes over with a nervous smile. He looks robust and healthy. "These detectives are here to see how the facilities for our workers have improved. Why don't you tell them how much you like the new accommodations?"

The man bobs his head agreeably and smiles. "It's very nice," he says in accented English. "Work is good. Mr. Mason is a good man."

"You like working here?" Joe asks.

"Oh, yes. It's very good. Everybody wants to work here. We are the lucky ones." He gives a crooked smile.

"Thanks, José," Mason dismisses him.

Mason turns to us. "We learned our lesson after the trial. Now we have field supervisors who make work assignments and oversee the work and breaks. Workers put in eight-hour days, six days a week, which is below the industry standard. Water is provided as well as hats, gloves, and sun protection. We even have rain slickers for rainy days. PPE is provided for chemical applications. There's also an on-site medical facility for any injuries or illnesses. I don't mind saying that the workers compete to come here since we changed our ways."

I'm impressed. It seems the orchard has really made

strides to improve the working conditions. I can't really see how a man like Greg Mason would continue to hold a grudge against the judge when things seem to have turned out so well for him. The tension I had coming out here to confront Mason relaxes out of my shoulders. It seems this is a success story.

Mason heads the golf cart back toward the stone building. As we pull up to the office, a worker is being made to leave the premises forcibly with two well-built men who appear to be security. Seeing us, the man pulls his arms away from the hold of security and fires rapid Spanish at Mason, his face pinched in distress.

Mason's face transforms to barely concealed rage and he returns with his own rapid stream of Spanish.

The man pulls at his hair and paces, avoiding our eyes. Joe and I glance at each other. *What the heck?*

The security guards regrip the man's arms and hustle him away.

"Do you mind enlightening us as to that exchange?" Joe confronts Mason.

Mason's face smooths back into the infomercial version. "Ah, just a routine issue. Nothing to concern yourself with. But I'm sorry, I'll have to cut our visit short. I have to help get things sorted out." His nonchalance doesn't quite ring true. He shepherds us to the cruiser and sees us off.

A couple of workers who must have accompanied the distressed man stand outside the office. When they see me looking, they turn away and rush off into the orchard.

Hmmm, it appears we may have just had a glimpse of something rotten under the carefully curated façade.

# CHAPTER THIRTEEN

It's late afternoon when we get back to the precinct. We give Garcia an update on our findings at the orchard, both its improvements and the strange exchange at the end of our visit.

A pile of paper awaits us on Joe's desk. Bob has collected everything he can find on Barry Greenworth, court transcripts, police interviews, the court file, and, of course, the threats we suspect he sent the judge.

I pull out the court transcripts to get a sense of the issues.

"It looks like Greenworth was accused of killing Matthew Speck because of a disagreement over some stolen jewelry. Stabbed him thirty times."

I pull out the crime scene photos and wince. "There's blood everywhere from all the stab wounds. Most of them are around the head and neck.

"The murder weapon was found in a nearby dumpster." There's a photo of a pocketknife and another of the gems. "The diamonds were in Speck's pocket."

I go back to the court transcripts and skim through. "The

assailant was right-handed, as is Greenworth. The case never went to trial because Greenworth confessed at the time of his arrest and at his arraignment, he pleaded guilty."

"What was the supposed disagreement?" Joe asks.

"The prosecution's theory is that they had an argument over the value of the diamonds and in the heat of the moment, Greenworth attacked Speck."

"Stabbing someone thirty times seems extreme if they just disagreed over the price," Joe comments.

I nod. It does seem excessive. Stabbing someone thirty times takes rage, passion. "There's got to be more to the story. Some shared history or something," I suggest.

"The prosecution would've needed to prove the crime occurred as they suggested, even if they had a confession," Joe comments.

"Right, the corpus delicti rule. They had to prove the confession fit the facts. Greenworth's confession was pretty vague, but they had all the evidence they needed, what with the money, the diamonds, Speck's blood on Greenworth, and the murder weapon nearby."

"How was Greenworth apprehended?" Joe asks.

"Someone called to report the altercation, and when the police arrived, Greenworth was fleeing the scene with ten thousand in cash on him. The diamonds were found on Speck."

"That sounds pretty incriminating."

"Right. And if that wasn't enough, they had the confession."

"So, if he confessed, why was Greenworth so angry with the judge?" Joe asks.

"It looks like the judge rejected the plea deal put forward by the prosecution. They recommended ten years for second-degree murder. They can ask for ten to twenty, so it was a minimum sentence. The judge said that since the murder occurred during the commission of a felony—purchasing stolen goods over a thousand dollars in value—that he would impose the maximum sentence of twenty years, no chance of parole."

"The judge can only change the sentence if he warned Greenworth and gave him the choice to withdraw his plea," Joe says.

I flip through the court proceedings. "It looks like the judge gave the warning but Greenworth didn't change his plea."

"He must've taken the gamble that it would only be a slight increase," Joe comments.

"But it turned into a maximum sentence. No wonder he was angry. But angry enough to kill him? And a quick bullet to the head is sure a different approach than the stabbing of Speck."

"True," Joe says. "But one was a crime of passion, the other premeditated. It could look different, even with the same killer."

"Bob's been trying to find Greenworth. I'll check on his progress." Joe gets on his phone and has a short conversation with Bob. Then, hanging up the phone, he shakes his head. "Bob wasn't able to locate him. He'll keep trying."

Blake and I decide to go out for dinner that night. It's his turn to choose and I find myself seated at an intimate table in a cozy Italian place. The smells wafting out of the kitchen are divine and I'm eagerly anticipating the pasta I ordered.

"This place reminds me of our first date. Remember we had Italian?" I ask Blake with a wry smile.

Blake chuckles. "I'm unlikely to ever forget it. All first dates tend to be memorable, but you really took it to the next level."

"What?" I say with mock-innocence. "Most guys would be attracted to a girl with a gun. You know, all that danger—most men love that."

"That might be true," he says, taking a bite of his pasta. "But they probably draw the line at having the gun pointed at them. And being accused of a crime on top of it."

I laugh. "You got me there." Not one of my finest moments. "So, you're saying that you prefer your extreme gestures to look more like John Cusack in *Say Anything*?" We'd watched the classic movie recently where Cusack's character stands outside the window of the woman he loves, after they've broken up, holding up a boom box and playing "In Your Eyes" in order to win her back. Blake thought it was corny, but I appreciated the vulnerability he showed...not putting any pressure on her, just declaring his love.

"I guess so," Blake laughs. "Although I feel like it would be a grand gesture for you to just come out to dinner with me and leave your gun at home." He winks knowingly.

Guiltily, I finger the firearm strapped under my blouse. "Got me there." He knows me too well. And he's right, I really should be able to lower my defenses enough to enjoy a meal with him without bringing my firearm. Admittedly, I have a problem with being too vigilant, even for someone who's seen the very worst of human behavior.

After we finish our meal, Blake takes my hand. "Come with me. I want to show you something."

Intrigued, I follow him. "Where are we going?" I ask.

"You'll see," he says mysteriously. He locates our waiter

and tells him, "We'd like to have a Tarot card reading."

This is news to me. I've never had a reading done, but I find the idea interesting.

"Right this way," our waiter says. He leads us up to a large mirror at the back of the restaurant and stops.

*What are we doing?*

He reaches out and pushes a button I hadn't seen hidden in the frame. The flat portion of the mirror slides aside to reveal a hidden room.

"A speakeasy!" I exclaim.

Blake winks. "I thought you'd like it."

The mirror is so large, we're able to step through it into the speakeasy. A few other couples are nestled into cozy booths in the small, dimly lit room. The ambiance is decidedly retro and cool. *I love it.*

We find an empty booth; circular with a small round table, perfect for a couple to sit side by side. A candle burns with an inviting flame in a glass jar on the tabletop. We snuggle in together.

Our waitress approaches. "Welcome to the Reading Room." She hands us drink menus printed on tarot cards held together with a metal ring. Each card features a different drink. Clever.

We each pick a craft cocktail. I love a good Dark and Stormy. Blake orders an Old Fashioned.

As we sip on our drinks, a woman approaches. She's dressed in a long flowing skirt, her hair tied back with a purple scarf, large gold hoops in her ears and layered gold bangles on her arms. She holds out a deck of tarot cards. "I'm Celeste, your tarot card reader for tonight. Would you like to consult the cards?"

I hesitate. I've never had my fortune read. *What if I find out something terrible is ahead of me?* But I'm caught up in the mystery of the moment, so I nod. *What harm can it do? It's only a fun diversion, after all.*

"You go first," I tell Blake.

"Okay." He nods, moving his drink to make way for the cards.

"Alright, sir. What can the cards help you find clarity on tonight?" Celeste asks.

Blake thinks. "Hmmm...I'm thinking of an upcoming occasion. Will it turn out like I hope?"

"Oh, so you're a man of mysterious motives." Celeste smiles, giving me a wink. She shuffles the cards, her gold bangles chiming softly as she moves.

"Now, tell me when to stop shuffling," she instructs Blake. He watches her shuffle a bit more and then says, "Stop."

Celeste places the four top cards on the table face down, in a cross. The candlelight flickers, casting shadows over the cards.

With a glance at Blake, she flips over the first card and smiles slightly. "The lovers. This occasion you're alluding to involves an act of love...of devotion. Someone you burn for... would do anything for. In this position, the card speaks of a blinding love. Possibly a dangerous love." She lets this hang ominously.

"Well, she better be talking about me or dangerous will just be the beginning," I joke.

Blake laughs, but it sounds hollow. *Something seems off but I can't put my finger on it.*

Celeste smiles serenely, unbothered by the tension she's creating, and flips the next card. "The knight of cups, reversed.

All is not as it seems. A misstep. You move too quickly—impulsively. Your actions disrupt the natural course of things, and the result is not as it is intended."

Blake's forehead knits in concern at her words.

"Ah, the seven of swords." Celeste shakes her head at the next card she turns over. "A hidden threat. A danger cloaked in darkness. You won't see them at first. They'll move quietly, stealthily...until the moment of attack."

*I'm not sure I like where this is going.*

Celeste turns over the final card, her bangles gleaming in the candlelight. "The tower. A confrontation. A flash of truth that burns away the illusion. It will change everything. Only what is real will remain."

Blake looks as confused as I am. "You are meant to act," the reader explains, "but not blindly. Love will call you forward. All will turn out well if you can overcome the hidden threat."

"Looks like you better not have that affair after all," I joke and we all laugh, dispelling the tension. *Is he thinking of a proposal?* The prediction is all wrapped up in elusive wording. It means nothing. *Or does it?* I shrug it off, dismissing it as the clever entertainment it's intended to be.

"I think it's your turn," Blake says.

With apprehension, I try to come up with something I need clarity on. "Okay. Tell me if I will discover the murderer in my current investigation." This seems a safe topic. She knows nothing about it. The answers will be vague and reveal the reading for the charade it is, a welcome distraction, but nonetheless, grounded in fiction.

Celeste begins shuffling again, her bangles tinkling. As indicated, I tell her the moment to stop. Again, she lays four cards out face down in the shape of a cross.

She flips over the first card. "The Moon." Her finger rests on the card. "The truth begins with a dream. All is there for you to see. A message half-buried in shadow. But dreams are tricky. What they show is truth wrapped in smoke."

Her words strike a nerve. *How could she know about my dreams?*

I duck my head to hide my confusion.

Unaware of my discomfort, Celeste turns over the next card. Her breath catches. "The hanged man, reversed. You want answers too quickly. You turn the vision upside down, trying to make sense of it—but in doing so, you change what it means. You mistake reflection for urgency and act before the dream has finished speaking."

I feel cold, as if ice is snaking down my back. *This is hitting pretty close to the truth of my reality.*

The next card is turned before I can process the meaning. "The seven of cups. Too many possibilities are at play. Too many dark shadows hiding in the mist. You follow the wrong one, and while you chase the mirage, the real danger walks free."

I'm afraid to see the last card. Slowly, dramatically, Celeste turns it over. The candle gutters and nearly extinguishes. I swear my heart skips a beat. "Justice, reversed. A judge undone. The scales tip. The wrong suspect, the right one unseen." Celeste glances at me. "The truth nearly lost. But reversed cards don't mean endings—they mean chances. The dream will return; you must have the courage to see it clearly this time."

Celeste raises her eyes to mine, as if she can see the truth mirrored there in the candlelight. But I know that she can't.

She doesn't know that her words speak of a truth that she can't possibly be aware of. She laughs mysteriously and gathers the cards again. "Follow your intuition and don't let the guilty go free, Detective," she says.

"How did you know I'm a detective?" I breathe.

She lets out a tinkling laugh. "Well, you did say that you're investigating a murder. A good tarot reader takes in all the information." She smiles. "Provided...or not."

Of course. She's just good at picking up on the details.

Celeste gives me a small smile. "May you have only sweet dreams." Indeed. She leaves the table and heads over to another couple.

Blake reaches out for my hand. "You okay? You look a little spooked. It's not real, you know?"

"Right. Of course." I smile to reassure him.

But the truth is, I'm stunned. It's going to take me a while to shake off this unsettling warning.

# CHAPTER FOURTEEN

*The crush of bodies jostling for position brings on a wave of claustrophobia. I breathe deeply to steady myself, but the smell of sweat and fear does nothing to dispel my sense of dread.*

*Enraged murmurs ripple through the restless crowd, escalating to angry cries in response to something I can't see. Ducking under the arm of the large man in front of me, I push my way forward, desperate to know what's happening.*

*And then, when I set eyes on her, I let out an involuntary gasp. There in the front of the courtroom, in the witness box, is Bethany. My friend. Only I barely recognize her after several nights in a prison cell. Her clothes hang limply, her face dirty, her hair greasy and tangled, eyes bright with fear.*

*"Bethany," I yell, to get her attention, to let her know that someone is here who believes her. Believes in her. But if she hears me over the noise of the crowd, she doesn't look up. Her eyes remain fixed in front of her, her lips moving in what can only be a last prayer for help. If only it didn't appear as if she's talking to herself, maybe even chanting a spell...*

*"Bethany!" Please look at me. Finally, she looks up, as if she heard my silent plea. "Sarah," she mouths, reaching a hand out toward me.*

*"Quiet now!" The magistrate's voice interrupts our silent communication as he attempts to regain control of the proceedings, his face scarlet with the effort.*

*The crowd finally quiets. Reluctantly. But the hush that settles over the courtroom is malevolent. The undercurrent of malice is almost tangible. Looking out over the seething crowd, I can barely recognize that it's made up of friends, neighbors—people I've known my entire life. There's the town barber, beside him the schoolmaster, and my neighbor the locksmith. I recognize their anger for what it is—fear.*

*Finding the proceedings back under his control, the magistrate takes his seat in a chair next to the accused. "Bethany Scott, you are here to answer for your crimes." She barely looks up to acknowledge him. Her eyes, wide with fear, stare forlornly at the floor.*

*The magistrate waves his arms dramatically. "Isn't it true that you are known for your pottage stew?" he asks, the question deceptively benign.*

*"Yes..." She hesitates. "But..."*

*The magistrate cuts her off. "Don't you use unusual seasonings? A secret recipe?"*

*Bethany shakes her head and glances wildly around the room in search of a friendly face. I try to get her attention, jostling to be seen over those in front of me. But her eyes don't find mine.*

*I know her stew. We all do. It's delicious, truly. I've had it many times at church gatherings, as have most present here today. Bethany is very proud of it. And that is where she went wrong...where she made a misstep that may claim her life. Pride. For pride is a sin in the eyes of the church. We all know this. Most of us are more careful to hide our vanity in these uncertain times.*

*"You must answer the question," the magistrate prods.*

*"Yes," she says so quietly that only those in front hear.*

*"Speak up, woman!" the magistrate lashes out.*

*"Yes. But everyone loves my stew! I bring it to all the church celebrations. It has never harmed anyone in all these past years!"*

*"Isn't it true that this is no mere stew, but a foul potion that is intended to bring about the demise of those who partake of it?" The magistrate is so emphatic that his spittle sprays outward.*

*"No!" Bethany shouts. She looks at the crowd desperately. "Won't anyone help me? You have all had my stew at one time or another..."*

Over here! *I will her to look my way, not daring to shout and draw attention.*

*The magistrate ignores her pleas. He knows what the crowd expects. He will see to it that they are not disappointed.*

*"We have a witness. Mrs. Granger, please come forward."*

*Lilly Granger pushes to the front of the crowd. She is dressed in black, head to toe, her face gaunt, her eyes red-rimmed. The very picture of grief. She points at Bethany. "That's her! The witch! It was her stew Robert was eating when he died in agony."*

*The crowd roars in outrage.*

*The magistrate again calls the room to order. After things quiet again, he addresses the witness. "Mrs. Granger, could you please tell us what transpired on the thirteenth of October?"*

*"My precious son Robert, barely three years old, was taken*

*early to his grave, a victim of this witch and her vindictive ways!" The words are flung out, spit out, Lilly's face wrung with anger and sorrow. A grieving mother. It's hard to imagine a more sympathetic figure. Her allegations have the backing of those assembled. They will brook no argument from the accused. The outcome of this trial has already been decided before it started.*

*"How did this happen?" the magistrate prods.*

*"He was so innocent! His only mistake was to eat Bethany's stew! But then he couldn't breathe. He clutched his throat and turned blue. He was sitting there—right beside me. Then he fell to the floor, and I tried to save him but...his little soul just slipped away!" She clutches at her own throat and lets out a high keening wail. "Why?" She drops to her knees, entreating the accused. "Why did you take my little boy from me?"*

*"Please, Lilly..." Tears stream down Bethany's face, she leans on the witness box, her legs giving way. "You know I would never hurt your son."*

*Lilly wipes the tears from her own face and, gathering herself, she stands back up in front of the accused. There is no understanding in her demeanor for the woman who used to be her friend. No forgiveness, only a determination to place the blame on someone, anyone, who may have caused this unthinkable event. Lilly hacks a glob of spit at Bethany, her face contorted in rage.*

*The crowd erupts, a live entity, ready to tear the accused to pieces.*

*The magistrate stands, his voice barely audible above the uproar. "You will be held until the governor can oversee your trial for witchcraft."*

*Overcome with anguish, I squeeze through the back of the*

*crowd to escape the room. I push open the heavy courtroom doors, desperately inhaling the fresh outdoor air.*

I awake with a start, taking in big gulps of air, just as in my dream. The feeling of grief sits on my chest, and I put my hands up to feel the tears on my cheeks.

*Was this a past life dream?* It definitely had the feel of one. This must be a past life I haven't encountered yet. My other past lives come to me often enough that I slip easily into their thoughts, like pulling on a pair of well-worn jeans. I may not always understand their perspective, but they feel familiar. This person's thoughts don't fit quite right yet. They leave me feeling off kilter, unsettled. And yet...it's a little like discovering a long-lost relative, leaving an expectation of future familiarity.

Up until now, I'd found America's witch trials to be a mysterious and fascinatingly tragic part of our history. Now, through this person's memory, encountering the frightening power of the mob mentality that dominated at the time, I have new insight into the terror that these trials instilled. The desperate need to fit in with popular opinion was more important for survival than a theoretical notion of justice for all. Having a view outside of the mainstream could mark you.

*We've come a long way...or have we?* Even in present day, while we think we've left these times behind, How we continue to allow prevailing attitudes to shape justice. I remember a recent case where a woman reported being stalked by a man she worked with. He was a respected member of the community and his influence with the mayor prevented a thorough investigation. The woman was ridiculed in the press as an oversensitive female making her colleague out as a villain to gain advantage in a competitive workplace. The case was dismissed. A few years later, the man was arrested for stalking and ultimately killing another woman. And conversely, I also know of cases where men were wrongly accused by women who knew the bias would be in their favor, only to be later disproven. *Will we ever be free of our own preconceptions?*

These gloomy thoughts weigh on me as I carefully get out of bed, leaving Blake to sleep a little longer. I shower, letting the soap and warm water slowly clear my thoughts.

I try to fit what my subconscious brought up with my current reality. An unfair trial. A little boy who likely choked or had an allergic reaction to the stew. But at the time, the fear of others' motives was so heightened that events without certain explanations found blame on the shoulders of those that the community saw as unusual. It was dangerous to be an outsider.

The trials had an expected outcome; the blame placed on a convenient scapegoat. *Is that what I am working through? An unfair trial? Perhaps that of Barry Greenworth? But he confessed, so that can't be right.* I'm mindful of the warning from the tarot card reading last night. Even if I don't believe in the validity of the tarot cards, I can't help but feel the need to heed the warning and not jump to a conclusion. The results of not proceeding carefully couldn't be demonstrated more clearly than they were in the events of the witch trial. A plaintiff wrongly accused, wrongly convicted.

# CHAPTER FIFTEEN

While I'm polishing off a quick breakfast of peanut butter toast, I look out my kitchen window and see that the weather looks like it's going to take a turn for the worse. Ominous clouds are gathering and heading inland from the Pacific Ocean. I leave Blake a quick note and then head to the precinct, keeping an eye on the incoming storm.

When I pull into the lot, Joe is already opening the driver's door of our cruiser, the wind whipping his coat around. His expression is grim.

"What is it?" I ask.

"Just got a call from dispatch. Some sort of altercation over at GuidanceLink. Someone called in, reporting shots fired."

*Yikes!* My heart rate ramps up.

I jump in beside Joe, slamming the cruiser door in my haste. We speed toward GuidanceLink, siren blaring and lights pulsing.

"Backup should be right behind us. I told dispatch we'll coordinate personnel, since we know the office layout," Joe says, slightly breathless from rushing. The sky is darkening with the oncoming storm, and a few scattered raindrops start to hit the windshield.

As we pull up to GuidanceLink, the storm is gaining momentum. Rain slices down in sheets and lightning forks across the sky. A lone figure stands out front, huddled under a tree in an attempt to escape the rain. As we approach, I recognize Adam, the receptionist. We usher him into the back of the cruiser.

Adam is soaked through, and his face is pale under the meager interior light of the cruiser. "I'm so glad you're here. I think someone might be hurt!" His voice is shaky.

"What happened?" Joe prompts.

"I was just getting the reception desk set up for the day. Then I heard raised voices and what sounded like a gunshot. I wasn't sure what it was at first. I was just about to go check and then I heard more shouting and another gunshot. That time, I knew what it was...I ran out here and called 911."

A flash of lightning illuminates the area, and an immediate rumble of thunder follows. The sky is so dark now that it's as if night has descended.

"Do you know how many people are inside the building?" Joe asks.

"No, I'm not sure but usually the only people here before me are Brian, Katie, and Andre."

"Could you tell who was shouting?"

"Two men. If I had to guess, it was Andre and Brian."

"Where in the building were they located?"

"It sounded like the food service area. Brian always starts coffee as soon as he gets in."

"I noticed some tension between the Lees and Andre last

time we were here. Is there an issue there?" I ask.

Adam nods. "Yes, you could say that. Andre doesn't think the employees should be made to return to the site. But the Lees are convinced that's the right approach. They've been arguing about it for months but now with all the new attention from the judge's death, it's heated things up again."

A report comes in from dispatch. "Backup is delayed by a tree down on the entry to GuidanceLink. They're going to have to clear it, there's no way around."

I glance at Joe. "Looks like we're on our own. I don't think we ought to wait if there's an active shooter inside, a possible injured victim, and others at risk."

"Agreed." Joe nods, resignation and determination etched in his features.

I swallow hard.

As we prepare to make a run through the rain, we see the lights flicker and then go out inside the building. A generator starts up with a whir but then it sputters and dies out. The emergency lights flash on for a moment and then it's black again. So much for the emergency generator. We grab our flashlights and dash through the driving rain to the entry doors.

The building's appearance is drastically altered from our last visit. It's pitch black with the power out. During the flashes of lightning, we glimpse the creepy arm-like branches of the treehouse structures high above us. At such a distance, our flashlights barely penetrate the darkness. It's like some eerie scene from Jurassic Park where a velociraptor pops out with the next lightning flash.

"This is the Seattle PD. Please come out with your hands up," Joe shouts into the darkness. We wait for a response.

Nothing happens. "Well, worth a try," he says quietly to me. "I still think we can diffuse this situation. Let's try to draw them out peacefully. There's at least one gun and potentially someone who is already injured." Joe peers into the darkness.

"Where do you want to start?" I ask, my voice also low.

"Let's head up to the food service area. That's where Adam heard the altercation."

Pointing our firearms ahead of us and scanning the darkness with our flashlights, we head to the stairs by the elevators. We are breathless by the time we reach the top of the staircase and emerge in the food services area.

We flash our lights around the grills and seating areas. No one's there. It's eerily quiet. *Where is everyone?* I experience a momentary shot of adrenaline when my light picks up a human, and I almost drop my flashlight. My breathing evens when I realize that it's a life-sized cardboard cutout of Brian that holds the daily menu.

Reaching the edge of the lofted balcony, we shine our lights down toward the open office platforms below. I'm too far away to be certain but nothing appears to move in the shadows cast by our lights.

As we head back toward the stairs, my light flashes on something dark on the floor in front of the coffee machine. "I'm going to check that out," I whisper to Joe.

He nods and whispers back, "I'll follow you."

Heading over to investigate, I get a whiff of the unmistakable smell of freshly brewed coffee. And a metallic tang of... *what is it?* My flashlight picks up the telltale red splatter at the same time as my nose recognizes the smell of iron. Blood. Just as we suspected, someone is injured. Searching around, I find a bullet hole in a nearby cabinet.

"Look," I whisper, pointing out the bullet hole and trail of blood to Joe. He nods grimly. We follow it to a another set of stairs leading down to a series of platforms below. We follow the trail of blood spatters down the stairs and platforms, carefully checking each area. No one is there. When we emerge on the main floor, we find ourselves in the exercise area.

Joe follows the trail of blood spatter leading down the stairs to the basement level with its aquatic theming. We peer down the stairs. There are no lights on down below and no windows to let in the occasional flashes of lightning. We're descending into complete darkness.

When we reach the bottom of the stairs, the narrow beam of my flashlight picks up movement as I train it into the room ahead of me. I gasp, flashing my light around to find out what caused the movement. But it's just fish moving in the enormous fish tanks. I force my tense muscles to relax again. In the central tank the jellyfish disturbed by my light cast a bioluminescent glow.

"Seattle PD. Come out with your hands up." Joe tries a third time.

"Thank god!" A response this time. Female. My flashlight picks up two figures rising up from behind a desk, holding hands. The Lees. Brian Lee is clutching his side, his hand covered in blood. The pair run toward us. We move past the jellyfish tank to come to their aid.

"Where is..." Joe never gets a chance to ask the rest of the question. Shots are fired. They hit the fish tank behind us with a deep thudding noise.

We all freeze.

For a tense moment, all is silent.

Then with a huge crack, the giant cylindrical tank in the

middle of the room erupts.

I'm hit from behind with an enormous wave of water. It washes over my head, throwing me to the floor. My flashlight is thrust out of my hand, but I manage to hold onto my gun. *Thank God!*

I stand back up drenched and peer through the darkness, trying to spot my flashlight somewhere ahead of me. There's no light, it must have been damaged. Crouching, I grope around on the floor in several inches of water but only find aquarium rocks, and yuck, is that a jellyfish? The sea creature glows in distress at my touch. I pull my hand back rapidly, unsure if these jellyfish sting.

In the chaos, I've lost track of the Lees. I hear a sob off to my left and reach out my hand, trying to locate Katie but I find only open space. The whine of a gunshot whizzes past my left ear. The shooter heard her too. *Joe, where are you?*

Two sets of footsteps slosh over the wet floor off to my left. I suspect it's the Lees making a break for the stairs. A bioluminescent trail of disturbed jellyfish follows their movement across the floor. Bullets hail in pursuit. There's a grunt as a bullet hits its intended target, but the footsteps only falter briefly, then continue upward until they clear the top of the stairs.

Still blinded by the dark, I move to my right as silently as possible, in the direction of the shooter. I holster my gun. I can't shoot without possibly hitting Joe. *Where is Joe anyway?*

*If I can just get around behind the shooter...* Water is dripping off my nose, my hair. My clothes cling to me. Moving slowly, I hope the jellyfish won't give my position away.

I bump into something solid. Squatting, my hand finds a suit jacket, and wait, yes, the slight rhythmic excursion of breathing. *Joe! And he's alive. Thank God!* He's lying on his back, his face out of the water.

A bullet whizzes over my head.

But this time, I saw the muzzle flash as the weapon discharged. Springing up, I detour to my right and, gauging the distance the best I can in the dark, I circle back around toward the firearm. Hearing my approach, the gun fires wildly at the spot I was standing when I bumped into Joe. Targeting the location of the muzzle flash, I tackle the gunman headlong. With my momentum, we both crash to the floor, landing in the water amid the aquarium carnage.

Using the moment of surprise, I manage to perch on the gunman's back and pin both of his hands in place long enough to attach handcuffs. He flails and attempts to buck me off but with his hands secured, he can't get leverage.

Hands come at me from behind, gripping my shoulder. *What? Another assailant?* Adam didn't know how many were in the building. I whip out my left arm reflexively, catching the person square in the stomach. There's a rapid intake of breath confirming I connected.

"It's me," comes the strangled response. *Joe.*

At that moment, the lights flicker and then come on. The room is drowned in the contents of the large fish tank. Jellyfish, plant life, and aquarium decor are strewn over the floor amid several inches of water.

I glance at my captive and confirm my suspicions... *Andre.*

Joe is bent over, clutching his stomach and taking large breaths. "Sorry," I say sheepishly. "Thought you were another gunman. Are you okay?"

He nods as he recovers. "I bumped my head on something when that wave of water hit us." Joe touches his head, wincing.

"Must've knocked me out. I don't have any bullet holes though," he says, as he looks over his wet clothing, pulling a long strip of seaweed off his pants.

After he recovers his breath, Joe helps me lift Andre to his feet. We march him out through the front door, all of us dripping with salty aquarium water.

The storm is blowing itself out, the clouds disappearing to the east, and the sun starting to dry the rain from the streets. As we emerge, the SWAT team and two ambulances pull up in front. I'm grateful they finally managed to get past the tree barrier to help us.

The EMS crew quickly assesses the Lees, stabilizing them and loading them in the first ambulance. It moves off quickly toward the hospital, sirens blaring. The crew from the second ambulance evaluates the three of us. Luckily, the fish tank was made of thick acrylic, and it broke into large pieces, so we don't have millions of pieces of glass embedded in our skin.

When I'm cleared by EMS, I call Blake. It's hard to believe it's only been three hours since I left him a note. He doesn't have a shift today, thankfully, but he won't be expecting a call from me in the middle of the day. He answers on the second ring. "Everything okay?"

"Yeah. But I've managed to get drenched in the course of things this morning. Could you pick me up?" I ask as cheerfully as possible. I don't want to scare him when there's nothing to worry about right now. The danger is over. I'm unharmed.

"Of course. Are you okay? How did you get wet?" He's not distracted by my upbeat tone. He knows me too well.

"Yes, I'm okay. I'll explain when you get here. I'll text you the address." I hesitate. "Oh, and bring me a dry sweatshirt, would you?"

The head of the SWAT team comes over to take Andre into custody. I recognize him from a past case.

"O'Sullivan?" I ask.

He nods. "Nice work, Kruse. Looks like you managed to avoid any casualties. I heard you tackled the shooter."

"I did what I could. We were flying blind down there," I reply. "How are the Lees?"

"Mr. Lee has two bullet wounds, one to the right side of his abdomen—it's superficial. And one to his left arm. He'll be okay."

It's not long before I spot Blake clutching a sweatshirt and searching the scene for me.

"Over here." I wave to catch his attention.

Blake approaches with a relieved smile and wraps me in a hug. "Are you all right?" he asks, pulling back enough to look me in the eye, searching for the truth. "I didn't expect to find a SWAT team out front."

"Yes, I'm okay. Besides being drenched by an exploding fish tank, I'm perfectly fine." I rest my head on his chest.

"What the hell happened here?" Blake asks.

"A man brought a gun to work and assaulted the owner. They had an argument over a lawsuit but I'm not sure yet what brought on today's shooting."

Blake's expression indicates he knows he's getting the PG version of events. He pulls seaweed out of my hair. "An exploding fish tank, huh?"

"Yes. Jellyfish everywhere."

"Your job—it could be a bit more boring. I'm just saying ... it would be better for my health, you know? When I pulled up here with the SWAT team and the ambulance and all the onlookers, I think my heart just stopped for a few beats."

I snuggle into his chest. "I wasn't really okay until I saw you, you know?" I let the tension leave my body and just lean into him.

He kisses my hair and says so softly that I barely hear it, "Me neither."

# CHAPTER SIXTEEN

When we arrive back at my apartment, I slump heavily onto the couch. Bone tired, mentally exhausted.

"Why don't you go ahead and get cleaned up? I'll make you something to eat," Blake suggests.

A warm shower is heaven. I take my time, letting the warm water run over me, clearing away the aquarium sludge and easing my muscles.

I wrap myself in a soft robe and plop down on the couch. Stalker jumps up beside me, purring as he curls up against the soft fabric.

Whatever Blake is making smells amazing. He comes out with a grilled cheese sandwich, oozing with sharp cheddar, and a bowl of tomato soup. The warm comfort food is heaven.

Blake sits beside me on the couch, his body angled toward me. "Want to tell me about it?" And so, I do. All the details tumble out. He listens, eyes widening at the dangerous parts. He says very little.

Talking through the event allows me to process it and I'm

reminded again how therapeutic it is to have someone to share these things with. I just hope I'm not worrying him too much.

I call my parents and Isabella to tell them about the day and reassure them that I'm okay. It's likely the shooting will make the news, and I'm always nervous that those I care about will hear about something that involved me before I have a chance to reach out to them.

I see my parents once a week for dinner, so it's only been a few days since I was at their home. "Are you really okay, dear?" My mother is worried. The endearment echoes the one from my dream of Abby.

My thoughts drift to the dream I had a couple of nights ago, and how very in love Abby was with her husband, Will. I'm lucky to have that kind of love again, with Blake, in my current life. I look over at him, feeling thankful that he seems to know just what I needed today. The repetition of relationships over past lives gives me an odd feeling of déjà vu.

"Kaitlyn?" My mother's voice brings me back to present day.

"Yes, I'm fine, Mom. And Blake is here. He can make comfort food like a pro," I reassure her.

Once my parents are content that I'm safe and sound, I call Joe. His wife, Sandra, picked him up after the crew diagnosed him with a mild concussion and advised him not to drive home. Another officer drove the cruiser back to the precinct. Sandra didn't miss the chance to fuss over me when she got to the site. I love that woman like a second mother.

"How are you feeling after being knocked unconscious by a tidal wave of jellyfish?" I ask Joe.

"A bit of a headache but I'm feeling okay. You?"

"Yeah, just a few aches and pains. Some scratches. Nothing that won't go away in a couple of days."

"Good to hear. Oh, and I heard from Garcia. They interviewed Andre and found out some interesting things."

"Oh yeah? What did he say?"

"He said he and Brian Lee have been increasingly at odds. Andre is against the lawsuit. He said that twice the arguments got so heated that it came to blows. According to Andre, Brian was the aggressor, and Andre was afraid of him. He started carrying a gun to work."

"That was a terrible idea."

"Looks like he found that out today. Andre said he was protecting himself but that doesn't fit the confrontation today."

"Right. It looked more like Andre was chasing Brian by the end of it. He made one mistake after another."

"And he wasn't the only one with bad judgment. Andre suggested that the Lees had offered the judge a bribe to find in their favor."

"You're kidding. The judge didn't seem like someone who'd take bribes. Just the opposite, in fact."

"I agree with you. So maybe Andre was wrong. He may have just suspected it," Joe says.

"Let's interview him again tomorrow. We need to know more about this."

"Good idea. I'll see you in the morning." Joe hangs up.

I contemplate the possibility that the judge took a bribe. Assuming he did, then who would have motive to kill him? A GuidanceLink employee perhaps, if they suspected it.

After the events of the day, my mind wanders and it's not long before I'm drifting off to sleep.

*Bethany stands quietly in the same wooden enclosure in the courtroom. Onlookers are jammed together and restless, but the courtroom is much quieter today. The governor has come to oversee the proceedings, and he has a much better command over the crowd than the magistrate did at the preliminary trial a few weeks ago.*

*Bethany is pale and distraught, wringing her hands in fright. She looks at me for strength. I nod at her from my place at the front of the crowd, encouraging her to be brave. She did nothing wrong. We all ate that stew...*

*"Joan Davis, please come forward," the governor calls the first witness. "Joan Davis?" he repeats when no one seems to respond.*

*"I'm coming. Make way." An elderly woman pushes through the crowd, so tiny that she isn't visible until she emerges from behind the taller people surrounding her. She shoves past me and approaches the front of the room.*

*"I'm here. I'm Joan Davis," she declares.*

*"What observation do you wish to relate to this court?" the governor asks.*

*"I saw her taking clippings from her garden..." Joan croaks.*

*The governor interrupts her. "Woman, you must speak up and indicate about whom you are speaking!"*

*Joan raises an accusatory finger at Bethany. "She did it."*

*When no contradiction from Bethany seems to be forthcoming, Joan gains confidence. "It was her!" she cries. "She was in her yard, finding bits of plants to put in that stew of hers. Poisons, you can be sure of it!"*

*Bethany gasps and takes an involuntary step backward. "Those are herbs...only flavorings, enhancements..."*

*"So, you admit you used enchantments!" Joan shouts.*

*"No! I said enhancements…" Bethany tries to interrupt but Joan is getting some momentum now.*

*"I know what you did! I saw you!" Joan flings the words at Bethany, who recoils as if the words indeed find purchase in her flesh. The crowd murmurs angrily. I meet Bethany's eyes. Hers are filled with terror. I hold her gaze, trying to give my friend what strength I can.*

*"She murdered him and she should die for it!" Joan shouts.*

*The crowd murmurs in anger. "She should die!" someone shouts. "Witch!" another voice chimes in. Others join in, taking up the chant. "Witch. Witch. Witch…"*

*"You will be quiet in this courtroom!" the governor shouts over the raised voices. The crowd reluctantly quiets but a current of malevolence is present now. They want blood. An eye for an eye. A life for a life.*

*The governor turns to the crowd. "Her fate is mine to decide. I will announce my decision tomorrow at precisely ten in the morning…"*

*They're going to hang her. If tomorrow's announcement finds her to be a witch, she will die. I feel tears on my cheeks. What will the governor decide? Who might influence him? There are rumors that he's been paid for his verdict.*

*"Wait," Bethany says desperately. A sudden change comes over her face. She's made some sort of decision. My stomach clenches. What is she about to do?*

*She straightens herself, stands tall. "You are right…I am a witch." She says it with determination. Owning it.*

*The courtroom erupts in angry cries.*

*"Silence!" the governor shouts over the noise. Reluctantly, the crowd quiets.*

*"So…you admit that you have partaken in witchcraft?" the*

*governor asks.*

*"I do," Bethany says quietly.*

*"Return her to the jail," the governor says. "We must know more about this witchcraft and who else might be involved."*

*I look at my friend. No witch. But now she has proclaimed she is one to save herself from hanging. She looks at me. There is strength in her gaze now. She has found the way out of her predicament. For the moment, she is saved.*

*Murmurs are heard around the room. It's occurring to those who accused Bethany that she holds the power now. She will be pressured to name others as witches. Who among them will she name?*

My eyes pop open in confusion. I've slept many hours and my limbs feel heavy and achy. Blake must've led me to bed last night because I'm in my room and the first rays of the sun illuminate the closed shades of my bedroom. I turn on my back, thinking about the witch trial. Why is my subconscious bringing up this memory? What am I trying to work through? Did the governor take a bribe to declare Bethany a witch? Certainly, it's plausible that the outcomes of the witch trials would've benefitted certain people financially either through property seizure or direct bribery.

And why would Bethany say she was a witch? What would she gain by that declaration? Maybe she knew there was a bribe involved and that the governor's ruling wouldn't be fair anyway? Or just that he would be motivated to please the crowd and find her guilty?

Does this relate to Andre? Is his accusation about the judge taking a bribe a false one? We need to talk to Andre to find out what exactly he knew about a bribe.

# CHAPTER SEVENTEEN

Feeling somewhat recovered from yesterday's excitement, I endeavor to make us some eggs and toast. When Blake emerges from the bedroom, hair still wet from the shower, I find myself watching him, admiring the view. Stalker winds around his legs in greeting and Blake reaches down and scoops up the cat, giving him a scratch under the chin. Stalker leans into Blake's hand and closes his eyes.

Looking up, Blake sees me watching him. "What?"

"Nothing. Just admiring."

He laughs. Seeing the food I've prepared, he pulls me into an embrace. "Thank you. That looks amazing," he murmurs into my hair.

"Just returning the favor from last night."

We eat together and then I give Blake a quick peck on the cheek as a farewell. "See you tonight?"

"No. Remember, I'm driving down to Portland tonight. Going to spend a couple of days with my brother. Go fishing."

Right. I'd forgotten. Thinking about it, I miss him already.

And, if I'm honest, I'm a little salty that he's going to be out of town on my birthday, which is tomorrow. But I push that selfish thought away. He should have his time with his brother. We can celebrate when he gets back.

"Okay. Just don't forget me while you're gone." I give him a long, lingering kiss.

"Hardly." He groans and pulls me closer. "You neither," he murmurs against my lips.

We're both breathless by the time he heads out the door. *Forget him? Not a chance.* My lips are still tingling when I leave twenty minutes later.

On my way out the door, I tear off a tiny piece from a napkin in my kitchen drawer. My low-tech security system. With Blake leaving, my defenses are up again. I've still never told him about the napkin. Recently I've found myself letting this habit slide when Blake leaves the apartment after me. Maybe I'm feeling a little more secure. The thought is welcome. Still...old habits die hard. I slip the napkin into the doorframe. Just in case.

As I arrive at the precinct, yesterday's events at Guidance-Link are weighing on my mind.

Joe arrives looking a little worse for wear after yesterday's events.

"How are you feeling?" I ask him.

"I still have a bit of a headache but the doctor cleared me to return to work. Just no running around after suspects until the symptoms go away."

I nod. I'm a little worried about him, but I've seen him shake off worse than a concussion. He'll be okay.

I bring up Andre's accusation that the judge took a bribe,

and we decide to have Andre brought up from holding so we can explore this further. While that's being arranged, we watch the recorded interview from the day before.

Starting the playback, we see Deputy Chief Garcia enter the room and sit down across from Andre. He looks distraught, constantly running his hands through his hair. When Garcia reads him his rights, he rocks slightly in the chair, holding his head.

"Andre, I'd like to know your side of the story." Garcia tries to draw him out. "Why don't you tell me what happened today?"

"Well...Brian and I, we aren't getting along too well lately," he mumbles, almost too quietly to hear, his gaze focused on his lap.

"Why is that, Andre?" Garcia sits back in the chair, indicating she has all the time in the world.

"We're fighting about the lawsuit." He shrugs, then restarts with more conviction. "Our employees started working from home during COVID, and...well, they want to *keep* working from home. And Brian...he and Katie, they want the employees to come back. The company invested a lot of money building that office, hoping that the natural setting would spark creativity. They don't want to give that up."

"And you disagree?" Garcia sits forward as if she's hanging on his every word.

"Well...I understand their perspective. I worked from home during COVID too. I really liked the flexibility just like the employees did. Some people even moved to another location...one they can't possibly commute from. The way I see it, why should they have to come back just because the company built some ridiculously expensive workplace and the owners won't give it up?"

"I see." Garcia nods as if agreeing with his perspective. "So, you and Brian have different opinions about the lawsuit. How is that affecting you at work?"

"I got sick of hearing Brian on his typical rants about the employees. And one day he started talking about offering the judge some incentive to find in our favor. After that, I just couldn't help telling him what I thought."

"How did that go?"

"Not real well. He was angry and told me I'd better decide where my loyalties lie. And then...I couldn't believe it; he took a swing at me. I had a bruise on my cheek for almost two weeks."

"Did the physical altercations continue?"

"Yeah...a couple more times, an argument ended up coming to blows. He's bigger than me, and I always ended up with the bruises. But I wasn't going to just back down because he thinks he's the boss. I helped start this company too. And I care more about the employees than he does." Andre's face reddens as he warms to his argument.

Garcia leans back in the chair again. "So why did you bring the gun to the office today?"

"To defend myself. I thought if he saw I had it, he'd lay off. I'm done being afraid at work." Andre pulls at his hair in distress. *Did he feel his own life was in danger?*

"I can see you felt the workplace wasn't safe." Garcia is thinking the same thing.

Andre nods.

"So, why don't you tell me your side of the story. What happened this morning?"

"I was minding my own business, getting my coffee, and

Brian came into the kitchen. He was already mad and he gave me a push. I didn't even say anything to provoke him. I spilled burning hot coffee all down the front of my shirt." He pulls at his stained shirt. "It still hurts."

"What was he so mad about?"

"He said, 'I found out, Andre! Not only are you a traitor to GuidanceLink but now I find out that you're screwing around with my wife!' His face was all red and his veins were popping out in his neck. His fists were bunched up. I thought he was going to kill me."

"Is that true about his wife?"

"Well...yes, it's true. But you have to understand, it wasn't my fault. Brian has been such an ass lately that Katie can't talk to him. She feels all alone. It was Katie who came to *me* and said she doesn't agree with him about the lawsuit either. Katie and I...we get each other. We started spending more time together, and one thing led to another. So, you see... Brian practically drove her away."

"So, he accused you of sleeping with his wife and he pushed you, spilling the hot coffee which burned you. And then what?"

"He was so angry, I'd never seen him so worked up. I was afraid for my life so I pulled out my gun, thinking it would make him stop, make him back off. But instead, he lunged for the gun and...I don't know...it just went off. And then he was bleeding..." Andre puts his head in his hands and rubs his eyes.

"Then what happened?" Garcia prods.

"He looked down and saw the blood, and it must have scared him. He ran for the stairs."

"And you went after him?"

"I just wanted to talk to him…to explain that I didn't mean to shoot him. So, I followed him downstairs. He went all the way down to the basement where Katie was working. She likes the quiet down there, so she's down there most mornings. I was scared he would tell her I did it on purpose… so I went down after him. They must've been hiding from me because I didn't see them when I got down the stairs. So, I was calling to them and looking around. Finally, they came out from the restrooms, with their hands up, looking really scared. I realized I still had the gun in my hand. The gun made me feel like I had control, so I pointed it at Brian. I just wanted him to explain what really happened to Katie."

"But he wouldn't?"

"No! He kept saying that *I* attacked him. But it was *his* fault. Then, suddenly, the lights went out because of the storm. It was all going wrong." Andre holds his head again. "I needed to fix it." He pulls at his hair. "I told them no one was leaving until he told the truth."

"So why didn't you stop when the police came?"

"I panicked, thinking Brian would make it sound like it was all my fault. I wasn't thinking straight. I felt…threatened." Andre is rocking again. "I just wanted to get out of there. I shot at the fish tank to cause a distraction. And then Brian and Katie ran off, and I wanted to stop them. I wanted a chance to tell my side of the story before they had the whole police force after me."

"Okay, Andre. Thanks for cooperating. It's helpful to hear your side. You'll be spending some time here before your arraignment." Andre nods, looking bleak. Garcia leaves at this point and the recording ends.

I look over at Joe. "There was a lot more drama going on

over at GuidanceLink than they told us about."

"There sure was. Now that we know things were getting that heated, I wouldn't be surprised if Brian offered the judge a bribe to make sure things turned out the way he wanted. He had a lot to lose if the employees didn't come back, not the least of which was his credibility."

"Did the interviews with Brian and Katie support Andre's side of the story?"

"Yes, Garcia told me that their stories were pretty similar, just varied on who pushed who first and when the gun was first drawn...that kind of thing. Each trying to make themselves look better."

Bob lets us know Andre is ready for us in the interrogation room. We head into the adjacent observation room to watch Andre for a moment. He's disheveled after a night in jail. His hair is messy, and his jawline has new stubble. There's a new look in his eyes—wild and desperate.

Entering the interrogation room, Joe and I take seats across from Andre.

"Andre, we have a few more questions for you." Joe says.

Andre barely nods, just sits there looking defeated and not making eye contact with us.

"Yesterday you mentioned that Brian had..." Joe looks at his notes. "...'started talking about offering the judge some incentive to find in our favor.' What did you mean by that?"

Andre rubs his face. "Brian was desperate to win the lawsuit. He thought I agreed with him—we hadn't had our first fight yet. He said we should find a way to influence the judge's decision."

"What do you think he had in mind?" I ask.

"We had an emergency fund of fifty thousand dollars

that he kept in cash in the safe. He said the lawsuit was an emergency and we should use the fund to sway the judge's decision."

"Did he actually try it?"

"I didn't think he would. I let him know that I didn't want any part of it. But then I was getting something out of the safe a few days ago, and I saw that the money was gone."

"Did you ask him about it?"

"I was going to yesterday, but I didn't get a chance. He barged in and started shoving me."

After the interview, Joe and I discuss the possible bribe money. There weren't any large deposits when we looked at the judge's bank accounts or in the home safe. Maybe Brian hadn't made the offer yet. Or maybe the judge refused.

# CHAPTER EIGHTEEN

As we're leaving the interview with Andre, Bob catches us to let us know that the judge's sister, Anna Shapiro, is home from Europe, and available for us to interview. Her family's home is just a short distance from the judge's house.

We pull up in front of a solidly middle-class, two-story brick residence with a white picket fence and a neatly trimmed lawn.

When we ring the bell, a dog barks and a light-colored golden retriever appears at the window beside the door, panting enthusiastically, its breath fogging the glass. The dog's whole body is moving with its wagging tail. I suppress a smile because the first thing that comes to mind is Bob.

Anna answers the door. She's a petite woman with short curly blonde hair. "Detectives, please come in. I've been expecting you." She opens the door for us to enter. "This is our dog, Aslan." The dog wags its tail in response. "He's friendly," she adds unnecessarily.

We follow her back to a round table in the breakfast

nook. A bay window behind the table looks out on a large backyard. Aslan pushes his nose into my lap, looking for attention. I give him a scratch behind the ears, and he lies down on my feet. It seems I have a new friend.

"I had my husband take the kids out for ice cream so we can talk more freely," Anna says. "It was very hard to get the news about Harry. All of us are shocked about his death. It was so sudden and so very sad someone did this to him." Her eyes are damp and rimmed with dark circles.

"Mrs. Shapiro, we spoke with Sofia Clifton, and she said you and Harry were very close," I say, easing into the interview.

"Call me Anna, please. Yes. We saw him regularly. At least once a month, he and Sofia would join us for Sunday dinner. The kids loved their uncle, and he never missed an opportunity to spoil them." She smiles through the tears. "I also had lunch with Harry sometimes, just the two of us. I knew my brother really well." She shakes her head wistfully.

"Mrs. Clifton said you two became very close after your parents' death. She told us that what you went through in court after they died was what led to Judge Harry's loathing for large companies that steamroll victims in court," I say.

Sofia nods. "Harry and I lost our case against the resort. It was never a fair fight. The resort had the nerve to claim that our parents ignored posted signs. We know that wasn't true because they were skiing with friends that day, so we had witnesses. You see, Mom and Dad were good skiers, so they chose a more challenging ski run. Their friends were worried the route was too difficult for them, so they took a different path down the mountain, planning to meet at the bottom. Their friends testified in court that no warning signs were posted at the point their paths diverged. The resort claimed the signs were there but may have been obstructed by new-fallen snow."

Anna's eyes flash in residual anger as she warms to the familiar story. "There was no proof on either side, but the ski resort had a huge team of lawyers on their side. They drowned us in paperwork. We were young and didn't have the money to hire expensive lawyers to stand up to the resort and their aggressive tactics. And to make matters worse, Mom and Dad's life insurance was delayed while their deaths were investigated."

She waves her arm in a circle to indicate her comfortable home. "We knew we would be well-off after the life insurance came through, so the lawsuit wasn't about the money. Not for us. We thought the ski resort should take responsibility. We lost our parents. They were our whole world." She sighs. "But, in the end, the resort was never held accountable."

"I'm so sorry it turned out like that. I know this is hard, but can you think of anyone that might have meant him harm?" I ask.

Anna thinks for a moment as she wipes her face with a tissue. "No. Not at all. Everyone loved him....Well, except some of those he had to sentence, of course. I really didn't know much about his court cases, other than what I saw on the news."

"How about Sofia? Did she and your brother get along well?"

"Yes, very well. Sofia is smart and spunky enough to hold her own and be a real partner to Harry." Anna smiles. "And I can tell she loves him—sorry, loved him," she amends, mumbling.

"How did Harry and Sofia meet?"

"It's kind of a cute story really. Harry loved to tell it. You see, there's a bar that some of the judges and lawyers hang out at called 'The Bar.'" She uses air quotes. "Harry met her there one night. As he tells it, she was walking by, tripped, and spilled a drink on him. She offered to pay for cleaning his shirt, but he refused." Anna smiles in remembrance.

"So, Harry thought that would be the end of it but then she shows up at his office the next day with a new shirt. He couldn't have been more surprised. But he tells her he'll make her a deal; that he would accept the replacement for his shirt if she would go out for a drink with him, and he could replace the drink she spilled. It was only fair, he told her."

Anna is laughing now. "Then...as he tells it—and you had to take all his stories with a grain of salt as he tends to embellish...at the end of the date, just as Harry is thinking that he's really taken with her, Sofia gets up, picks up the last of her drink, and slowly pours it down the front of his shirt. He said he just sat there in disbelief, but that it was the 'sexiest damn move he ever saw'—his words. So, he asks her what exactly she's doing, and she says that this time, she'd like to clean the shirt herself...back at her place. Well, he took her up on it and the rest is history."

"It sounds like they had some chemistry." I can't help but chuckle. "Were they pretty close?"

"Yes. They were." She sniffles.

"Was Harry excited about Sofia's pregnancy?" I ask.

"Sofia is pregnant?" Anna's eyes widen in surprise. "Oh, that's such a gift! I love that he'll leave a part of him with us." She smiles broadly through happy tears.

"You didn't know?"

"No, but that's not surprising. She can't be very far along or I'd have noticed. When I was pregnant with each of the kids, I didn't tell anyone until the end of the first trimester. Many women keep it to themselves until they're certain the pregnancy is viable."

"Would Harry have been glad to be a father at his age?"

"Why? Because he was in his fifties? Oh, sure. He never did act his age. And he always wanted to be a father. He would've been thrilled."

"Did he and Sofia have any problems?"

"Like what?"

"Oh, like financial concerns or personal issues with neighbors or friends."

"Not that I can think of. And I know they must have been doing well financially because, just the other day, he offered to set up a college fund for both the kids, twenty-five thousand each."

I blink in surprise. *It looks like we might've found the fifty thousand from GuidanceLink's emergency fund.*

I head home from the precinct that night looking forward to a nice relaxing night to myself with Blake out of town. Don't get me wrong, I love having Blake around but a night to myself is such a rarity now that I covet it.

I stop by the grocery store to pick up a few things. A tomato-basil marinated chicken breast catches my eye, so I pick out some fresh vegetables to stir fry for a side dish. I don't get the time to cook myself a meal very often, but I can handle a little pan frying. One of my favorite bottles of Sauvignon Blanc should pair nicely, I think, picking it up off an end-cap. On a whim, I select a new book—a bestselling thriller. Ah, and some lavender-scented bubble bath. *All the makings of a heavenly evening,* I think as I go through the self-check-out.

I'm already anticipating the delicious meal and a long soak in the bubble bath as I take the stairs to my apartment two at a time. I'm distracted and it takes me a minute to register that the napkin isn't in the door frame where I left it this morning.

The hair on the back of my neck stands up and my hands tingle in alarm. I know this isn't a normal reaction but it's not long ago that I had a serial killer stalking me, and if that wasn't enough, someone broke into my apartment during a past case to confiscate evidence. Admittedly, I already had this tendency toward hypervigilance long before I had actual reason for it.

Whether it's warranted or not, all my senses are now on high alert. I search the floor and there it is—the napkin that used to be in the door frame. Someone has opened the door. Blake is the only one with a key. And he's out of town. *Who got in? And are they still there?*

Quietly and carefully, I put my grocery bags down on the floor.

I listen at the door but don't hear anything.

Inserting my key, I slowly turn the lock. To my ears, the click of the lock unlatching is disconcertingly loud.

With my hand on my gun, I slowly open the door. I'm greeted only with darkness and silence. Something smells unusual. *Someone has definitely been here.*

I don't want to alert an intruder, so I walk slowly, carefully, in the dark.

There's no sign of the cat. *Did he get out? Or maybe he was locked in the bedroom.* I head for the bedroom.

Suddenly, I hear a noise from behind the couch. It faces

the entry door and there's a large space behind it allowing access to the balcony. Crouching, I grope blindly behind the couch and feel...a foot!

With speed born of many years apprehending perpetrators on the police force before I made detective, I tighten my grip on the foot and yank hard, pulling the person toward me and keeping them off balance. I hear a muffled male grunt as I pounce, pinning the person and yanking their hands backwards, securing them with zip ties from my work pants. "Don't move!" I yell. "I'm a trained police officer. You're trespassing and you're under arrest."

With the threat neutralized, I head for the light switch by the kitchen to find out who I'm dealing with, leaving the invader lying flat on the floor, bound. My fear-numbed brain registers that he's saying something, but I'm too intent on identifying him to pause.

I smash into something that isn't usually in my path from the living room to the kitchen. *What the heck?* In my haste to get to the light, I hit the object with my hip and send it flying. It sounds like glass and objects hitting the floor.

I flip on the light and see...*what?* My mind can't assemble the pieces.

A small table with a fancy tablecloth lies flipped over. Food is strewn across the floor in a splatter of potatoes and peas. Spilled red wine looks like a swath of blood splattered across the mess. The glasses and dinnerware that held the meal lie shattered amid the ruined meal.

*Oh no! Oh no!* I'm registering what this must be...what it was meant to be. And somehow while I was neutralizing the threat, what I felt was adrenaline powered by fear, but now... now I experience pure terror. Somehow this is worse. So much worse than what I thought. Because now I have handcuffed my boyfriend and destroyed what was intended to be an intimate dinner. *A dinner for what? Oh...for my birthday... which is tomorrow.*

I now decipher what the person was trying to say. The person who is now silent on the other side of the couch. I peek around apprehensively and see Blake all dressed up and zip tied on the floor behind the couch.

"Blake! I'm so sorry, I'm so sorry!" I run to the kitchen and grab scissors from the drawer. Running back, I kneel and clip off the zip ties. Blake sits up.

I've never seen this expression on his face before. He's angry. And disappointed. And maybe a touch humiliated. He'd been going for the grand gesture, and I managed to ruin it.

*Shit! How am I going to make this up to him?*

He rubs his abraded wrists and dusts off his suit jacket. He can't even look at me. I can see him tamping down the anger. When he stands, all that's left is the disappointment.

"Kaitlyn. We're done." Now he looks at me, and I see the finality written there. There's no coming back from this.

Instantly, I feel my insides crumple in acute loss. Tears spring to my eyes. "No, wait..." If I can just get him to stay, maybe I can explain.

I try to grab his hand, but he pulls away and heads toward the door. When he reaches it, he turns to look at me for what I know will be the last time. "I just can't be with someone who keeps putting me at risk like this. It's just bruises...this time...but what about next time?" He says it quietly, sadly, but there is steel there too. He means it. This was the line, and I crossed it.

He's right too. I'd had my hand on my gun when I entered,

after all. What if he'd jumped up in the dark...

I can't even complete the thought.

Blake leaves and closes the door behind him. I sink to my knees in the gravy and mashed potatoes. There's a slight nick as a small piece of wine glass embeds itself in my knee, but I don't even care. The pain of his leaving me is so large that I don't even feel the cut.

# CHAPTER NINETEEN

*"I've got a surprise for you, George." Shirley ushers me into the living room of her family's home, her face alight with excitement.*

*Shirley is a fetching girl. Her honey-colored hair is pinned up under a bonnet, but a few short strands curl around her pretty face. We've been courting for a few months now and we've been getting on well. I've mostly been tolerant of these little games. Being patient is a small price to pay to see her radiant smile when I play along.*

*She pulls out a wooden box and a square of dark fabric. She hands me the box, and I'm about to open it when she stops me. "No! Don't peek, George!"*

*I leave the box on my lap, unopened, while Shirley folds the square of fabric to make a blindfold, placing it over my eyes.*

*"Now you can open it. See if you can guess what's inside," she says, her voice pitched high with excitement.*

*Blindly, I reach into the wooden box as instructed, groping around to see if I can identify what it holds. I run my fingers around the edges of the box, feeling where the sides meet the smooth bottom. The tip of my finger snags on a latch, distracting me momentarily, but then I find what I'm looking for. My fingers close around a smooth object. I run the tips of my fingers over it, getting the shape of it. It's circular with a helix spiraling outward. It has some weight in my hands.*

*"So, what do you think it is?" Shirley prods.*

*"It's a stone." I purposely guess wrong.*

*She giggles. "Nope! Try again."*

*I pretend to investigate the object further, turning it in my hands. "It's a seashell!"*

*"Close...but wrong again!" She laughs. She doesn't know I've dug dozens of these out of the ground. I knew exactly what it was the moment I held it in my hand. I'm a field assistant to Mary Anning; I dig up fossils for a living. I've tried to explain what I do to Shirley, but she doesn't really understand fully.*

*"It's...a fossil!"*

*"Yes!" she cries. "Now go ahead and have a look if you like."*

*I pull off the blindfold and examine the fossil. It's a fine specimen. Often part of it will be broken off before the shell becomes fossilized, but this one is completely intact.*

*"Do you like it?" she asks shyly. Her cheeks are rosy and her lips full. I pull my eyes away from her lips, trying to think about something else.*

*"I love it," I tell her.*

*"I thought you would. I saw it and I just had to buy it for you."*

*"Thank you," I tell her sincerely. It's sweet that it made her think of me. I give her a quick peck on the cheek.*

*She blushes furiously.*

*I glance into the box, wondering what I felt jutting out from the smooth bottom. Shirley takes the box out of my hands before I can get a good look.*

*She grabs my hand and leads me out into the garden, away from the watchful eyes of her mother, where I can kiss her properly.*

I awake from the dream as blissfully happy as George was in this moment. He was an assistant to paleontologists on the Jurassic Coast in England in the early 1800s. He would've seen a lot of shell fossils, but instead of saying so, he made sure his girlfriend knew how much he appreciated the gift. *That's so like George.*

In the glow of first love leftover from the dream, it takes me a moment to come back to my own reality. *Blake left me last night. I screwed up.* I'd spent the past evening cleaning up the ruined meal and shattered dishware. And what's left is my shattered heart. I cry messily as a new wave of grief washes over me.

Well, the message of the dream is obvious. Clearly, George knew better how to appease his love interest than I do. If only I'd been able to anticipate Blake's surprise. He was just a little too good at pulling it off—saying he was going out of town, sneaking back into the apartment while I was out. He really did surprise me.

I call Isabella and pour out the whole heartbreaking story.

She exclaims in all the right places. "Kait, you two were meant to be together. Just give him some time to get over this. He'll be back."

"I wish I agreed with you. But you didn't see his face."

"Yeah, well...you did tackle the man and zip tie him. His male ego is bruised as well as possible other parts. Not to mention you destroyed a dinner that he worked hard to prepare. It might take him a minute to get over it. But in the end, he'll remember how lucky he is. You're worth it."

"Yeah, we'll see."

"It sucks that you're sad on your birthday. And I know you can't take a break from your work right now. Just try to believe, as I do, that this will sort itself out. Give Blake some time. And we'll have a drink in honor of your birthday at the bachelorette tomorrow. We'll all help you forget about it for a bit."

When I get off the phone, I have a message from my parents wishing me a happy birthday. I return their call and give them the unhappy news about Blake. They weren't expecting him at dinner tonight since I told them he was supposed to be out of town, but I know I won't be myself. Better to explain it now. They have a lot of questions, most of them regarding my wellbeing. I reassure them that I'm okay.

I can't help myself. Against Isabella's advice, I leave several voicemails on Blake's cell phone apologizing. He doesn't pick up. Okay. Message received. He's not ready to talk yet.

It's Saturday, and my birthday, but the new case still needs our attention. No weekends off right now. And today I could really use the distraction. I head to the precinct to meet up with Joe.

# CHAPTER TWENTY

Joe is at his desk when I arrive. He's brought cupcakes and one has a little candle stuck in it. I notice his shoelaces are yellow today—very festive. The day is looking up.

"Aww. For me?" I say, picking up the cupcake and candle before he can light it and make a big deal.

"Yeah…happy birthday." He smiles.

I do my best to smile back. "Thanks. Did Sandra make these?"

He nods. "She knows you love the chocolate cupcakes with hazelnut frosting."

"That's really sweet." Truly, Sandra and Joe are as kind as they come. I'm really touched.

"Bob found Barry Greenworth's son, Sean Greenworth," Joe says. "I contacted him. He's a firefighter, but he's off shift today. We can head over there now."

On the drive over, Joe gives me a long look. "You're awfully quiet today, Kruse. What's up?"

"You should really be watching the road," I snap, annoyed

that he's noticed so quickly that I'm out of sorts. And that I'm going to have to tell this embarrassing story. *Again!*

"Not ready to talk about it yet?"

"It's Blake. We had a fight. He won't answer my calls. And, yes, I'm not ready to talk about it."

"Gotcha," Joe says. "When you're ready…"

"Sorry. I don't mean to bite your head off…I'll tell you the whole sordid story later. Today, can we just focus on work? I need to think about something else."

"Of course. Say no more."

Sean Greenworth's home is a modest but cheerful yellow two-story. A tricycle is abandoned beside the driveway as if a child jumped off just minutes ago. I almost expect to see the wheels still spinning. Wind chimes are hung by the front door, tinkling slightly in the breeze. Flowering shrubs flank the entryway.

The man that answers the door appears younger than I expected, mid-twenties, tops. His tight t-shirt strains over toned shoulders and biceps.

We introduce ourselves and show our badges.

"S'up, detectives?" Sean juts his chin as he says this. It's a greeting, not a question. He stands aside as we enter and indicates a couple of overstuffed chairs in the small living room.

The home is tidy, but everything appears a little faded and worn. When I sit down, I sink so far into the chair that I wonder if I'll be able to get out again. Seeing my predicament, Joe gives me a hand up. I struggle to pull myself out and sit perched on the front edge of the chair. Joe hides his smile and wisely sits on the wide arm of his chair instead of trying to sit in it.

Sean takes a seat on the sofa across from us, elbows on his thighs, his arms and shoulders relaxed, the picture of nonchalance. But he picks at his cuticles, betraying that he's a little more nervous than he's letting on.

"Sean, we'd like to ask you some questions about your father. We've been trying to locate him. Do you know where he is?" Joe asks.

"I'm afraid not. Haven't heard from him in months. I've been checking the homeless shelters every few days, but no one remembers seeing him. After he got out of prison, things didn't go so well for him. Couldn't hold a job. He got real effed up."

"Did you have contact with him when he was in prison?"

"Yeah, me and my mom went to see him every Saturday when she was still alive. She said he saved my life, and it was the least we could do. She died from cancer a few years ago. But I kept going to see my dad every Saturday. It was a habit by then."

I have to admit, I'm surprised. "What did she mean that he saved your life?" I ask.

"Well, I know that he confessed and all but he never killed that guy. He just said he did because he was protecting me." *What? Is this just something his mother told him to shield him from the truth of his dad's past?*

"How so?"

Sean seems to consider carefully what he says next. "Well, it's been so many years, I suppose it won't hurt to talk about it now, but it's always been this big secret." He pauses, seemingly still conflicted about discussing a long-held family secret. Then he nods, making the decision that the secret has been buried long enough. "The way my mom tells it, on the day of the murder, she and my dad got a real scary phone call. The caller said he'd taken me, and they needed to bring ten thousand dollars to a specific location or they'd never see me again."

"Someone kidnapped you?"

"Yeah. See, a man came up to me on the playground at school and asked if I wanted to see the puppies he had in his van. He said my mom's name and told me that she said it was okay. I know...it's exactly what kids are warned about nowadays. But I was only six, nothing in my sheltered life had taught me to be suspicious. I thought all adults were trustworthy. I went right off with the man. When I didn't come back after lunch break, the school called my mom. But she'd already talked to the kidnapper by then and they told her not to tell anyone what was going on."

"So, your parents find out you were kidnapped and there was a ransom demand. What did they do?"

"My dad went to the location they gave him with the ten thousand dollars...all of their savings...and all he sees is this guy lying on the ground in a pool of blood. My dad wasn't sure what to do but he thinks maybe it's the kidnapper, like maybe there were two of them and they had a disagreement or something, so he better check. He looks the guy over, trying to find some sign of where I might be. But there's nothing on him except some diamonds that my dad doesn't dare mess with. By then, my dad has the guy's blood all over him...he was stabbed so many times, there was blood everywhere. It starts to hit my dad that the whole situation is off. Maybe he's being set up. So, he takes off running. He calls my mom while he's running away to tell her it's a trap."

"So why didn't your parents call the police?"

"My parents, they don't trust the police too much and, well, the killer already called my mom while my dad was going to the meet up. They put the fear o' God in her. Told her that if my dad doesn't take the blame for the murder then they'll kill me. So, my dad is fleeing the scene and my mom is screaming at him that he has to say he committed the murder or they'll kill me. Meanwhile, someone saw my dad at the scene and called the police. They picked him up and took him in for questioning, let him know there's a witness, that he was there messing with the body. He's so scared that he does exactly what my mom told him to do—confesses to everything."

"So, your dad was afraid you would be killed if he didn't do what they asked, so he lied in his confession? He was protecting you?" Joe asks.

Sean nods.

"So why didn't he say he was innocent after you were returned to your mom, safe and sound?"

"Whoever set my dad up was really slick. They left me on my own front porch with a note pinned to my shirt. My mom didn't show me what it said at the time but years later, she pulled it out. The note said that if my dad ever took back his confession, they would off me and my mom."

Indeed. Whoever was behind this seemed to have all their bases covered. It was a well thought out plan. All the parts had to be put into place and the right pressure applied at the right time. They must've targeted Barry for some reason. Maybe they knew how much he loved his son. Whatever motivated them, it's a sad story. If it's true, then Barry spent twenty years in jail for a crime he didn't commit.

"So, your dad kept this all to himself and decided to take the fall for the murder in order to protect you and your mom?" I ask.

"Yeah, he thought it was his only choice. But one thing he was counting on, he thought if he confessed and made a deal, that he'd get a light sentence, since he cooperated. They offered him ten years, so he thought I would still be a kid when he got out. But when it came to it, that didn't happen."

"And, let me guess, Judge Harry was the reason it didn't happen."

"Yep. The judge refused the deal. Since my dad brought money, it was assumed he planned to exchange with the man that was killed. See, the dead guy was a known jewel thief, so the theory was that they met to exchange the money and the jewels and then had some argument over what the diamonds were worth. So, my dad went along with their story since he couldn't tell the real story. But then the judge pointed out that if my dad was buying ten thousand dollars in stolen jewels, then the murder occurred during the commission of a felony. So, the judge rejected the deal and gave him twenty years. My dad was furious with the judge. He cursed him every time we visited him in prison. I think he was almost angrier at him than he was at the person who set him up."

"But the judge never knew the real story—that your dad wasn't planning to buy the jewels. That he was set up."

"Right. My dad knew that. I think he just wanted someone to blame for his shitty situation."

"Did Barry know who set him up?"

"He never knew for sure...but he suspected. One of his cousins was associated with a gang and he always thought it was him. But he knew he couldn't prove it."

"He had the letter. Couldn't that have helped him?" Joe asks.

"At first, he was too afraid and told my mom not to show the note to anyone. He told her to burn it. She didn't though, she just hid it. He always thought my mom and me were in danger. Told us to watch out."

"But no one ever came after you?" I ask.

"No. But then my dad never told anyone, so I guess they had no reason to."

"And you don't know where Barry is now?"

"No. I haven't been able to find him on the street. I'd like to bring him back here and give him a place to live. He could be a grandpa to my kids, and I could pay him back for what he did for me and my mom. But he's too proud. Won't let me help him out."

"Do you think he's still angry with the judge, even now? Angry enough to hurt him?"

"He was pretty bent out of shape about the long sentence, but I think he got over it as time went by."

It's a sad story if it's true.

"Do you still have the letter?" Joe asks.

Sean nods. "Yeah. My mom gave it to me before she died. Said it was proof of my dad's love. She wanted me to keep it somewhere safe."

"Could we have it to see what evidence it might provide?" Joe asks.

Sean looks hesitant.

"We might find something that helps us discover who was behind this," Joe says.

"I'd sure like to see the guy pay for what he did to my dad," Sean says. "I'll go find it." He goes to the second floor and is gone a while.

He returns with a note in a large Ziploc. I perk up when I

see it—a note saved like that might still have DNA and fingerprints. We'll submit it for forensic analysis.

Joe and I thank Sean and head back to the precinct.

"Barry seems a long shot for the murder. I just don't see a homeless guy being that prepared. He wouldn't have the means to hire someone, and the killer we observed is way too slick. He had resources and access that Barry just couldn't have," Joe says, glancing at me.

"True. What about the person who set Barry up? Could he be the murderer? Could he have been afraid the judge knew the truth, or was about to find out the truth?"

"Maybe. But why go after the judge? If anything, I could see him going after Barry to keep him from telling his story."

"Maybe he couldn't find Barry. Even his son doesn't know where he is."

"Or maybe he already found him and eliminated him as a threat." Joe says grimly.

"We better have a look for him tomorrow," I say.

It's not until I'm driving home that it hits me. *A false confession.* That's what the witch trial dream was trying to tell me. Bethany confessed she was a witch when that seems to go against her self-interest. How did this benefit her?

I pull over and research it on my phone. It turns out that it wasn't unusual for accused witches to confess. If they went to trial and were found guilty of witchcraft, which most were, then they would be sentenced to death. Those that confessed lived, though they typically were sentenced to jail time and were often encouraged to implicate others as a sign of their sincerity.

I guess I missed the message that dream was sending me. It makes me think of the tarot cards. They were right after all. I missed the point. Too distracted with the situation with Blake, I guess.

Feeling discouraged about my misinterpretation, I get back on the road, heading to my parents' home for dinner to celebrate my birthday. After my breakup with Blake and my obvious oversight on the case, I just want to crawl into a hot bath and drink a glass of wine alone. But I know I need to show up and try to seem engaged, instead of wallowing in self-pity at home. My parents will help lift my spirits.

When I arrive, I head out to the back patio. My parents have the outside table set with good dinnerware and candles. Shrimp skewers are grilling on the barbeque and a huge spinach salad with strawberries and slivered almonds sits on the table. *If only I had an appetite...*

Dad waves to me from behind the barbeque. He has an apron on that says "The Grillfather. The man, the myth, the legend." I internally roll my eyes. *Are all dads masters of the dad joke?*

"How are you doing?" Mom asks, giving me a hug.

"I'm okay," I say, but I have to grit my teeth to prevent traitorous tears.

"I'm so sorry. Do you want to talk about it?" Mom asks.

"Not really. I'd just like to enjoy the evening and forget about it right now."

"Of course."

Overhearing, my dad comes over and gives me a long hug but doesn't say anything.

We sit down to dinner and to my parents' credit, they distract me with stories and news, and I almost manage to forget about the last couple of days as I attempt to eat the nice meal they prepared. I even find myself laughing when they light candles on a cake and sing "Happy Birthday" off key.

After the meal, Dad presents me with a small gift box tied up with ribbon. Inside is a very expensive gold charm bracelet. The charms are all items that make me think of my childhood, a fish reminding me of visits to Pike Place Market, a crab for the rocks we looked under at the Seattle shores, a ferry boat, and a Husker 'N' for Thanksgiving football games with my Mom's family in Nebraska. It warms my heart.

It's not until I'm alone again in my car, heading home, that I think about Blake and feel the pain of the loss so acutely again. I detour on the way home and end up at Isabella's apartment. She opens the door, and I don't say anything. I just start sobbing.

"Oh dear," she says pulling me inside. "I know." She sits me down on the couch and just holds me until the sobs become hiccups.

She gets me a cool washcloth for my face and a glass of water.

"Better?" she asks.

"Mu-ch," I say but I manage to hiccup right in the middle of the word, which makes us both laugh.

"Where's all the wedding stuff?" I ask, looking around the room. All the sequins and glitter are gone.

She sighs. "The centerpieces are done. They're in my mom's garage waiting for the wedding. I was tired of tripping over them all the time."

"Are you ready for your bachelorette party tomorrow?"

"Yes! I can't wait. And I think it will do you good too, to get out and forget about Blake for a bit."

"Agreed." Honestly, going out to a bar is not what I want to do at all right now, but she's right, I need to think about something else, and focusing on her sounds perfect. I'll have my game face on by tomorrow night.

When I get home, I crawl into bed, emotionally drained.

# CHAPTER TWENTY-ONE

*It's early evening, the shadows are already starting to lengthen but the air is still comfortably warm. I take my time walking through the meadow, collecting flowers as I go.*

*Arriving at the front of the stately home, I thump the knocker against the plate. Shirley opens the door, flinging it wide, a broad smile on her face.*

*"George!" she exclaims as if I'm the person she most wants to see. And maybe I am that person. One can hope.*

*I offer up the bunch of flowers I collected for her.*

*"Daisies! My favorite!" she grins. I know she said the same about the posies I brought her last week, but I'm just gratified to see her smile.*

*"Come in, come in. Why don't you wait here while I find some water to put these in." She indicates a chair in the parlor and then takes the slightly crumpled bunch of flowers, bustling off toward the kitchen.*

*As I wait, I can hear Shirley's mother instructing her to recut the stems and put some sugar in the water so they'll last longer.*

*This may take a bit. Gazing around the room for something to occupy the time, I spot a wooden box on a low shelf. I recognize it as the box Shirley used a few weeks ago to surprise me with the fossil. It had something in the bottom of it.* What caught on my finger? Was it a latch?

*Curious, I pull the box out and open it. Some yarn and knitting needles are stored in it now. I remove them and examine the bottom edges. Sure enough, I find a latch at the back. Turning it, the floor of the box raises up on that side.* A false bottom! How clever!

*I pull it open and see some papers underneath. I'm so taken with examining the mechanism of the latch that it takes me a moment to register that I've probably invaded Shirley's privacy. I start to put the papers back but the words "My dearest Shirley, the object of my undying affection..." catches my eye. I'm no expert when it comes to the written word but that sounds a bit familiar for my taste.* What does this mean? Does she have another suitor? Surely not.

*Before I can read more, the letter is snatched out of my hands. "George! How dare you!" Shirley is glaring at me, hands on hips.* I'm in for it now. *Speechless for a moment, I rub a papercut inflicted by the quick removal of the letter from my hands.*

*"Who is that letter from, Shirley?" I finally manage.*

*"It's none of your business. You should never have been snooping in my things," she says haughtily, trying to make me out to be the one in the wrong. I'm incredulous that she is shouting at me for impropriety when clearly, she's corresponding with Mr. Undying Affection.*

*But somehow, my mouth won't work. I'm not sure whether to explain why I was looking in the box or shout back at her for her duplicity.*

*I stand and hand back the box. "You have another suitor," I say simply.*

*"What if I do?"*

*At this inopportune moment, Shirley's mother appears in the doorway, having overheard our heated conversation. I see in her shrewd eyes that she's already assessed the situation.*

*"Shirley, you will say nothing more. Now go to your room. I will deal with you later," her mother says,*

*Shirley balls her fists and huffs like a chastised child. But she complies, rushing out of the room without a backwards glance.*

*Her mother turns to me. She raises an eyebrow. "Mr. Smith. It seems my daughter's attention is easily won. Perhaps it is time that you state your intentions so that she might be obliged to make a choice. Hmmm?"*

*"Do you think her choice will be in my favor, ma'am?" I'm no creator of poetic discourse as is her other suitor.* Am I merely a diversion? Will she turn me down?

*"Let's just say...she'll never marry that scoundrel if I have a breath left in my body, I'll make sure of it." It's said with a touch of menace, but then her face transforms into a bright smile. "I wish you a good day, sir, and may your proposal be rapidly forthcoming."*

*She ushers me out the door.*

*After it closes behind me, I stand for a moment, feeling like the mere pawn that I am in this matrimonial chess game. Suddenly, I'm not so sure why I've been spending my time trying to win the affection of this girl who so clearly has her sights elsewhere. I suspect I dodged a bullet, as they say.*

I wake chuckling, amused by George and Shirley. But then,

it dawns on me what this dream is pulling from my subconscious; I'm afraid that Blake will find someone else before this rift between us can be repaired. In my heart, I haven't accepted that we're broken up. I'm hoping that when Blake cools down, he'll want to reconcile. And I'm ready to promise remediation of my hypervigilance in whatever capacity he demands. But what if he moves on? Then I'll never have a chance to win him back.

The thought is like ice forming in my heart. I can't let that happen. I grab my phone and proceed to construct...and amend...not less than a dozen texts to Blake before I think better of it...and send nothing.

*He needs space and time.* I sigh. *Patience is not my virtue.*

To calm my restless mind, I head out for a run. The cool air, the rhythmic movement, and a beautiful sunrise all help to soothe my thoughts. By the time I return, I'm ready to focus on the day ahead. I'll need to have my wits about me for today's plans.

# CHAPTER TWENTY-TWO

It's the start of a beautiful sunny Sunday. We don't want to call any extra officers in on their day off, so instead we issue a BOLO for Greenworth so all those officers on the Sunday shift will be on the lookout for him. All we have for the BOLO is his most recent prison photo, so it's likely he'll look very different if he's living on the streets and hasn't shaved or cut his hair in a while. I try to imagine the clean-cut features with a beard and longer hair.

We visit a few shelters but none of the staff recognize the man in the photo. We face the fact that we'll need to search the homeless encampments. The fairer weather of summer means thousands will be on the streets. The number of homeless in Seattle has been increasing in recent years. Though sweeps and removals have attempted to reduce the number of encampments, they've more likely just relocated them temporarily to reform again at a later time. Seattle will have to come to terms with the lack of affordable housing available before this situation is likely to change.

Parking by T-Mobile Park, we walk down the encampment of RV's and tents, packed together closely for maximum two-block-long occupancy. Many of the inhabitants are sitting in the sunshine, some on overturned crates, others on discarded lawn chairs. Dogs sit with their owners, tongues lolling.

We are respectful. These are people coping in the only way they have available to them. Some just don't have the means to pay for housing. Others have personal issues such as mental illness, PTSD, drug addiction, illness or injury. Whatever the underlying reason, these arrangements function as people's homes, so we treat them as such.

An assortment of items are scattered among the shelters, each no doubt providing some usefulness to its owner. The utility of some items is obvious, such as coolers, camp stoves, tarps, blankets, shoes, and articles of clothing. Other items have a less clear purpose, such as ski poles, garden rakes, and bike wheels. With some creativity, I can imagine how these items might be repurposed. Mixed in with the useful items is a profusion of trash. Some of the occupants have made an obvious effort to keep their area clean, others…not so much.

We don't flash our badges, not wanting everyone to scatter, thinking we're there to remove them. We go "door to door" showing Greenworth's photo. Some occupants shy away but many are interested and willing to engage with us. Still, we get only shakes of the head in response to our inquiries.

A woman walks by with all her belongings in a shopping cart, searching for items she might trade or sell. When asked to look at the photo of Greenworth, she takes her time examining it. Noticing his prison jumpsuit in the headshot, she comments, "Them ex-cons, they're at the Jungle. That's where you'll find him." It's said with certainty. She then turns and shuffles off down the street again.

The Jungle is a homeless encampment on Beacon Hill with notorious criminal activity. Attempts to relocate its residents have been numerous, but ultimately unsuccessful. We aren't anxious to venture into that territory if we don't have to. Instead, we move our search to an encampment under a nearby overpass.

Several tents are huddled together, each in a different bright color. Some occupants are sleeping on mattresses in the open, some are sheltered under repurposed street signs or wooden pallets. Chairs, fire pits and a few bicycles are scattered about. Belongings are clustered inside and in front of tents.

Stepping around and over mounds of trash and a few discarded needles, we show Greenworth's photo to whoever will take a moment to look at it. Many in this encampment are strung out. Those whose attention we catch all shake their heads no when asked if they've seen him.

Finally, one man with plastic sunglasses and a baseball cap worn backwards takes a closer look. "I saw that guy at the Jungle a few weeks ago," he says. "That place is scary, man. I was glad to get out of there."

As we walk back to the cruiser, Joe comments, "Well, we've heard it twice now, it looks like all leads are pointing to the Jungle." Reluctantly, we head to the encampment by I-5.

The number of occupants seems sparse. A recent sweep is probably responsible. This should make it a little less dangerous. Still, Joe says, "Stay sharp here, Kruse..." He's interrupted by his phone ringing.

After a short conversation, he hangs up and tells me,

"Bob and Sally saw our BOLO and found Greenworth by the pergola in Pioneer Square. He must've been relocated in a recent sweep." What a relief—we won't have to navigate the Jungle.

"That's right by the courthouse," I comment. "I wonder if he was watching the judge."

"Possibly. But it's a ways from the judge's home where the murder took place. I don't see him getting there easily."

"True. Are they bringing Greenworth to the precinct?" I ask.

"No. Instead they're going to help him gather his things, then take him to his son's house to get cleaned up. They contacted Sean and he asked them to bring Barry there. Let's meet them at the house so we can talk to Barry there, instead of taking him in. The last thing I want to do is remind him of his past interrogation. I think we're more likely to get him to talk if he's comfortable."

"Do you think he'll tell us anything? He spent twenty years in prison for a crime he didn't commit, just to keep his family safe. Why would he change his story now?" I ask.

"Yeah, I thought of that too. Assuming the story Sean told us was the truth, repeating that now could put his family at risk again. I think we have to approach this as an opportunity to get justice and at the same time protect him from any retaliation. If the murderer is behind bars, then Greenworth and his family would finally be safe."

When we reach Sean's home, Bob and Sally haven't arrived yet. This time I sit on the arm of the chair offered. Sean is pacing nervously. For the second time in two days, his kids are with his wife getting ice cream. Bet they can't believe their luck.

"Sean, when is the last time you saw your dad?" I ask him.

"Right after he got out of prison. Told him he could stay with me, but he was too proud. Wanted to make it on his own. Only, it was too hard for him after all that prison time. He got fired from his job at a fast-food restaurant. I went by looking for him one day and the restaurant owner told me he had complaints from customers that my dad was rude, so he was fired. After that, I lost track of him. He'd moved out of the halfway house when I went by. I think he was embarrassed. Didn't want to face me." His voice breaks as he says, "As if I would've cared after all he's done for me."

The cruiser pulls up out front of the house and Sean heads outside. Joe and I hang back, just inside the door. The moment is tense. I'm not sure if Barry wants this reunion as much as his son does.

Sally gets out of the passenger side and opens the rear door of the cruiser for Barry. He gets out, blinking in the bright sun. His hair and beard are long and tangled, his eyes a little wild as he scans the yard for threats. He's a large man, broad in the chest and tall. His clothing is dirty and appears to consist of many layers. A plaid button-down shirt is open over a couple of scruffy t-shirts. A green vest sits on top of that. His jeans are frayed and caked with dirt. Likely it's the only clothing he owns. Gloves with the fingers cut out are on his hands—good for cool nights—and he wears large work boots, loosely laced.

Bob gets a knapsack out of the trunk. It's only slightly larger than a child's school backpack. *This is all he owns?*

I find my hands are clenched in anticipation of the meeting and I purposely relax them.

"Dad." The word comes out slightly strangled as Sean

fights back tears.

Barry looks at his son, his eyes squinting to focus on him. All of us hold our breath.

A minute passes. Then another.

I can see the moment that Barry's expression softens. "Son …" he says, barely louder than a whisper.

Sean rushes to close the distance between them, and my heart rate spikes, anticipating that Barry might find this threatening given his background: a lifetime spent in prison and on the streets. But Barry stands his ground and embraces his son. After a moment, he holds Sean at arm's length. "I need to get a good look at you," he says gruffly. His eyes search his son's face. "You still got your mother's eyes."

"So I'm told."

"Sean, I…"

"You don't have to explain, Dad," Sean interjects.

"I know I don't. And don't interrupt your father." He looks sharply at Sean, but then his expression softens again. "All these past weeks and months I've been on the streets, I've had a lot of time to think 'bout what I wanted to say to you…if I ever saw you again."

He takes a deep breath as if to steel himself. "So here it is. All those years I was in prison…every week, I couldn't hardly wait to see your face, to see how you'd grown and how you'd changed."

He pauses, gritting his teeth. "But I felt…ashamed." He shakes his head. "I hated bein' on the other side of that glass. It broke my heart for you to see me that way."

"But it wasn't your fault."

"Maybe not, but I felt the shame, just the same." Barry pauses again. This is clearly a difficult moment for him.

"And then when I got out…I couldn't face you as an ex-con. I wanted…well, I was thinkin' I would get a job, some money… then come find you when I felt like a man. A man worthy of your company. But…well, look how that turned out." He spreads his arms and shrugs.

"I just wanted to see you, Dad. You didn't need to do all that."

"I did need to. For myself," Barry says gruffly. "But now… now I know what rock bottom feels like and, well,…that will knock the pride right out of a man." He looks sheepish, his face coloring in mortification. "Will you forgive me?"

Sean nods. "There's nothing to forgive. Now, come inside." He steers his dad toward the front door.

I sigh in relief. Silently I'm rooting for these men to find each other again. If Barry's story is true, then they deserve a second chance.

When Barry sees Joe and I, he stops short.

"Mr. Greenworth, I'm Detective Riley and this is my partner Detective Kruse. We're sorry to interrupt your reunion but we'd like to speak with you when you've had a chance to get settled."

"You're wastin' your time, detectives," Barry says, pushing past us.

"Do you want…" Sean indicates the bathroom. Barry nods. "Just a minute," Sean says.

Going into the bedroom, he returns with a clean set of clothes and a razor.

While Barry is cleaning up, I look through the front window and see Joe talking with Sally and Bob and then they head off to return to their duties. Then Joe and I wait with Sean in the living room for Barry to be done in the bathroom.

It takes a while.

"What did those cops tell my dad to make him come with them?" Sean asks Joe.

"They said his son wanted him to come home."

"Home." He repeats. "That has a nice sound to it. I hope I can get him to stay."

Just when I'm thinking we need to check if Barry climbed out through the window, he emerges from the bathroom, a noticeably better odor accompanying him. His hair is damp and still long and pulled back in a ponytail. He's shaved his beard off. The combined effect takes years off his appearance. "I'll never take a shower for granted again," he says, grinning at Sean.

Noticing us still in the living room, Barry comments, "I see you didn't take your cue to leave."

"Mr. Greenworth, we'd like to speak with you about your relationship with Judge Harold Clifton," Joe says.

Barry sinks onto the couch opposite us. "That's easy, there's no relationship. I got nothin' to do with him. That man cost me ten years of my life. When I heard that he was killed, I thought, *He must've pissed off the wrong guy.*"

"He increased your sentence. I can see how that would make you resent him. I have to ask, do you have an alibi for last Monday night, the night he was killed?"

"No, I was on the streets." He shakes his head as if the question is ridiculous. "I don't remember what day that even was. I heard a rumor that the judge was shot in his home. Do I look like I had the green to buy a piece and get a lift to some fancy neighborhood to off someone? That just don't make no sense."

I tend to agree, but the question had to be asked. And he's not off the hook; there are ways he could've made it happen.

*If there's a will, there's a way*, so they say.

"Fair enough," is all Joe says. "Listen, we have reason to believe that you weren't able to be completely honest in your original confession. Would you like to discuss it?"

Barry gives his son a long searching look. Trying to determine what he's said, no doubt.

"Nope. Nothing I wanna to say 'bout it..." Barry starts.

"Dad, you don't have to protect me any longer," Sean says.

"Sean! What did I say about interrupting me!" Barry says angrily. He turns his attention back to Joe and he chooses his words carefully, meting them out in a measured, even tone. "What I said before...in my confession...was the truth. I. Killed. Speck. But now I done my time, you see? And I don't have to answer any more questions. So, with all due respect, I think it's time for you to leave."

Ignoring what Barry has said, Joe tries again. "Are you sure you don't want the true killer to pay for what he did? You spent twenty years in prison serving his time. Don't you want justice?"

"Detectives, I don't know what you think you know, but you're dead wrong. I did it. End of story." So, he's not done protecting his son and his son's family. That's how he's going to play it. Or maybe, just maybe, he really did do it, and this is just the story that Sean's mother told him all these years. A story of sacrifice and love that she thought would open her son's heart. Maybe Barry really is a killer. I want to believe in the hero protecting his family but perhaps it's a myth after all.

"If you change your mind." Joe hands him a card.

"I won't," he says to our backs as we leave.

# CHAPTER TWENTY-THREE

I set a smoked Old Fashioned in front of Isabella. It's an inside joke; once, her fiancé Darius said he thought it was sexy when the smoke from the drink made her voice raspy. Tonight is Isabella's bachelorette party. She teaches third grade so she's off for the summer; she's not worried about celebrating on a Sunday night, and it was the only time the both of us and all five bridesmaids could make it. I'll have to watch out not to drink too much or tomorrow's going to be rough at work.

We're at our first stop, Bar None, the bar where I've met Isabella for a drink many times. The waitress brings me a Dark and Stormy without even asking. I'm about to decline, thinking I'll pace myself, but decide to just go with it. I've arranged a limo to take us to the bars on our list and then to take everyone home after, so no one has to worry about driving. I could use a drink to drown my sorrows about Blake anyway. I'll just let this first drink take the edge off, then I'll take it slower.

As if reading my mind, Isabella asks, "Any word from Blake?"

"No. Not a word," I say with a sigh.

"He'll be back," Isabella says sagely. It's hard to take her seriously with her "Bride to be" sash and tiara. "It's only been two days," she says. "Give it time."

"I'm not so sure. I had a dream last night about someone finding out their girlfriend was seeing someone else. It made me worry that he might move on before I have a chance to smooth this over."

"Well, then, you just need to make sure that doesn't happen," Isabella says, winking at me.

Isabella's five bridesmaids return from the bar. "Ready to get this party started?" Ivy asks, as she and Taliah set seven shots on the table.

"Let's do it!" I agree, picking up a shot glass. All of us whoop like sorority girls even though we're all in our thirties. Yep, we aim to be as embarrassing as possible tonight. We clink our glasses and I toss one back along with the rest. The shot is some sweet concoction that probably has a flirty name, and it burns just slightly going down.

I'm ready to have fun with Isabella tonight. I want this to be the sendoff she deserves.

Draining my first drink in record time, I start to feel a little buzzed, but pleasantly so. My resolve to watch how much I drink is swiftly going out the window.

"It's time to test your knowledge of your husband to be," I announce, pulling out a list of questions about Darius. I've asked him the answers already.

"Do your worst," she challenges me. "I know him better than he knows himself."

"Cocky, huh?" I laugh. "So what is Darius' favorite late-night snack?"

"Easy," she says. "He loves whipped cream straight from the can." She wiggles her eyebrows suggestively and is rewarded with hoots of laughter from the bridesmaids.

I start to look up his answer. "But..." she says, holding up a finger for me to wait. "He won't admit that. He'll say, his favorite late-night snack is the chocolate dipped pretzels I make. He knows just how to butter me up."

I look down at his answers, as the bridesmaids do an imitation of a drum roll. "His response is...Isabella's chocolate pretzels." She raises her hands as everyone cheers.

"Okay, smartass," I tease. "Here's one you won't get. What does Darius pretend to like but secretly hate?"

She thinks for a minute. "He hates it when I order light and then steal his food at a restaurant. He pretends that he doesn't mind but I can see he's thinking—'order your own.'" She laughs.

The drumroll resumes. I look down and begrudgingly have to admit, she knows Darius pretty well. "He said: 'Sharing my french fries.'"

The game continues with Isabella getting more right than wrong. She's tripped up by his favorite book turning out to be *The Da Vinci Code*, when she thinks it's *War and Peace*.

And she has no idea that his guilty pleasure is once a month going to the arcade when he says he's at the gym.

"Well, it wouldn't be a guilty pleasure if you knew about it," I point out.

"I guess he'll have to pick something else to feel guilty about now," she says and everyone laughs.

The next bar stop goes by in a blur of laughter and shots

all around. After some coaxing, we manage to get Isabella up to the microphone to sing karaoke. She picks "Single Ladies" by Beyoncé, pointing out all her single friends to the crowd and then showing us the ring on her finger as she belts out the lyrics. We all cheer her on and she nails it, even if she's a little tipsy. She has a great voice.

Several bridesmaids pick a song, but I'm not nearly drunk enough yet to take the mic. I'll probably never be that drunk. I don't sing in front of people.

By the third stop on our bar tour, I'm feeling no pain. We're at a country bar and I'm dancing every song with Isabella and her other friends. It's a great group of women and we are having an excellent time. Now, several drinks in, I've finally forgotten that I have anything to be sad about.

I get another round of shots from the bar, and everyone gathers around to take one. Our whoop is getting louder as we lose any inhibitions. I'm sure we're drawing some amused and maybe some annoyed glances from others in the bar, but I'm past caring.

The music changes and a line dance starts up, but it's a couple's dance and I don't know the moves, so I take a seat at the bar. Isabella takes a seat beside me.

"Having fun?" I ask.

"So much fun," she says. "Have another drink with me?"

Just as I'm about to hail the bartender, I feel a tap on my shoulder. Looking around, I see a handsome man in a cowboy hat. "Dance with me?" he asks.

"You should ask this gal here," I say pointing to Isabella. "She's the bride. She'll be off the market soon. Now's your chance."

He laughs and says, "I'm asking you."

Overhearing our conversation from her seat beside me, Isabella turns and pushes me off the bar stool. "Go have fun," she says. "Oops!" she says giggling as I almost fall. Mr. Handsome grabs my elbow and keeps me upright.

*Right, I should go have fun,* I think. Blake wants me out of his life, so why shouldn't I?

We head out onto the dance floor, joining the other couples. I manage to pick up some of the moves by watching the other couples, and Mr. Handsome guides me through the rest, leading me and spinning me in time to the music. *I'm starting to feel dizzy.*

"You've done this before," I comment inanely.

"Guilty as charged."

"Do you come here often?" *Why am I resorting to pick up lines in place of conversation?* My brain is searching for something more intelligent to say but the alcohol in my bloodstream is making it a challenge.

"I do," he says, laughing and placing his hand on my back to steer me the correct direction. He catches me as I trip over my own feet. I laugh at my own inability to follow the moves. It's freeing to feel so out of control. Flirting with this man makes me feel desired again. Just for the briefest of moments.

He spins me again and then dips me back, his face coming inches from mine. My eyes wander to his lips. He pauses briefly, tantalizingly, before righting me.

The room is rotating slightly, and I feel more than a little off balance.

*This isn't what I want. I don't want this man to get the wrong idea. What I want is Blake. Even through the fog created by the alcohol, I know this to be true.* Suddenly my head hurts and I feel nauseated from all the turns.

The dance ends. "Another?" he asks.

"I think I better sit this one out," I say and turn to head back to the barstool.

"Aw, come on," he says and grabs my arm, pulling me backward. With my current lack of balance, I slip and fall back, landing in his arms. I'm trying to stand back up again when I hear someone say, "I'll take it from here." Strong arms lift me back on my feet. I struggle against this new person, feeling manhandled and disoriented.

Mr. Handsome doesn't back off. "She's with me," he says... *but that's not right.* My mouth won't form the right words to protest.

"It sounds like she was ready to sit this one out," says my rescuer.

Mr. Handsome backs off, hands lifted. My face is pressed against my rescuer's chest as his one arm pins me against him. *Out of the frying pan, into the fire. Did this new guy just see how vulnerable I am and swoop in? The way he's holding me so close feels like the beginning of an abduction. I'm no longer sure if the confusion I'm feeling is just the alcohol. Did someone put something in my drink?*

I struggle out of the arms of this new man. He lets me go. I squint to bring his face into focus, not sure if I want to thank him or tell him to leave me alone. *And....Oh my God! It's Blake! How is he here? And he had to pull me literally out of the arms of another man. How could this be worse?*

"Blake, what...?" is all I can come up with.

"I just wanted to make sure you were okay," he says and even though the room is spinning, the anger in his tone registers. He turns and walks out of the bar. I'm left with my mouth literally hanging open. *How did I let myself get so out of control? This is so unlike me.*

I find my way to Isabella. "Was that really Blake?" I ask, wondering how he could have possibly been here. *Did I just imagine him because he was who I wanted to see?*

"What? Where?" she asks, whipping around. She's in no better shape than me.

"Why was he here?" I ask, as if she could possibly know.

"I think...I think I texted him," she says blearily.

I grab her phone and scroll back a ways. Sure enough. She told him where we were and that he better come make things right with me if he didn't want to lose me. *Drunk texting. Never a good move.*

*But he came to the bar. To make things right with me. Maybe I do have a chance to get back with him...or did. Before he found me in the arms of another man.*

*How do I keep screwing things up?*

Suddenly, I'm mortified. I just want to be able to think straight. I ask the bartender for water and drink it down without a pause, then ask for more. I need to sober up.

The rest of the night passes without incident and I start to get my head straight. I even manage to wrangle a gaggle of drunk women back into the limo and safely back to each of their homes.

Isabella is the last to be dropped off. She's very drunk, but in a happy way.

"I love you!" She throws her arms around me.

"I love you too!" I hug her back and accompany to her door, her arm flung over my shoulder.

"I'm shorry if I meshed up things with Blake," she slurs. So, she does remember, I wasn't sure.

"It's okay. You meant well."

"I did!" she exclaims, gesticulating wildly.

"You did," I agree.

I help her find her key and get safely inside.

I sit quietly in the back of the limo, heading home, unsure if my actions have now pushed away the love of my life... for good this time.

# CHAPTER TWENTY-FOUR

*It's lunchtime.* Finally. *This morning's patients were challenging, and I've worked up an appetite.*

*As I'm heading to the break room, I notice my hands are clammy.* Calm down, Sam, *I tell myself. I haven't found a note in my lunch for a couple of weeks now. But every day, I'm afraid that I'll find another one.*

*I can't believe I've let Devin get under my skin. My mind reels, recalling the events of the past few months. Ever since the bomb threat and the note Devin left—"Be careful when you eat your lunch"—I've been on edge.*

*I got the first note in my lunch bag a few weeks after the fake bomb. I'd almost forgotten about Devin and his threatening package. But then, one day I opened my lunch and found a note inside nestled among the food I'd brought. It simply said, "Enjoy your lunch." Such a benign sounding note. The kind of message a mother might leave for her child in a school lunch. Only, it's not benign.* Not even close.

*When I found that first note, I involuntarily pushed back*

*from the break room table, shoving my lunch bag away from me. I used a paper towel to pick up the bag and threw it in the trash. I washed my hands thoroughly, concerned that the note might not be the only thing placed in with my lunch. Was there poison in my sandwich? Was this the first time someone messed with my lunch, or could previous lunches have been tampered with? In my state of uncertainty, it wasn't until the next day that it occurred to me that I should've called the police … had the lunch tested. Only—would anyone take me seriously?*

*I'd called the prison and was told that Devin had been released after completing his sentence the following week. He'd still been inside when the package was sent, so either he had an accomplice at the time, or he'd managed to send it while he was still in prison. But now he was out there—somewhere.* Would I ever feel safe again?

*I keep scanning the office visitors for someone with Devin's appearance. For a while after that first note in my lunch, I bought my lunch at the sandwich shop on the corner. Eventually I felt ridiculous and went back to bringing my own lunch again. But then, a couple of weeks later, I found another note. Out went the lunch again.*

*Since that time, I've found a few notes. And every day, I wonder if one will be there. I've taken a couple of lunches, both with and without the notes, and had them tested for cyanide—Devin's poison of choice. I have a friend who works at a forensics lab, and she ran them for me. To my extreme relief, no cyanide was detected. I just hope Devin hasn't graduated to a new form of poison. The food tastes fine, but that's no guarantee. One thing I know for a fact is that he's gotten in my head with just a few innocent-sounding notes. Some days, I feel like I'm going crazy.*

*Bringing my thoughts back to the present day, I pull my lunch bag out of the fridge. Bracing myself, I peek inside, anticipating a slip of paper with a deceptively cheerful message. Today there's nothing. Only my lunch. Relief courses through me.*

*I'm taking an early lunch so there's only two other people in the break room. I glance around. I don't know either of the other employees very well so I find my own table.*

*Pulling out the contents of my lunch bag—a sandwich, an apple, and a piece of cake—I immerse myself in a copy of a research article I brought with me, while I eat. The sandwich is ham and cheese, my favorite, so I'm glad there wasn't a note today. When I finish it, I pick up the apple. Distracted by the article, I'm just about to bite into the apple when I notice that it looks like it's been cut into. It's subtle, a thin line, barely noticeable.*

*I take the apple to the break room counter and pry the slit open with a kitchen knife.*

*The hair on the back of my neck stands up.*

*I pull out a tiny note that has been slipped into the apple, and unfold it.*

*"Enjoy your lunch."*

*Involuntarily, I throw the apple away from me.*

*It rolls down the counter, coming to rest with the opposite side toward me. There's another slit. With shaking hands, I use the kitchen knife to pry it open.*

*What I find makes me jump backward in alarm. I cry out as the knife and the apple drop to the floor with a clatter.*

*Hearing my distress, the others in the room rush over to assist me.*

*"Are you okay?" asks Drew, the janitor, at the same time*

*that Becky, the receptionist, asks, "What happened?"*

*I point at the apple on the floor.*

*Becky reaches down to pick it up.*

*"Be careful!" I shout in alarm.*

*She looks at me strangely, then carefully picks the apple up. Looking in the slit she sees what made me cry out...the item nestled in the flesh of the apple.*

*"A razorblade!" she says, incredulous.*

Waking from the dream with a jolt, it takes me a minute to quell the fear that gripped Sam when she found the razorblade in her apple. The memory is so disturbing, and as fresh as if the event only just occurred. I reexperienced Sam's fear that someone was watching covertly, wanting to cause her harm. The death threats Barry sent to the judge must have brought this memory to the surface. With this experience of Sam's fresh in my mind, I'm amazed the judge was able to ignore the threats and go about his day without always looking over his shoulder.

I wonder if Sam ever brought this to the police. Surely, she would've after she found the razor blade. And did they catch Devin? It's surprising that he was able to slip into the office without Sam recognizing him. I could see it happening once, but for it to happen multiple times seems improbable.

My head hurts this morning, thanks to last night's celebration. Crawling out of bed, I stumble to the bathroom. With my eyes scrunched shut against the light, I take some ibuprofen and drink a couple of glasses of water. It's a while before I begin to feel human again.

# CHAPTER TWENTY-FIVE

I order two extra espresso shots in my latte from Barrett's, drinking half of it before I even get across the street to the precinct. It helps some, but I'm dragging a bit. *Ah, regrets.*

Joe looks up when I arrive with the coffee and bagels. He chuckles. "Late night last night, Kruse?"

"Is it that obvious?" He knows it was Isabella's bachelorette party last night so I'm hoping he just expected that I'd be tired today, not that I look like something the cat dragged in... although admittedly I *feel* a little like that.

"You just look tired."

*Nope, I guess I actually look it.*

"Well, I'll be better after a nice caffeine jump-start," I reply, holding up my coffee cup.

"Hey, look at this." Joe pulls out a couple of reports. "I had the lab put a rush on the analysis of the note that was pinned to Sean when he was a kid. When I took it over, they said it was pretty old and not to expect much in the way of fingerprints or DNA, but since it was stored in a Ziploc, they would do what they could. It looks like they actually found one partial print, and they got DNA as well. They just had to exclude the other two sources of DNA: Sean and his mother."

"How did they exclude them? Did they have their DNA?"

"No, but they had Barry's since he was incarcerated, so they were able to figure out which DNA was Sean's since he was a fifty percent match, and from there, his mother's, since she was a fifty percent match to Sean."

"Sounds complicated, but that's good news. What did they find in the remaining DNA?"

"I'm running the print through the system now to look for a match. But the DNA came back as a male with a ten percent DNA match to Barry."

"So, a relative."

"Yep. Remember Sean mentioned that Barry suspected a cousin might be behind the murder cover-up? Looks like he was right."

Joe's computer chimes to signal the end of the fingerprint search. He turns the monitor so we both can see the results. No match. *Darn.* So, Barry's relative is not in the system.

"Barry was so insistent on telling us that he was the murderer. It made me wonder if it really was him and maybe his mother made up the whole story to preserve his legacy in the eyes of his son."

"I wondered that too," Joe says. "But now it seems his mom's story is supported by this. Someone else was involved."

"Do you want to go back and interview him again?"

In answer, Joe grabs the cruiser keys off his desk and we head off.

When we arrive, Sean answers the door. "Detectives, I wasn't expecting you."

"Hope you don't mind. We have some more questions for Barry," Joe says.

"We're just getting the kids ready. You can come in. My wife and Barry are in the kitchen."

He steps back from the door to let us in, and we step into a very different scene than on previous visits. The whole family is present and getting ready for the day ahead. Chaos reigns.

Joe is almost impaled by a small girl who comes flying around the corner with a backpack in hand. "Here it is…Oh, sorry!" she yells as she speeds by into the kitchen.

Sean's wife is busy preparing sandwiches. "Put it on the chair there," she tells her daughter. "Hello, detectives, Sean has told me all about you. We'll be out of your hair in a minute," she says to us, looking up from her position at the island as we enter.

A slightly older boy comes running down the stairs. "I can't find my insect book, Mom."

Barry is standing at the sink, clearing up what looks like a pancake breakfast. "I know where we put it. We were looking at those dragonflies with it last night. It's on the table in the other room there." The boy rushes to the next room to get the book.

Sean's wife finishes the lunches and stuffs them into backpacks. She glances at us. "They're in camp this week. I'm taking them over now on my way to work." She picks up both backpacks and her own work bag and heads out the front door, calling back over her shoulder, "Come on, kids, it's time to go."

The kids trail after her, each trying to find matching shoes on the way out the door.

Barry looks up from the sink, his expression somewhat overwhelmed. "Never a dull moment around here." He chuckles. He's cut his hair short, and the transformation is remarkable.

Sean takes a plate from him. "Go ahead and talk to the detectives, Dad. I'll finish up."

Barry dries his hands and heads for the living room where we all find a seat.

"I told you all I had to say," Barry says, his tone firm. He's not changing his mind.

"Right, but now we have some new information that we thought might be relevant," I say.

Now we have his attention. "What information?"

"Well, Sean gave us the note that was pinned to him when he was returned home."

"I told my wife to burn that," Barry says, looking up at the ceiling as if asking for patience with his late wife.

"Well, it's a good thing she didn't. We ran the DNA on it and the result was interesting."

"Yeah? What did it say?"

"When we excluded your wife and son's DNA, the only other DNA on the note was from a male that has a ten percent match with your DNA, meaning it was a relative that was involved."

"That son of a bitch!" Barry jumps up from the chair, clearly agitated. He clenches his fists.

"You know who it was," Joe comments.

Barry sits back down and I can see him struggling to decide what to do with the information. Does he tell the truth now and put himself and his family back in the crosshairs? Is getting justice worth the risk of tipping off the kidnapper that Barry might expose him?

He sighs heavily. "My son told me what he said to you. Let's just say, for argument's sake, I went to jail to protect my family. Do you think...after I did twenty years in the slammer...after I did my time...that I would change my story now? Now, when I just met my grandkids and have even more to protect?"

*He has a point.*

"I understand your concern," Joe says. "If you can identify who it is, we can put a protective detail on you and your family until we can put him in prison and away from your family."

"Not good enough." Barry shakes his head. "You don't think someone could threaten my family from prison?"

"Fair enough," says Joe. "Like you said, you've done your time. Or the way I see it, someone else's time. If you don't want the person who separated you from your family for twenty years to get what's coming to him, I guess we can't make you. We don't have enough for a case without your testimony."

Barry nods solemnly. "My family is too important. It's not worth it." He's made his choice and he's at peace with it.

As we're getting ready to leave, Joe remarks, "I have to say, Barry, having met you, I'm surprised about the violence you promise in the death threats you sent the judge. It doesn't really seem your style. They sure were creative, though." He arches a brow, inviting comment.

Barry looks at Joe blankly. "What death threats?"

"Oh, okay, I'm sure you don't want to admit to threatening a judge..." Joe starts.

Barry shakes his head. "I didn't send any death threats. It's true, I told my son and my wife I hated the judge for givin' me double the time. But I didn't put it in writin'. I'm not that stupid."

I'm not sure whether to believe him. *If he didn't send them, who did?*

It's my turn to drive. I take the wheel and turn the cruiser back toward the precinct.

"We could look into Barry's family. If we can figure out who the murderer was, we could bring them in for questioning and maybe, if we're lucky, they leave some DNA on a coffee cup," I say.

"Yeah," Joe replies. "But I'm not sure it's worth putting Barry's family at risk." Even though I want justice for Barry, I have to agree with him. The only thing worse than spending twenty years in jail protecting your family is having it turn out to all be for nothing by putting his family back at risk.

Joe's phone rings and he puts it on speaker.

"This is Detective Riley," he says.

"Yes, Detective, this is Dr. Clive Ogilvie. I'm the Chelan County Medical Examiner."

Joe glances at me, a quizzical look on his face. Chelan is in the middle of the state. *Why would they be reaching out to us?*

"What can I do for you, Doctor?"

"I understand you and your partner were in the Wenatchee Valley this past Wednesday, is that correct?"

"Yes, we were there."

"Well, an event occurred on one of the orchards that day and I sure could use your help looking into it."

"Which orchard?"

"Apple-a-Day," he replies. Joe arches a brow at me.

"We weren't aware of any 'events,' Doctor."

"I suspected that."

"Could you be more specific? What does this relate to?"

"I'm afraid not. I'd prefer to discuss it in person. Could you both make a trip back out here?"

*Well, that's odd.*

"We could come out tomorrow morning," Joe replies, looking at me to confirm. I nod.

"I sure would appreciate it, Detective."

"Okay, we'll see you then."

Joe hangs up. "Well, what do you think that's all about?" he asks me.

"You got me. I'm not sure why he would reach out to us. How did he even know we were there? That's a little spooky."

"There was that one incident that occurred with the worker, just as we were leaving. Greg Mason tried to downplay it but maybe he's not treating his workers well or something."

# CHAPTER TWENTY-SIX

The dream about the razor blade in the apple from last night has been on my mind all day. I just have to know how it turned out for Sam. Did they catch Devin? How did he get the notes in Sam's lunch without being seen? If only I could just call up a memory at will so I could answer some of these questions. After having these dreams of my past lives for years now, I've come to recognize that I dream about whatever is currently troubling my subconscious. So, while it's possible that if I concentrate on the dream from last night when I go to bed tonight, that I might have a related dream, there's no guarantee.

Luckily, I have another way to find out what happened.

After work, I head over to visit Sam's sister, Tina. I know her from dreams of my past life as Sam. But while Sam passed away in her late thirties from melanoma, Tina is still alive now in her late sixties, or maybe early seventies now, come to think of it.

After a couple of previous cases took me into Sam's past,

I reached out to Tina for more information. At first, I didn't tell her about my dreams, explaining my knowledge of Sam's life by saying that my mother was a friend of Sam's. But once I came to trust Tina, I came clean and admitted the lie. She was understandably unhappy about the deception, but she was able to see past it to recognize the gift our connection provided: that of sharing our memories of Sam.

It was a huge relief to reveal my ability to Tina. She's the only one I've ever talked to about my strange dreams. Over time we've become great friends, almost like sisters really. Since I was Tina's sister in my past life as Sam, it's not surprising we both feel the connection.

I text her to make sure the time is okay and she responds, "Come on over, I have a chicken pot pie in the oven."

My mouth waters. Tina is a great cook.

When I knock on her door, I still feel the same sense of déjà vu—Sam's memories make this house feel like the home I grew up in, even though I've only recently been here as Kaitlyn.

Tina greets me warmly and ushers me back to the cozy kitchen, where I take a seat at the familiar table. She pulls the pie out and dishes some out for both of us. I decline wine. My head still hurts from last night. I dig into the flaky pot pie. It's heaven.

"You have another case that relates to Sam's memories?" Tina guesses.

"Yeah, I might. I'm not sure exactly why I'm dreaming about this particular memory, but I had to know how it played out in Sam's life."

"Wow. Must have been a dramatic one," she comments.

"It was. I dreamed about a man that Sam treated for a

while. I was wondering if she told you about him. I've had dreams about him before."

"She was pretty careful about confidentiality but there were a few patients that ended up being known publicly for one reason or another, and those I knew about."

"Well, this one would've definitely been known publicly. He was arrested and convicted of attempting to poison his coworker by putting cyanide in his lunch."

"Ah, yes, hard to forget Devin."

"What did you know of him?"

"I remember that he blamed Sam for his conviction and he began threatening her. He sent her something in the mail that looked like a bomb. She had the whole building evacuated. Scared her to death."

"Yes, I've had that dream." I grimace. "But then last night, I had another one where she got notes in her lunch saying, 'Enjoy your lunch,' and when she found out he'd been released from prison, she was worried he was sneaking in and poisoning her lunch."

"I remember." Tina sits back in her chair and shakes her head at the memory. "Devin was something else. He liked to toy with Sam. Make her worry. Putting little notes in her lunch. Sam met me for lunch one day and I could tell she was really shaken. It was right after she found a razor blade in an apple. She barely touched her lunch even though we were at a restaurant. She lost some weight during that time. Even just the memory of finding the notes and the razor blade made her lose her appetite."

"I woke up shaking just from dreaming about it. I'm just thankful she didn't get hurt. But my dream ended before I could learn what she did about it. Do you remember?"

"She went to the police with the apple. They were very concerned about her safety and set up surveillance to monitor the fridge she put her lunch in. It was all done very hush-hush so that Devin wouldn't know they were watching. She said they installed the surveillance equipment at night when all the employees had gone home. Sam had never spotted Devin in the office so she figured he must have disguised himself."

"I wondered about that. So, what happened? Did they catch him?"

"They watched for a few days and then sure enough, one day someone came in before lunch and took Sam's food out of the fridge. They put a note in and sprinkled something on her sandwich."

"Did they catch him?"

"Sure did. Caught him right in the act. The powder he sprinkled on was cyanide, just like he used before on his co-worker. Only...it wasn't Devin."

"What do you mean? Someone else was poisoning her?"

"Yes, Devin was paying someone to do it all for him because he knew Sam would recognize him. Turned out it was the janitor."

"The janitor? Drew? He was in my dream. The day the razor blade was in her lunch, he was in the break room. That asshole! He acted so concerned about Sam, and all that time, he was the one who put it there. He must have wanted to watch and see if she bit into it. The gall of that man!"

"I remember it really shook Sam up."

"I could feel how scared she was." Then I remember something from my dream. "Sam had her food tested for cyanide, but it came back clean."

"The police thought he wasn't poisoning it every day."

I mull it over for a bit. "But why did I have this dream now? What is my subconscious trying to process?"

"Anyone at the precinct poisoning lunches?" Tina jokes.

"I don't have time to bring a lunch with me. We usually eat out. I'm not worried about my lunch."

"In your murder case, did someone get poisoned?"

"No…but someone did write notes…death threats. In fact… I think that's it!"

"What is?"

"We found out today that the person who we thought was sending threats to the victim wasn't the person we assumed it was. At least, that's what he claims. The notes had a vague signature—a dollar sign, which we thought pointed to a man named Greenworth. You know, a dollar, implying money, 'green'. I thought we made an incorrect assumption, and that they were from an entirely different sender, someone else who felt represented by a dollar sign. But maybe the sender actually wanted us to suspect Greenworth all along and throw us off the trail. Now I'm even more convinced that if we find out who wrote those notes, we'll find the killer."

"Just like the janitor actually wrote those notes that seemed like they came from Devin. He was the real stalker."

"Right."

"Thanks, Tina, that was very helpful." I give her a big hug.

"I'm so glad."

She gives me what's left of the pot pie to take home.

Before I go to bed, I try Blake's cell phone again.

He's still not answering.

It's not looking good for us.

# CHAPTER TWENTY-SEVEN

*Glancing around in the dark to ensure no one is watching, I descend the stairs leading to the basement access behind the hotel. I knock twice on the rough wood of the non-descript door. Pause. Then twice more.*

*The door cracks open. It's a new guy. I've never seen him before. He's bigger than Bill, the usual door guy. His biceps are at risk of ripping his skin-tight shirt.*

*"No entry," he says gruffly. "Go around to the front."*

*"I need to get out of the rain," I reply. Though the night sky behind me is clear, the stars twinkle overhead.*

*He steps back and swings the door wide, allowing me entrance to the speakeasy. Several small tables are scattered about the small room, the rough wood bare except for candle stubs flickering in tin cans. Men are clustered around the tables, drinks in hand. A group at the back of the room erupts in raucous laughter as one of them tells an energetic story. I recognize a couple of orderlies from the hospital in the far corner, bent over a game of cards. They give me a nod of acknowledgment.*

*I nod back but head straight for the bar and slide onto a barstool.*

*"Abrams!" The bartender gives me a crooked smile. "What'll it be tonight, Doc?"*

*"Old Fashioned," I reply, going straight for the hard stuff.*

*"Bad day?" Leo raises an eyebrow.*

*"The worst."*

*Leo pours the amber whiskey into a glass, adding sugar and bitters, then slides it over.*

*I take a sip, resisting a cough, as the bootleg liquor burns down my throat, its raw taste barely masked by the sugar.*

*"That good?" He chuckles.*

*I raise the glass in response. "I'm just glad to have a drink tonight. After the day I've had, I'll take the whiskey however it comes."*

*"Want to talk about it?" Leo asks, leaning on the bar.*

*"Not tonight. Tonight, I'm drinking to forget." I throw the drink back and this time I can't resist the cough. Leo doesn't comment, just pours me another one.*

*I look around the room for Suzie, the usual waitress. We've had a bit of a thing going for a while. She's placing drinks on a table. When she looks up, she catches my eye and winks. She's headed my direction when suddenly the door at the back of the room bursts open.*

*"Is there a doctor? Marco's hurt real bad…"*

*I spring off my chair. "I'm a doctor." It's an innate reaction, part of my bone marrow. Despite my aching back and tired limbs, the part of me that took an oath responds before I even process the possible danger.* Who exactly am I getting mixed up with? A bootlegger? Worse? *But I push those thoughts away.* Someone needs my help.

*"Come with me," the man gestures anxiously. I follow him back through the door and find myself in a long tunnel. I've heard about these tunnels under Sioux City. Supposedly, they're used by the bootleggers to supply spirits to the speakeasies. I've never been in one…until now. The man runs down the tunnel, turning right at the end.*

*Following him around the corner, I come upon a group of men standing over someone on the ground. He's little more than a boy, lying on a makeshift stretcher. He's holding his right shoulder and whimpering.*

*I kneel, the healer in me taking over. "I'm a doctor," I tell him, reaching to look at the wound he's covering. He hesitates. "Let me see," I urge him.*

*He removes his hand, soaked with blood. I pull back his shirt so I can get a look. A small hole mars the skin. It's a bullet hole. No doubt about it. This is why he hesitated. The small hole speaks volumes.*

*It's one thing to buy bootlegged liquor in a speakeasy, quite another to get involved with the illegal activity. Removing this bullet is going to put me in league with this group of criminals. But there's no going back now. If I back out, they won't take kindly to it. I've seen too much, as they say.*

*Avoiding eye contact with the watchful group of co-conspirators, I continue examining the wound as if I hadn't noticed it holds a bullet. Surreptitiously, I note the telltale lumps under the clothing of the assembled men.* They're all armed.

*"I need pure alcohol, clean bandages, needle-nose pliers and a torch. And a needle and thread if you can get it." The leader of the group dispatches a couple of the men back to the speakeasy to get supplies.*

*A man hands me a flask of moonshine. I pass it to the kid and tell him to take a few good swigs. He takes a few mouthfuls, swallowing it with a grimace.*

*In doctor mode now, I instruct a man to sit behind the boy with his upper body supported by his own.*

*"James, hold his arm," the leader instructs the man beside him.*

*The boy is looking at me with eyes slightly glassy from the drink, but there's trust there too.*

*"This is going to hurt," I tell him.*

*He nods, bracing himself.*

*I glance up at the leader for the first time. Somehow, I feel I need his permission. The man looks me in the eye and gives me a clear nod of consent. But I barely notice it because my brain is suddenly buzzing with a new recognition.*

*This man, the leader, he's a renowned mob boss.*

*So, the rumors are true....Al Capone does hide out here when things get too hot in Chicago. Clearly, he's up to the same illegal endeavors here. And James must be his brother—James "two-gun" Hart.*

*I will my hands not to shake. "Hold him tight," I instruct my two helpers, and they tighten their grip. I pour the raw spirits over the wound, and the poor kid screams himself hoarse. Sweat prickles on my brow, but none of the men do more than wince. They've seen this before and know how it goes.*

*The men return with the requested supplies, giving me the opportunity to concentrate on the task at hand and forget that I'm doing it under the watchful eyes of the notorious mobster.* What will he do if I botch the job? Better not find out.

*I pass the needle-nose pliers through the flame of the torch to sterilize them. "I'll be as quick as I can," I say to the kid as I wait for the pliers to cool.*

*"Hang on," Capone says, and my entire body tenses.*

*He pulls a leather glove from his pocket and places the edge of it in the kid's mouth. "Bite on that," he instructs, and the kid complies through his haze of alcohol.*

*I try to relax again, focusing on the task at hand. Inserting the pliers into the wound causes the boy to buck and scream into his leather gag. The men grunt with the effort of keeping him still. I want to just grab the bullet and pull it free in one motion, but it's deep. I have to fish around. Sweat breaks out on my brow again, but then finally—mercifully—I find the bullet and manage to pull it free. I hear the collective exhale of breath as I pull it out. Seems I wasn't the only one holding my breath.*

*Blood wells up out of the wound, and I hold pressure with a clean bandage. Then I sew up the wound, using the pliers to drive the needle and tying it off neatly. I take my time applying clean dressings. I'm dreading the moment when I have to make eye contact with these dangerous men again, but eventually, my task is completed.*

*The time has come. I stand, making only the briefest of glances their way, and then turn to leave.*

*Capone grabs my shoulder, turning me back. I brace, uncertain what to expect.*

*He gives me a lopsided smile and extends his hand. I take it somewhat reluctantly and he shakes it with a steel grip. "Doc, you done good here." Keeping my hand in his, he adds, "You probably know how much we appreciate discretion. It keeps everyone living a long life."*

*Threat very much intended.*

*Capone claps me on the shoulder with his other hand. "We take care of those that take care of us." He releases my hand finally and I flex my fingers to get feeling back to them. He hands me a wad of cash that is likely more money than I will see over the whole next year from the hospital.*

*I nod, speechless and terrified, and turn numbly to walk back to the speakeasy.*

*Leo wordlessly sets out a whiskey on the bar for me. I slump onto the barstool, pick up the drink with shaking hands, and down it in one swallow.*

I wake from the dream with my hands trembling. Dr. John Abrams worked as a physician in Iowa in the 1920s-1950s. I've dreamed about his brushes with Prohibition in the past, most recently regarding a car accident with a suspected bootlegger at the wheel. But I've never dreamed about Capone until now. My limbs are liquid with relief to be back in my own timeline. The man sure knew how to instill fear. And yet, I have to admit…he had a certain charm.

What a contrast the rough, crime-adjacent speakeasy of the past was with the one Blake and I visited. Today we find it retro and cool to revisit this part of our history, but the reality was truly dangerous. Sort of like our fascination with witch trials. And pirates, for that matter.

Why am I having this dream now? Is my subconscious connecting to the bullet wound? The boy's clean entry wound did resemble that of the judge's. Or is it the association of Barry's cousin with a criminal gang? I can't help but feel like I'm missing something.

# CHAPTER TWENTY-EIGHT

After we clear it with Deputy Chief Garcia, Joe and I head out to Wenatchee. Garcia is just as curious as we are about what the ME has to tell us.

As we make the long drive, Joe broaches the subject I've been avoiding. "Are you ready to talk about Blake now? It seems like you're doing okay but I've noticed you're distracted sometimes."

"Yes. You're right, I'm trying to keep my head straight but sometimes it sidetracks me. My parents and best friend keep checking in with me too, so you're not the only one." I sigh and relate the disastrous event, yet another time. My mortification at what happened hasn't eased at all yet. All the feelings come back to the surface.

Joe is silent, allowing me the space to tell him about it without passing judgment.

When I finish the story I add, "So Blake broke it off, but it was completely my fault. I feel terrible, and I'm not sure I can fix it."

"Time has a way of bringing what's important to the surface." Joe says. "I think he'll find it in himself to forgive you, but you might need to make some uncomfortable changes and commit to them."

"Like leaving my gun at home on dates?" I joke, with a subdued chuckle.

"Like leaving your gun at home," he agrees. "And maybe giving up the napkin security trick."

"Right."

"Look, no one understands better than I do what it does to a person's sense of security to face murderers down every day, but for the sake of those in our lives we have to be able to put it aside."

"I know. You're right," I acquiesce. "Did Sandy ever get mad at you for something like this?"

Joe laughs. "Did she ever. Just ask her about the time I almost handcuffed the caterer because he took the liberty of entering the backyard early one morning to set up before a party."

"You did?"

"In my defense, the man had gang tattoos and didn't come to the front door."

The time passes quickly as Joe relates the humorous story and before I know it, we arrive at the Chelan County ME's office.

A portly man in his forties greets us in a white coat and scrubs. "Clive Ogilvie," he says, shaking our hands. His hand is cold and damp. I resist wiping my hand on my pants.

"Thanks for coming out. If you'll follow me," he says.

He leads us back into the morgue, and I brace myself for whatever post-mortem gruesomeness he's going to show us.

But to my surprise, he keeps on walking through the morgue, past the offices, and exits the building. I glance at Joe and he shrugs as we follow Ogilvie outside.

"We can talk back here," he says mysteriously.

"Why can't we talk inside?" Joe asks, his voice friendly but with a hint of unease. We don't know this man. Who knows what he might be mixed up in. Did he lure us here for some reason? *No, Kruse,* I tell myself, take it easy, *there's no reason to think he has bad intentions.*

I wonder for a second who knows we drove out here today? *Bob? Garcia? How long will it take them to start looking for us if something goes wrong?* My senses heightened, I notice that Joe has his shoes with orange laces today. His lucky color. *Good, we may need the luck.*

"There are cameras in the lab and I'm not sure who might be listening," Ogilvie says, pacing and obviously agitated.

"Everything okay, Doc?" Joe asks. "Maybe just take a few deep breaths."

Ogilvie nods and visibly shakes himself, but he continues pacing. "Sorry, detectives, I just never thought I would be mixed up in this kind of thing."

"Whatever is going on we'll help if we can," Joe reassures him. "Maybe just start with why you reached out to us, instead of your local PD."

Ogilvie nods gratefully and stops pacing. He looks at us, pausing a moment before he gathers himself sufficiently to explain. "I contacted you because Greg Mason, the owner of the Apple-A-Day Orchards, mentioned that you were here to check on the conditions of the farm on the day one of his workers died. He gave me both of your names, indicating that the death was observed by law enforcement, so there was no need to look into the circumstances surrounding it."

"We weren't aware a death occurred while we were on the farm and we certainly didn't observe it. Maybe you better start from the beginning," Joe says.

I think back to the day of our visit to the orchard. At the end of our visit, there was the altercation between Mason and one of his workers. *Was that related to the death?*

"Okay, I guess I should go back a bit." Ogilvie wrings his hands, thinking. "It all started a few years ago. We were getting the occasional immigrant worker who was killed on the job while working for Apple-A-Day Orchards. It's not unusual, accidents happen occasionally on all the orchards. Farming is dangerous work, and the workers died from the usual dangers found on orchards: falls from picking platforms, injury from equipment, that sort of thing. But it seemed to happen more regularly at Apple-A-Day." My mind goes straight to *Apple-a-Day didn't keep the doctor away.*

Ogilvie continues, "Most of their workers are immigrants from Mexico in the US on visas, so it falls to us to document the death, notify the consulate, and manage the exportation of remains if the family requests it. Documentation of the loss of a worker allows the orchard to request additional visas to replace workers."

"So far it all sounds legitimate," Joe says.

"I thought so too. Apple-A-Day is a large orchard so if they had a few more deaths than the other orchards, this didn't trigger any concern, so in the past, we would just document the death. We don't do a full autopsy unless something seems suspicious, you know, like if there's a bullet wound, that sort of thing."

I perk up. This strangely echoes my dream from last night.

"Did you get any suspicious injuries? Any bullet wounds?" I ask.

"No, we didn't..."

"So, what's got you worried, Doc?" Joe raises an eyebrow at him. It's taking this guy a long time to get to the point.

"Well, the most recent worker that they brought in...the injuries...well, they fit falling off a ladder while pruning trees, just like they said happened. But it struck me that it looked like the worker made no attempt to break his fall. It was more consistent with being *dropped* off a ladder than *falling* off one."

"How so?"

"Typically, it's instinctive to protect our head from injury, so we put our hands out when we fall. Usually, we see fractures of the wrists and forearms, but this guy fell right on his face. It seemed suspicious. So I did a tox screen."

"What did it show?" Joe asks.

"It came back with such a high level of fentanyl that he could never have survived. He wasn't just so high that he fell without trying to break his fall, it was a massive overdose. I think they inflicted the injuries to cover the overdose."

"Wow," Joe says. "That's certainly concerning. Do you think the orchard has an issue with fentanyl use among the workers? It's highly addictive. Maybe they're trying to sweep it under the rug."

"I wondered that. At least at first. I looked back at the photos of the bodies from the other deaths. Even though they weren't full autopsies, we documented the injuries. None of them had forearm fractures or other defensive wounds. None of them attempted to avoid injury."

"A pattern."

"Right."

"So, you think maybe there's a drug problem at the orchard?" Joe asks.

Something isn't adding up. These workers hardly seem like they had the money to spend on drugs. Was the employer supplying them as some sort of method to control them through addiction? That seems unlikely. Unless... "Had the workers been in the US for long when they died?" I ask.

"I can see you're thinking what I was thinking, Detective. I checked the visa dates for each of the deaths over the past few years. All but one of the deceased workers were recent arrivals."

"They were drug mules."

"That's what I think." Ogilvie nods. "If one of the drug balloons they trafficked in their GI tract burst, they'd drop them off a ladder to make it look like an accident before the worker died of an overdose. They had to do it before the person died, so there was typical bleeding or bruising. Only, the person is too far gone to respond to the fall."

"Did you look for the hidden drugs?" Joe asks.

"I looked, but there was nothing there. I'm sure they would remove the drugs before releasing the body to us."

We all stand in stunned silence for a moment. I think of my dream last night. The organized crime, the bootlegging—my subconscious had already been exploring the idea of a drug-ring operation. It was leading me in this direction. *But why? Maybe the similarities between the mob boss and Mason? I'm not sure.*

"So, let's work this through," Joe says. Now he's the one pacing. "The man we saw talking to Mason at the end of our visit was possibly telling him that another worker was dying because of a suspected rupture of a drug balloon. Mason knew he had to set up a fall before the man died because a dead man doesn't bleed or bruise. So that was why he basically sent us packing."

"Right. Post-mortem injuries wouldn't appear the same as those prior to death, so they had to act fast," says the ME.

"So, if that's true, the orchard is a front for a more lucrative operation—trafficking fentanyl into the country. That's where the real money is," Joe says, and I can see his face transform as the pieces drop into place. "Now it makes sense that the orchard seems to be doing unbelievably well after it acquired its new 'investing partner.' It's probably a Mexican drug cartel. The visa holders come to the US with balloons of fentanyl contained in their GI tract. They return at the end of the season and then come back again the following year, with more drugs. It's a self-perpetuating operation."

I nod. "And a clever front. Those poor immigrants are taken advantage of by both sides of the border: the drug cartel on one side and the orchard on the other. And once they're in, they can never get out." Echoing my dream, I say, "They know too much."

"Let's not get ahead of ourselves, though. We don't know the extent of it. Maybe it was just one worker that had an addiction or maybe the orchard leverages fentanyl addiction for another reason. We need to find out more," Joe says. "Did you go back and look for overdoses in the other deaths?" he asks the ME.

"Those bodies aren't here any longer, I only have the photos to go by. Unfortunately, it's too late to check for overdose on those deaths."

"We're going to have to talk to Mason," Joe says.

# CHAPTER TWENTY-NINE

Pulling up to the information center at Apple-A-Day Orchards, we park and head inside. Joe and I discussed tactics on the way over and agreed we'll have to press Greg Mason hard to get him to come clean if he's involved with the cartel. I'll follow Joe's lead on this one.

Mason comes out of his office to greet us. Clearly, we showed up on his surveillance.

"Good morning, detectives. How can I help you?" He sounds irritated but is at least making an attempt to cover it.

"Good morning, Mr. Mason. We have some more questions for you," Joe says.

"I think we covered everything when we spoke before," he replies. He's not going to play ball.

"Well, I thought we'd about covered it as well...only... it seems you forgot to tell us that your business partner is a drug cartel," Joe provokes him.

The blood drains from Mason's face. He looks around to makes sure no one is nearby to overhear. "Why don't you come with me to look at what we're doing in the fields right now?" he says pointedly, gesturing to the nearest field.

Looking behind him, I spot a camera above the entrance to the information center. Ah, he's afraid the cartel will overhear us. I guess we're not the only ones under surveillance. Obviously, Joe hit a nerve. *We're onto something.*

We follow Mason down a row of trellised apple trees. He stops a good distance from the office building, out of hearing range and view of the camera. Mason is cornered. He's either going to confess or try to get us off his trail in some way. And one of those ways may be by making us disappear. My hand drifts toward my firearm.

"I don't know what you think you know," Mason says. "But I assure you, Apple-A-Day Orchards is a legitimate and profitable business. We don't have any interest in illegal operations."

"That's what they all say," Joe shoots back.

"Who says that?"

"All the shady business owners like you."

"You're wrong."

"This is your chance to come clean, Mason," Joe says. "If you tell us what you know then we may be able to get you some lenience from the DA in exchange for your testimony." He cocks an eyebrow. "And maybe protect you from your new *partners*."

"You can't possibly have any proof of what you claim, or we wouldn't be having this conversation." Mason juts his chin and crosses his arms defensively.

"We have a worker who died of a fentanyl overdose. One you dropped off a ladder and claimed he fell. Only you didn't know that dead men really do tell tales."

"That's ridiculous," Mason splutters.

"It's true. The lack of defensive injuries tells us that he wasn't conscious when he fell."

For once, Mason is at a loss for words. The conflict plays out in his features. He's trying to decide if the gig is up and if so, if he dares rat out his partners. It's a crucial decision—the wrong move could cost him his life. I don't envy him the choice.

He sighs and puts his hands on his hips, looking up to the cloudless blue sky as if for guidance. Finally, he looks at Joe and says, "I'll need protection. For me…and for my family."

Joe nods. "We can provide police protection for now. For all of you. Witness protection would have to be arranged with the DA. It would be up to them."

Mason takes a large breath, as if to find strength for the task ahead. "They bought me out before I realized what was happening."

"Who did?"

"The cartel. They swept in like vultures when they sensed the death of my business. They preyed on my vulnerability. I was up to my eyeballs in debt from the lawsuit—the legal fees and fines ruined me."

"Served you right for how you treated those poor workers," I say.

He glances my way, then looks down. "I was just trying to survive. The farm had such a narrow profit margin back then. The cost of labor went up and took every last penny of my profits. Something had to give. I couldn't afford to have workers taking days off for a cold or for doctors' visits. Hell, I never took a single day off myself. It was just the reality of the situation."

"You could've sold the business or closed it down. What you put those workers through was inhumane."

"It was no worse than what I personally endured every day, I assure you. But whatever you believe about the working conditions, the lawsuit left me with nothing. I had no choice but to look the devil in the eye and sign my soul over. And the devil was Gabriel Manteris."

I know the name. And it's not associated with anything good. He's involved in the highest circles of illegal drug supply from Mexico to the U.S. His reputation is that of a merciless drug lord. If he's involved in this operation, then we have a formidable foe on our hands.

Sweat breaks out on Mason's forehead as he relates the rest of the story. "He saw the opportunity to expand his empire by partnering with me. I would continue to grow apples, and he would use my workers to smuggle drugs into the U.S. 'Win-win,' he said." Mason uses air quotes. "With the money he invested, I was able to bring the orchard into the modern era and make it profitable. Adding the tours was his idea. He thought it looked wholesome. A family-friendly activity as a front, while right under the tourist's noses, the drugs were coming into the country. Manteris loved the irony of it."

"Drugs coming here to ruin families with addictions and overdoses," I say with disgust. "So, I suppose that's really why you don't use the automatic pickers. You need the constant flow of immigrants to keep bringing the cartel's drugs into the country."

Mason nods.

"Selling your soul is a high price to pay for the rescue of your business," Joe says.

Mason looks deflated. "It was. It is. I know this, of course.

At first, I tried to resist, not wanting to be controlled by them. But then I came home one day to find my daughter..." His voice breaks.

"What happened to your daughter?" I ask with a sense of foreboding. Joe said she died of suicide when he read the case file.

"She was just seventeen," Mason continues with a shaking voice. "She was home alone after school. My wife was in town picking up groceries and my son had activities after school. I was working in the field, as usual. She was alone. All alone..." His voice drifts off.

We wait in silence for him to find the strength to continue.

Mason looks up as if he's just remembered that we're there. He clears his throat. "I came home to find her..." He takes a deep breath. "She was in the bathtub. Her wrists slit. And the blood. There was so much blood. The water was red. There was blood on the floor..." He breaks off again, tears filling his eyes.

"How did you know it was Manteris and not...?" Joe asks quietly, unable to say the word "suicide" to the girl's grieving father.

"On her forehead..." Mason is barely holding back sobs now. He whispers, "On her forehead, written in her own blood, was 'GM.'" He looks at us. "His initials."

Mason wipes his face and gathers himself. "I realized then that they could get to my family any time. Since then, I've never stepped out of line, and my wife and son have continued to live and breathe. The cartel has eyes everywhere. They watch everything I do with cameras and drones, and who knows what else."

"I'm sorry about your daughter," Joe says. "Did you tell the police it was a suicide because you were afraid of the cartel?"

He nods. "I…I cleaned the blood off her forehead, and told the police she slit her own wrists. They never questioned it. Even my wife and son don't know the truth."

"Do you think the cartel was involved in the death of the judge?"

"I can't really see what motive they would have to kill him. But I've learned never to underestimate the reach of the cartel. Even though Manteris lives in Mexico, he has people everywhere. In my most paranoid moments, I even suspect they may have had a hand in starting the lawsuit against me. It tore my business down and made me vulnerable to their attack. Maybe they set it up. I don't really know." Mason's bravado is gone. He looks like what he is—a broken man.

A shadow passes over us as a drone zooms overhead, disappearing off down the row.

Mason's eyes widen. "Those drones are surveillance. Now they've seen us talking!" He grabs the front of Joe's jacket. "I told you everything! Now you have to protect my family!" he cries, sinking to his knees.

Joe grabs Mason's hands, prying them off his lapels.

"Calm down, Mr. Mason." Joe pats the shoulders of the man on the ground before him, placating him. "Of course, we'll protect you. Let's go get your family right now. If Manteris knows we're talking, we need to bring them in right away."

Mason puts his head in his hands, visibly relieved. Joe reaches out a hand and helps Mason up, and we head down the row back toward the end of the field. Manteris has a scary reputation, sure, but I can't help but think Mason is playing up the drama so we'll feel he had no choice in his actions. I'm not convinced he's so innocent in all this.

Also, although I agree with Joe's choice to give Mason and his family protection, even if Manteris' surveillance caught us talking, he can't possibly know what it was about. It does look a bit suspicious that we went into the field, away from the cameras, but as far as Manteris and the cartel know, we just came out to ask Mason more questions about the judge.

I'm telling myself all this to keep from going down the rabbit hole of worrying what Manteris might put in motion if he did get suspicious.

It's then that I hear the whine of the drone returning.

The machine slows as it approaches us. We continue walking, acting as if we don't really notice it, as if we're just discussing apple growing, the weather ... nothing of importance.

The drone moves on, over our heads, barely high enough to avoid missing us, its propellers whirring. I duck involuntarily, feeling the wind caused by the propellers as the drone passes over. Goose bumps prickle the back of my neck.

I turn and watch the drone disappearing, feeling relieved. We continue to walk down the row. Maybe we convinced whoever was watching that we don't know too much. I feel the echo of last night's dream—maybe we *do* know too much now.

That thought has barely formed when I hear the whine of the drone, yet again. Only it's louder this time. The sound causes a thrill of fear to zing down my nerves, making my fingers tingle.

We all turn.

The drone is coming back.

But now it has friends. There must be at least ten drones heading our direction.

I see flitting shadows over the far reaches of the field as

more come to join them.

"Are the drones armed?" I yell to Mason over the noise.

"No, of course not," he replies, but then amends, "But I'm sure it'll hurt to get hit by one." His eyes are wide as he takes in the cloud of drones hurtling toward us.

We turn and start to jog down the row, still not really believing we're running from farming drones.

The first of the drones swoops down, smacking Mason in the back of the head. He cries out, reaching back with his hand. It comes away bloody.

"Run!" he yells and the fear in his voice makes my adrenaline surge.

We run in earnest now as drone after drone swoops down behind us, buzzing by our heads. One comes so close, I feel its propeller tug a chunk of hair out of my ponytail.

"Get down," I yell. We hit the dirt as the rest of the drones sail over our heads. There's more than twenty of them now. Once they pass, we get up, brushing dirt from our clothing, taking stock. Other than the cut on Mason's head, no one is injured. Yet.

"Look." Joe points. The drones are circling back. And more are joining them. *How many drones does this operation have anyway?*

Joe and Mason take off running again, and I follow just a few steps behind. My breath is coming hard, my muscles screaming as I head for the end of the row.

I hear the menacing buzz coming behind me and I will my legs to go faster. Mason and Joe are just ahead of me as they round the row end, taking shelter behind the last trellised apple tree.

Joe turns back. "Hurry, Kruse!" he yells, reaching out.

I grab his hand, and he pulls me past the last tree and out of the path of the accelerating drones. They whizz past one after another, so close I feel the wind of their passing. There are way more than twenty now.

"Hurry. Let's get to the cruiser," Joe pants, out of breath.

Wordlessly, we follow him in a sprint toward the cruiser.

In the distance, the drones circle back toward us once again.

Though I'm moving as fast as I possibly can, I feel like I'm wading through mud. Every movement is too slow, like a bad dream. *We aren't going to make it.*

The noise of the drones is deafening now as they head full speed at us. Somehow, we get to the cruiser just before the cloud of drones is upon us. We fling the doors open. Joe slides into the driver's seat and I push Mason into the back seat and jump in beside him.

I slam the door shut just as Joe yells, "Duck!"

I put my hands over my head and duck down on the seat as the first drone hits the window. It crumples like a bird hitting glass, then drops down and flops around on the ground, crippled. The drones pelt the cruiser, one after another, crashing at full speed. I cringe as more hit the window, but the bullet-proof glass holds.

When the rain of drones finally stops, I tentatively lift my head and look out.

A final drone smashes into the glass beside my face, and I jump back in surprise. It skitters against the glass and then careens off.

The ground is littered with wrecked drones. They lie crumpled, several still fluttering around. Broken, like crushed bugs.

Joe starts the cruiser with shaking hands.

"Let's get out of here!" he yells back at us.

I couldn't agree more wholeheartedly.

"Where's your wife and son?" Joe asks Mason as he punches the accelerator.

"At the high school," Mason says, breathing hard.

"Both of them?" Joe asks.

"Yes," Mason confirms. "My wife volunteers there and my son is in class."

"There are more drones coming!" I yell, spotting more heading out of the fields.

Joe speeds down the drive, taking a sliding turn onto the road and accelerating away from the orchard. Looking back, I see the drones come to a halt at the end of the drive, hovering at the transition between the drive and the road, like sentries. Though I know they are inanimate objects controlled remotely, I can't help but see them as menacing insects, watching us retreat.

"What in the hell was that?" I exclaim between breaths, turning to Mason.

He slumps back in his seat, head against the backrest, his breath coming in gasps.

"That...that was Manteris," he says, closing his eyes.

I look around at the three of us. Dirt is caked on the front of our shirts and pants, and we have smudges of it on our faces. I'm bleeding from my palms where I went down on the orchard path. Mason has blood trickling down the back of his head.

It seems Mason's fear of Manteris wasn't so overblown after all.

# CHAPTER THIRTY

Joe pulls the cruiser over once we're a safe distance from the orchard. The drones don't seem to be following.

He turns back to look at us. "Everyone okay?"

"Basically intact," I say. "Mason has a wound on the back of his head, but it doesn't look like it needs stitches."

Joe nods.

"We need to get my wife and son," Mason says, his voice still shaky.

"Call her and tell her to get your son and we'll pick them up," Joe says.

As Mason pulls out his phone, I get out to check the cruiser. The side assaulted by the drones is dented and scratched as if impaled by a hail of rocks. I shiver, thinking that could've been us.

I dust off my clothes the best I can, then go around to slide in beside Joe.

We look at each other, our expressions silently communicating our disbelief over what has transpired over the past couple of hours.

"How are we going to explain the damage to Garcia?" I ask.

Joe shakes his head. "I better talk to her about what is going on anyway and have her set up a safe house for the family, so I'll let her know about the damage…unless you want to tell her." He flashes me a quick grin.

"Not on your life."

"What? You don't want to?" he jokes. He chuckles as he dials his phone.

Sinking back in my seat, I listen to Joe and Greg Mason making arrangements. When Mason hangs up, he says, "My wife and son will meet us out front of the school."

As we pull up to the front entrance, I see a woman in her forties with long red hair standing beside a tall teen boy with the same red hair. As soon as the vehicle stops, Mason jumps out and embraces them. I suspect they know very little about what has been going on.

I get out and hold the back door of the cruiser open for them. The sound of a drone buzzes in my head. I must be having some sort of PTSD. *Get a grip, Kruse,* I think, *they're gone.*

Only, they're not. Off in the distance, I spot a drone approaching the school. My body goes rigid with dread, my instincts registering, even before I can identify the reason, that something is different about this drone. It's bigger than the ones on the orchard and looks military grade. And there it is…the cause for my fear, the unmistakable contour of a gun muzzle. *It's armed!*

"Get in, quickly," I say to the family, my voice pitched unnaturally high.

Mason looks quizzically at me.

I point to the approaching drone.

He needs no further encouragement; he quickly shepherds his family toward the cruiser.

The whine of a bullet passing close makes me duck instinctively, pulling the Masons down behind the cruiser as another shot skims off the top of the vehicle.

I shove the Masons into the car and, staying low, scramble into the passenger seat.

"What's going on?" Joe asks, looking around frantically. "Where are the shots coming from?"

"There's a drone over by the parking lot," I exclaim, pointing. "And this one is armed!"

As if in confirmation, a bullet hits the rear window, causing the glass to shatter with a loud crack. The Masons scream at the sound. A large circular area of fractured glass is left where the bullet was absorbed.

Joe accelerates, shooting out of the lot and onto a side street. The drone drops down low and follows. A bullet hits the back window as the Masons cower. Joe swings around corners, trying to shake off the drone. His quick maneuvering takes us out of the drone's sights so it can't make another shot.

The drone starts to fall behind.

Then I no longer see it.

We make a few more turns and it doesn't seem to be following.

"I think we lost it," I say, peering out the shattered back window. "I can't see it anymore...." The sentence dies in my throat as I turn back around, and the drone drops down in front of us. It must have followed our route from higher up.

Joe and I both yell at the same time.

He brakes and swings the car around just as a bullet cracks my side window. I'm thrown against the side of the car by the quick turn.

So far, the bullet-proof glass is holding up but its protection becomes less with each hit. It won't hold out forever.

Joe straightens out the car and guns it down the road.

This time we find ourselves on a major street.

Joe flips on the lights and siren and heads for the highway entrance. "I should be able to outrun it if I can get up enough speed," he says, his eyes never leaving the road. He dodges in and out of lanes staying out of the drone's sights. Luckily the traffic is light.

We hit the highway entrance and Joe accelerates. Once we get over fifty miles per hour, we start to leave the drone behind.

Joe looks in the rearview mirror. "I think we finally lost it," he says, shaking his head in amazement. He turns off the lights and siren to make it harder for the drone to follow us.

I look back in the rear seat. The Masons are clustered together low on the seat, arms around each other, their eyes wide.

"Is everyone okay?" I ask.

Greg looks his family over. "It seems like it," he says, sounding dazed.

Joe navigates the highway toward Seattle.

I continue to scan the sky for the drone. A couple of times, I swear I see something high above us. But thankfully, we don't have any more close encounters as we climb out of the Wenatchee Valley. I'm not planning a return trip anytime soon.

We make the two-hour trip back to Seattle without further incident.

The Masons have been talking in the back seat as Greg fills them in on the events that transpired at the orchard. I notice he doesn't tell them about the cartel, only that the orchard is under attack. He says their safety is in question and they need to find a place to hide. We hear many exclamations as his wife and son absorb the news. At one point, his wife starts to cry. I'm glad Greg hasn't told them everything. The less they know, the less motivation the cartel will have to get them out of the picture.

I can't imagine how Greg Mason must be feeling. Having to leave the life you knew and start over, always in the shadow of a vindictive man like Manteris—that's hard. He may never feel fully safe again. And he's chosen to bear the weight of it entirely himself.

Through secure comms, Deputy Chief Garcia sends us the address of the safe house she's arranged. When we arrive, Bob and Sally are already on site. She must trust them as much as Joe and I do, to involve them in this. While that may seem a given, recent events at our precinct established that not all officers are worthy of such trust. I'm sure she chose carefully.

Bob and Sally have aired out the rooms and brought a few groceries and toiletry kits for the Masons since they literally had to leave with only the clothes on their backs.

Bob collects their phones. He gives them to Joe to take to the precinct so they can't be traced here by the cartel. And so we can look through them for evidence. We also don't want the Masons trying to contact anyone.

"Here, Mr. Mason," Sally gestures to a kitchen chair. Mason pauses, knowing what's coming, but the look Sally gives him says she isn't taking no for an answer. He sits obediently while she places ankle restraints, and fingerprints him, putting him under house arrest. We'd typically book him at the station, but we can't take that risk.

"Now, let me take a look at that head injury," she says, taking out a first aid kit. She puts on some gloves, and goes about cleaning and bandaging the abrasion. I don't dare show her my hands or she'll be after me too.

By the time we get the Masons settled, it's getting dark and Joe and I are exhausted and ready to call it a day. We'll have many questions for Greg Mason in the days ahead but for now we leave the family in the capable hands of Bob and Sally.

When we arrive at the precinct with our severely damaged cruiser, Joe gets a text from Garcia instructing us to stop by her office. Her window looks out on the parking lot. She's probably seen the state of our vehicle.

We head toward her office, dragging our feet a little as we anticipate a grueling debrief.

But as we approach her open office door, we hear Garcia on the phone with someone and it's obvious she's getting an update she didn't expect. Joe and I exchange half smiles. *Saved by the bell.*

Or so we thought.

As we enter her office, we're expecting her to signal us to come find her tomorrow but instead she ushers us inside.

Joe and I exchange another glance, this time perplexed.

Garcia stands, leaning her hands on her desk, phone still pressed to her ear. Her face registers concern. "Close the door," she mouths to us.

Now alarm bells are going off in my head. She doesn't

want someone to overhear our conversation. *Why? What news is she getting?*

We can only hear her side of the conversation.

"...stabbed how many times?"

"Out of surgery now?"

"Make sure there's a protective detail in the room."

My heart rate picks up. Did someone get to the Masons already? *That seems impossible.*

Garcia gets off the phone.

"Who was stabbed?" I ask.

She looks at us gravely. "I didn't see this coming," she says.

# CHAPTER THIRTY-ONE

"Sofia Clifton was stabbed," Garcia tells us. "She must know something that the judge's killer wants to bury. Maybe something she doesn't even know that she knows. Or maybe they just think the judge shared something with her. I need the two of you to go over to the hospital to talk to her now."

We both nod. If this is the cartel, the vast tendrils of their reach are revealing themselves. And the extent of their influence is truly terrifying.

I mentally shift, shaking off the fatigue. I need to stay alert. It seems the cartel will stop at nothing to stamp out awareness of their involvement with fentanyl trafficking. Knowledge that Joe and I are also now in possession of. We're entering dangerous territory. We can't let our guard down.

As we turn to leave, Garcia says, "And detectives..."

Joe and I turn. Garcia lobs a set of keys for a new cruiser at Joe. "I saw the condition of your cruiser. I'm going to need a rundown on exactly what the hell happened out there." She pauses to give us a look. "But I'm glad everyone was okay.

Try not to destroy your next vehicle inside of five minutes, okay?"

While Joe and I are enroute to the hospital in our unmarked replacement cruiser, Garcia obtains Sofia Clifton's room number and sends it to us securely. Sofia is registered under an alias—Garcia made sure of it. She's taking no chances that someone might make another attempt on her life.

We go directly to the room, knock twice and wait. An officer opens the door from the inside, blocking entry until he sees it's us, then stands aside.

"Officer Lowrey." He shakes each of our hands, talking quietly so as not to disturb Sofia. "You must be Riley and Kruse. Garcia messaged me that you'd be coming by. The victim's sister-in-law, Anna, is already here with her." He gestures to the bedside.

Anna lets go of Sofia's hand and gets out of the bedside chair to join us.

"Hello, detectives. I wish we were meeting again under better circumstances," she says.

"How's Sofia?" I whisper, looking at the patient. She's sleeping, her long, dark eyelashes a stark contrast to the pallor of her face. She looks ghost-like against the white sheets. The monitor above her beeps steadily, tracing her heartbeat from the telemetry leads attached to her chest. An IV-line threads into her arm. She looks...vulnerable.

"She was stabbed in the stomach. She lost a lot of blood. They're giving her IV fluids now. The surgeon said she was lucky the knife missed her internal organs. He says she'll be all right. She's getting antibiotics every few hours to prevent infection. She needs rest," Anna says.

"The baby?" I ask in a whisper.

Anna grabs my hand and takes Joe and I out into the hall, closing the door behind her.

"She told me she lost it," Anna says with tears springing up in her eyes.

"Oh, that's horrible!" I exclaim at the same time as Joe says, "How sad."

"How is she coping?" I ask Anna.

"She's sad and I think a little numb still. I don't think she's processed it all yet," Anna says. "Who would do this? Stabbing her in the stomach seems so intentional."

Anna has no idea about the cartel, but she's right on the mark. Someone knew she was pregnant and wanted to give her a very specific warning. It definitely seems like the cartel's handiwork, warning her not to say anything she shouldn't or next time it will be her own life on the line. Still, it seems particularly cruel to target the baby. My estimation of the cartel's ruthlessness ticks up a notch.

"We'll be looking into it," I tell Anna.

"I'm glad," Anna nods.

"Until we know who did this, make sure not to let anyone know where she is," Joe advises.

Anna nods, her eyes welling up. She wipes tears off her face. "The poor thing," she says, voice breaking. "What she's been through. I just can't imagine."

"We need to speak to her," I tell Anna.

"She just got out of surgery a little while ago. She's pretty groggy still. Except for telling me about the baby, she's barely spoken. The doctor said she needs rest and I don't think she'll be much help right now anyway," Anna says.

As if conjured by our conversation, a nurse heads down

the hallway in our direction, her expression registering her annoyance. "You all need to leave now," she says, ushering us off with her arms. "The doctor was very clear that the patient needs to rest. She's barely out of surgery."

We leave quietly, returning to the precinct for our cars in a sort of stupor, fatigue setting in.

When I finally reach my apartment, there's no napkin in the door jamb. I'm trying to change my ways—I didn't put it in this morning. The timing seems ironic, what with a vicious drug cartel likely knowing my identity now. But I need for Blake to see that I can change. I need to prove it to him…and to myself.

I heat up something that comes in a frozen plastic container and eat it without tasting it, while I respond to messages from Isabella and my mom. They've been checking up on me, worried I'm alone and sad about the breakup. It's sweet. They don't know that right now I have more than enough distractions to keep my mind off my own issues. I reassure them that I'm doing okay.

Struggling out of my work clothes, I tumble into bed, exhaustion taking over.

The events of the day are still swirling in my head as I go to sleep.

# CHAPTER THIRTY-TWO

*It's late at night when I finally leave the hospital. My walk home is short but it takes me through a rough area of town, so I keep my wits about me.*

*Shadows seem to move in my peripheral vision, and I whip my head around, trying to catch someone lurking in the dark. But no one is there.*

*Even with my heightened awareness, I don't see it coming when they jump me.*

*Hands reach out and pin my arms while others firmly clamp over my mouth. I struggle with seemingly no effect on my attackers.*

*"Don't be stupid, Doc. The boss just wants to talk to ya," comes the hoarse whisper in my ear. A blade pressed against my throat nicks me.*

*The man's accomplice drops a hood over my head, and I'm pushed roughly into the back of a vehicle.*

*"Good man, Abrams," a man beside me says as the car lurches down the road. I know that voice; it instantly instills*

*fear in and of itself.*

This situation is not good, not good at all. *Because that voice...it belongs to Al Capone...I remember it from when I took a bullet out of one of his henchmen.* Or henchboy, *if I'm honest.*

*I'd hoped to never to run into the man again but now, here I am, in the back of a car with the notorious mob boss, a hood over my head. I'm sure there are worse situations to be in, but I can't think of one right now. I guess I could have my feet encased in concrete and be hovering over a body of water. That would be a little worse.*

*Capone probably thinks I'm going along with this abduction because I'm so paralyzed with fear that I can't respond. But I'm* decidedly not *going along with it! If only I could find something adequate to say.*

*We bump along for a while in silence. Then the car comes to a stop, and everyone gets out. I'm hauled out of the vehicle by my arm and marched up some stairs and into a building.*

*It's warm inside and I smell wood smoke through the material of the hood.*

*I'm pushed down in a chair, and the hood is roughly pulled off my head. Static crackles as it pulls free, causing my hair to stand on end. I probably look as frightened as I feel. I put my hand up to the place at my throat that the knife nicked me. There's only a small trickle of blood, thankfully.*

*The room I find myself in is mostly bare except for a smoldering fireplace and a small table and chairs with a few lit candles. Capone is seated across from me. Three of his men stand behind him, arms crossed, legs wide.* Not too subtle a threat, boys.

*Capone chuckles as he takes in my appearance. "Nice hairdo, Doc. Looks like you got hit by lightning."*

*I pat my hair down. "I guess that's what happens when you kidnap someone right off the street and put a hood over their head," I say before I have a chance to think better of it.*

*Capone's eyes narrow at me, and I feel my stomach clench in fresh terror. But then he smiles. "Well, now, Doc, we wouldn't want you to think we were inhospitable. James, get the man a drink, will you?" He turns to a man I've met before and suspect is his brother, James Hart. He exits to an adjacent room and returns with two glasses of whiskey, placing them on the table. Not daring to turn it down, I take a small sip. I need to keep my head clear.*

*To my surprise, the whiskey is smooth, nuanced even. My eyes widen.*

*"I see you can appreciate good whiskey," Capone chuckles. He takes a large swig from his own glass. "See, Doc, we're not barbarians." Capone laughs and the men behind him all laugh along with him.*

*"Why am I here?" I manage. I haven't seen any injured men in the room, but maybe they're close by.*

*"Well, I was just getting to that. See I have a problem." Capone's smile twists into a menacing grin.*

*I'm about to ask what the problem is when a man is brought in from another room, a hood over his head and a blood-soaked bandage on his left arm.*

*"This is Tony. He's one of my guards," Capone says with deceptive civility, gesturing at the man. "Now...here's my dilemma. A whole shipment of whiskey went missing...and the thing is..." Capone sits back, narrowing his eyes again. "You see, that whiskey, it was under Tony's care. He was* responsible *for it."*

*The emphasis on "responsible" makes me afraid for Tony.*

Why has Capone brought me here? Is the wound infected? Does it need sutures? How can I possibly help this man?

*Capone goes on. "Well, it seems Tony here, he was injured protecting my whiskey. So, I owe him a debt of gratitude, wouldn't you think?"*

*I nod, but I'm not understanding. The man has a hood over his head. Doesn't seem much like gratitude to me.*

*"Yes, you would think so." Capone answers his own question, finding my mute response inadequate. "Only...see, now we are getting to my problem. One of my men says he saw Tony here put that knife wound right in his own arm."*

*Capone sits forward suddenly and grabs my arm. "Can you believe that, Doc?"*

*Terrified, I shake my head no.*

*"No." Capone releases my arm and sits back. "No. Me neither. A man putting a knife wound right in his own arm. And it's a doozy too, you should see it. Yeesh. Putting a gash in your own arm. That's a story. Right, Doc?"*

*I'm not sure how to respond, but Capone isn't waiting for my reply anyway.*

*"But then I get to thinking. If I'm Tony and think I might just steal my boss's whiskey....Well, what's one little knife wound to my arm to take the suspicion off of me?"*

*I don't say anything but I'm thinking,* Who would steal from Capone? A dead man walking *is all that comes to me.*

*"So, I'm thinking to myself, how am I going to know if Tony here is telling the truth? Don't you see? That's when I think of you, Doc. I think, Dr. Abrams, now there's an honest man. He'll tell me the truth of it."*

*My hopes of getting out of here unscathed sink. I'm about to be put in an impossible position where I'll either have to lie to Capone or get this man killed. Unless, of course, it wasn't self-inflicted.* Please don't have inflicted this wound yourself, Tony, *I plead silently.*

*The man is shuffled over to the table and forced to sit.*

*"Have a look, won't you, Doc?" Capone tears the bloody bandage off Tony's arm with one movement. The man screams underneath his hood.*

*Reluctantly, I examine the wound. No signs of infection, but the edges are gaping. It needs to be sutured.*

*The cut on his left arm is smooth, a controlled line that is at the right angle to have been inflicted by a knife held in the man's right hand. The location...on the inside of his lower arm with the gash going toward his elbow could be inflicted by an assailant. But typically, as the attacker slices the victim's raised arm aiming for the face, the gash goes the other direction... elbow to wrist.*

*In a defensive fight against someone wielding a knife, it's also unusual to see a single wound. What I've usually seen is multiple shallow slices on the forearms and involvement of the hands as the victim attempts to grab the knife. Wounds would be irregular, not smooth, as the victim struggles.*

*Even more incriminating, I see blood spattered on the man's pants. This is not where it would be if he had his arm raised defensively. It looks more like he cut his own arm as it rested on his leg.*

*In my opinion, this man really did inflict his own wound. But I'll be damned if I'm going to get this man killed. Keeping him alive is going to be tricky though. I'll have to be very careful. If Capone suspects I'm lying, I could end up six feet under.*

*"Take off this man's hood, please," I say. "I need to look him in the eye."*

*James yanks the hood off. The man's dark hair is damp, his eyes wild. I look at him steadily, willing him to trust me.*

*"Raise your left arm over your head," I instruct Tony. "Like this," I demonstrate, putting my left arm up like I'm shielding my eyes from the sun.*

*He hesitates but complies. I pick up a pencil from the table to serve as my knife. "It looks like the wound was inflicted like this." I make a slow-motion slicing movement like I'm going to stab sideways with my right arm. Intentionally, I move in the direction wrist to elbow. It's possible.* Maybe the guy really is innocent. *I choose to believe my own lie.*

*"This is how the wound was inflicted. Tony was defending himself. His story is true."* It could be. *I pray they won't notice the blood spatter on his pants.*

*Tony nearly collapses in relief. His life has been spared. "See, Boss, it's true," he says weakly to Capone.*

*Tony doesn't look me in the eye. That's when I know for sure that I'm lying for him. I hold my breath.*

*Capone sits back with a look of incredulity on his face. For a heartbeat, I think he's going to contradict me. His henchmen will stick me in the ground for lying and no one will ever find my body.*

*"Well, Doc, it looks like Tony was telling the truth," Capone says reluctantly. "I'm sorry we snatched you off the street like that, Doc. My apologies. James will take you back home. No harm done, right, Doc?"*

*"Of course not," I reply congenially, my own limbs weak with the relief of being free of this mobster again. I stop short of saying I'd be happy to help out in the future. The truth is, I'd be glad to never see these men again.*

The frightening dream has me tossing and turning in my sleep. When I awaken, my comforter is on the floor and I'm all tangled up in the sheets.

I extricate myself from the bedding and flop back on my pillow. Sometimes my dreams have more subtle messages, but this one seems pretty clear. My subconscious is picking up on something that suggests Sofia's injury is not what it seems.

Sofia was so invested in her baby; there's no doubt in my mind that she would never have done anything to put her pregnancy at risk. It must be something else about her injury that's bothering me.

The dream clearly ties a mobster to an injury that occurred conducting his line of business. Is Sofia maybe unwittingly tied up in the cartel's activity? Could the judge have been involved with them and now they're trying to get her to complete his responsibility?

We better find out what Sofia Clifton knows.

# CHAPTER THIRTY-THREE

As we return to the hospital, I run my thoughts by Joe.

"Do you think Harry Clifton could've been involved with the cartel?" I ask him.

"Wow, interesting idea," he says, giving it some thought. "It's possible, of course, but it sure doesn't fit with his persona."

"Right. If anything, I see him as a sympathizer with the immigrants and their terrible working conditions. I can't see him going along with putting them in danger trafficking drugs, even if he was corrupt."

"Who knows, though? With enough pressure, people will agree to almost anything. Maybe someone was threatening his wife, and he went along with it. I can't see him caving without some significant pressure though," Joe says.

"I agree. I was wondering if he might have been involved in something and now the cartel is trying to threaten Sofia into completing whatever he was involved in."

"It's possible. Let's keep that in mind. But I get the impression she has no idea about the cartel."

"Me too. If she's involved in any way, I think it's unwittingly. I'm worried she's in a lot of danger. We need to make sure she's fully protected."

"Agreed," Joe says.

When we arrive at Sofia's room, all seems quiet on the ward. We knock twice again and a new officer opens the door to confirm our identity.

"How's Sofia doing today?" I ask.

"She's still in a lot of pain but she seems fairly coherent when she's awake."

"We hate to disturb her," Joe says. "But we need to ask her some questions. It's important."

The officer nods.

Joe and I sit at the bedside. Sofia looks a little better. She's not as pale as she was yesterday after surgery. I take her hand; it's cool in my warm one.

"Sofia, I'm sorry to wake you. It's Detective Kruse. Detective Riley and I need to talk to you."

Sofia's eyes flutter open. The way she looks at us reminds me of rising to the surface after diving into a lake. The surroundings come into slow focus, confusion and fear plain on her face. When she reaches the surface, her eyes clear in recognition.

"Detectives..." She attempts to sit up in bed and then winces in pain, grabbing her right side where the bandages are.

"Don't try to move," I say.

She nods and reclines carefully back against the pillows, her lips pressed thin from pain.

"I'm so sorry to disturb you, but we're worried about your safety, and we need to find out who attacked you. Do you remember what happened?" I ask.

She thinks for a moment. "I was outside taking the empty trash bin in from the curb. That I remember clearly. I grabbed the bin and started for the house. I was just getting to the garage when I heard my name." She stops to take some deep breaths as the memory overwhelms her. "I turned around and a man with a hoodie was right there and then I felt... the pain." She reaches down again to touch the bandages and then stops herself. "I guess that's when he stabbed me."

"Did you know him?" I ask.

"No. I didn't recognize him. I've never seen him before."

"He said your name?"

"Yes. That stands out. It wasn't just some random attack. That just makes it so much worse." Her eyes tear. "Who would want to do this to me? And to the baby?" she asks miserably.

"I'm so sorry this happened," I say. "But we need more information if we're going to find your assailant. Could you tell us height, build, anything else?"

"He was just under six foot, and had a slim build." She pauses. "Sorry. He was so quick, I barely remember." She thinks for a bit. "Oh, his voice was deep when he called my name."

Maybe we finally have a lead. He might be the same person who killed the judge.

"Is there anything that you might know about the judge's cases that someone wouldn't want you to?" Joe asks.

She looks at him. "What kind of things, Detective?"

"Do you remember we asked you about the Apple-A-Day Orchards case?" When we interviewed her after the Judge's death, she definitely knew something about the trial and felt strongly in favor of her husband's ruling. *But does she know more?*

"Yes," she nods.

"Did you ever hear what happened to the orchard after the trial?" I ask.

"I have no idea. I guess I didn't care to check."

So, she doesn't know anything about the current situation. If the stabbing was ordered by Manteris, he may think she knows more than she does.

"I'm so sorry, detectives," Sofia says feebly. "I'm so tired..."

"Of course," I say, letting go of her hand and tucking it under the sheets. She's already sunk back into sleep before we leave the room.

As we step out into the hall, we see Anna coming toward us with an overnight bag. "Good morning, detectives. I brought some clothes for Sofia. The doctor said she can go home as long as she has someone to care for her. She's going to come stay with us for a while. It's the least I can do after everything Sofia did for us."

Her comment seems odd and niggles at something that's been bothering me, I just can't put a finger on what it is. Then it comes to me. Doesn't she mean everything Sofia *and Harry* did? Like the money Harry gave her sons. The money we think came from GuidanceLink.

"That reminds me," I say. "I've been meaning to ask you. Did Harry ever say where the money came from that he gave you for your sons? Even with a judge's income, it seems substantial."

"Well, it was actually Sofia that gave it to us. She's always been so generous. She said not to say anything to Harry. He'd given her some cash to spend on some very expensive jewelry pieces as an investment, but Sofia wanted his nephews to have it." Anna smiles. "That was so like her."

"I see," I say to her, but the new information has me reeling. I wonder if Joe is having the same thoughts. We glance at each other. Yep, he is.

"Well, I'm just going to go get Sofia a wheelchair," Anna says, turning.

"Just one more thing, Anna. Until we know who attacked Sofia, she'll need protection. The officer watching her here can go with you and keep watch outside your home," I say.

"Of course, that makes sense," Anna responds.

As we exit the hospital, Joe turns to me. "So, it was Sofia who had the bribe money from GuidanceLink," he says.

"Right," I say, trying to process what this means. "We don't really know that for sure but it sure sounds like it. The exact amount of the supposed cash bribe from GuidanceLink ended up being gifted from Sofia to Anna's sons. In cash, no doubt. A clever way to hide the money. But I don't know what that would mean. Was she paid to influence the judge? And did she just give the bribe money away or did she plan to take the money back at some point?" I'm more confused than ever about who was involved in the judge's death and why.

Joe looks as perplexed as I am. "Okay. We have suspicions but no proof. Maybe we better go talk to Brian Lee about this supposed bribe and see what he did with the fifty thousand dollars in the emergency fund. We never really tied up that loose end. Maybe GuidanceLink is where we should be looking, rather than at the cartel. Maybe they were the ones that hurt Sofia. If she took the bribe but couldn't make good on her promise to influence the judge, then they might want their money back."

"Oh, what a tangled web we weave..." I say under my breath.

Joe chuckles. "This has certainly gotten complicated. And we don't even know who hired the assassin yet, let alone who it was."

"I'm beginning to feel like we may never untangle this. But maybe we'll find something to trace her attacker. We should go back to the home after we talk to Brian."

"Right, we're going to have to loosen this knot one strand at a time."

Arriving at GuidanceLink brings back unpleasant memories. But today the sun is shining brightly, no storm in sight. *Sunny with no chance of gunfire,* I think. *At least, I hope.*

Adam greets us at reception and tells us Brian is "in his office." Which means he's on the platform he works from.

"Come on up, detectives," Brian says, his head poking over the railing of the platform above us. No privacy here with all the open space.

We head up the stairs to his location.

Brian Lee greets us with a smile and firm handshake, clapping us each on the shoulder familiarly. His movements only seem slightly stilted from his recent injuries. I notice he's not using his left arm, the injured one. "Detectives, I owe you a debt of gratitude. You probably saved my life last week. I haven't had a chance to thank you. I'm so glad you came by today so I could," he says congenially.

"It was an unfortunate situation," Joe says, deflecting the praise. We're not on Brian's side here. He was just as much a cause of the altercation as Andre, and we suspect him of bribery. *We aren't friends.*

"Andre is out on bail now. Have you had any contact with him?" Joe asks.

"Yes, through our lawyers. We came to a mutually beneficial arrangement. He agreed to sell us his portion of the company, and we agreed not to press charges or sue him for damage to the property."

"Sounds like it worked out for all of you," I comment.

"Yes, we're happy with how it turned out."

"How are your wounds healing?" I ask.

"Pretty well," he says, touching the bandage under the right side of his shirt and the one under his left sleeve. "Just flesh wounds, you might say. Still hurt like a hot poker, but I'm told I'll heal up okay."

"We have a few more questions for you," Joe says, gesturing to the desk and chairs. "Can we sit?"

"Yes, of course," Brian says and heads for the chair behind his desk, but not before I see a shadow cross his features. He wasn't expecting more questions. *Is he hiding something?*

"Andre told us that you have an emergency fund. Fifty thousand dollars held in cash."

"Yes, that's right," Brian says warily.

"He said he noticed it was missing from the safe. He thought you were planning to offer the judge a bribe to find in your favor. Is there any truth to that?" Joe asks pointedly.

Brian looks defeated. "I'm afraid there is." He takes out a key from his desk and inserts it into a locked drawer.

Joe and I tense. What is he about to pull out? A gun? We've had too recent a brush with gunfire in this building to not have the thought.

My hand moves toward my sidearm automatically. Out of the corner of my eye, I see Joe do the same. "Mr. Lee, please raise your hands and let me open the drawer," Joe says.

Brian looks up at us in surprise. Seeing our posture, he

pales and raises his hands as instructed. "Detectives. I don't have a weapon, if that's what you think."

Joe moves behind the desk and opens the unlocked drawer. He pulls out a thick manila envelope and looks inside.

"Cash?" He looks quizzically at Brian.

I release my held breath.

"Yes," Brian says, feeling it's safe to put his hands down. "It's the fifty thousand. I didn't bribe the judge. I guess I might've tried if the judge hadn't been killed, but his death changed my plans."

"What do you mean?" I ask.

Brian sits down and leans back in his chair. "I decided that the bribe was misplaced. Instead of bribing the judge, I bribed our employees."

"You bribed your employees?" I'm confused.

"Yes. I bribed them to come back to work. I doubled their salaries. The money was less than the lawyers would have charged for the lawsuit. All but two of our employees agreed to come back to the office at the new inflated salary. The other two accepted a ridiculously large severance package to find other employment."

It's a good solution. But, not for the first time, I'm struck by the contrast between these two companies: GuidanceLink and Apple-A-Day Orchards. The extreme wealth of the tech company versus the struggle of the orchard that left its workers vulnerable to the Mexican cartel. What a different world GuidanceLink's employees live in. Their extravagant salaries and luxurious work environment versus that of the poor immigrants, who barely have rights and face one peril after another, whether abysmal working conditions or being enslaved as drug mules. In my line of work, I see how often migrants are the victims caught in the middle as they try to escape appalling situations in their home country, only to come here and find themselves in an exploitative relationship. And if that wasn't bad enough, they're often blamed for causing the situation, on one, or even both, sides of the border. *We have to do better.*

As we leave GuidanceLink, hopefully for the last time, Joe says, "Was it just a coincidence that Sofia offered twenty-five thousand to each of Anna's boys?"

"Seems like it was. I'm not sure how much I believe in coincidences though. Maybe Brian had reached out to her to influence the judge, and she thought the money was coming. I'm not sure, but it seems odd."

Thinking about the judge being influenced by Sofia makes me think about their relationship. They seemed so much in love. It's so sad that she lost him. It makes me think that a love like that should never be taken for granted. You have to enjoy every moment you have together.

It's time for me to attempt to repair my own love life. Even if it requires extreme measures.

# CHAPTER THIRTY-FOUR

I'm thankful the Emergency Room isn't seeing a lot of traffic in the early evening as I stand just outside the entrance. Waiting.

A man heads toward the doors from the parking lot, a bloody bandage on his hand. He glances my way, curious, but not enough to ask what I'm up to, thankfully. He has his own issues to attend to.

As the automatic doors whoosh open, I catch a few notes of music playing overhead. It's started, I think, sending my nerves into a tailspin. No turning back now.

I lift the poster-sized cards I've prepared, readying them. A woman carrying a sick child hurries past and the door opens again. A few strains of Peter Gabriel's *In Your Eyes* floats out before it closes.

I've enlisted the help of one of the ER nurses to get the music to play overhead. He was thrilled to help. "Maybe he'll stop moping about. *Finally,*" he'd said. "The man's been a bear to work with for the past week. Now it all makes sense."

I only hope Blake remembers the movie *Say Anything* that we watched together, and the discussion we had about grand gestures. *That he thought was corny,* I think. *Is he going to hate this? Oh god, please let this work.*

The door opens and my heart skips a beat. Is it Blake? A woman walks out with a bandage on her head. No, not him.

I watch the woman get in her car, thinking, *Should she be driving with a head injury?* From beside me comes a voice. "It took me a minute to figure out where you were."

*Blake!* I was distracted by the woman and missed him coming out. He sounds...*uncertain.* Well, that's better than angry or disappointed. *I'll take it. And does the man have to look so damn sexy in scrubs? It's distracting.*

I heft the stack of cards up in front of me, facing toward him. *Here goes.*

His expression is...*slightly frosty. Damn. Please let this thaw him out.*

I show him the first poster which says, "You made a grand gesture."

He reads it, then looks at me, raising an eyebrow. Maybe amused by the cards, maybe interested in what I have to say. I push on, hoping both are true.

I flip to the next card. "Which I ruined."

He's still watching.

Flip. "So here I am."

Flip. "Making mine."

The ghost of a smile tugs at the corner of his lips.

Flip. "I choose you." I'm watching him intently and I see a very slight thawing of the frost. Enough to give me hope. I've moved the man at least a little bit.

Flip. "I *can* change."

Flip. "I *will* change."

Flip. "I *need* to change."

He rolls his eyes at the over-emphasis.

Flip. "Even if you don't choose me."

Flip. "But please do."

Flip. "Please."

Flip. "Choose me."

I've never felt so vulnerable. My heart is out there, waiting for him to accept it or crush it.

I can see him wrestling with the choice and it breaks my heart. *Is he going to say no?* Unexpectedly, he reaches for the cards. Unsure what to expect, I hand them to him.

He pulls one out and turns it back toward me.

"I choose you," it says.

My heart soars and I burst into happy tears. I leap into his arms. He lets the cards go and pulls me to him tightly.

"I'm so sorry," I murmur against his chest. "I do solemnly swear that I can undergo remedial training." I push back from his chest so I can look him in the eye. "I can be a normal person. I swear I can."

"I need that, Kaitlyn. If I say I can be with you without a change, I'd be lying. I just can't be in constant dread of what you might misinterpret. I keep thinking about what might've happened that night if you'd thought to shoot first and ask questions later."

"I know. I think about that too, believe me."

I crush myself against him again.

He wraps his arms around me. "When I saw you with that other man..." His voice breaks.

*This has been really hard on him too,* I realize.

"I wish that never happened. I'm so sorry." I pull back to

look at him again. "You're the only man I want. He was just a guy who asked me to dance." *A guy with really bad timing...*

Blake brushes the hair back from my face, looking at me intently. My knees melt with anticipation as he eyes my lips. Then his lips are on mine. The kiss is as good as only make-up kisses can be. I sink into it.

The clearing of a throat interrupts us.

"Doctor, you have other hearts in need of attention."

It's the nurse that helped me. I grin at him like a fool. He gives me the thumbs up behind Blake's back, then jerks his hand down as Blake turns toward him.

Blake chuckles. "I guess I'd better get back."

I nod, still somewhat dazed.

"It seems *some* of my coworkers have been conspiring behind my back," Blake says pointedly as he walks past the nurse, toward the entrance.

Looking my way, the nurse dramatically puts a hand to his mouth, as in, *Oh no, I've been discovered.* He winks at me and I laugh at his antics, allowing the tension I've been carrying for days to finally start to melt away.

# CHAPTER THIRTY-FIVE

*My maid hasn't come up to dress me yet this morning and I have a few minutes to myself. I flop onto my back in bed and place my hand just below my belly button, where I imagine the baby is growing. I'm not showing yet, but my courses are two weeks late.* Two weeks! And I'm never late.

Don't get ahead of yourself, Abby, *I chide myself. I may not turn out to be with child, but I can't help but be excited, can I? A baby is all I've been wishing for over the past many, many weeks.*

*I can't wait to tell Will, but I'd decided I wouldn't say anything until I'd missed a full fourteen days. No use getting him all excited if it didn't turn out to be true. But now...now I feel more certain.*

*A sudden wave of nausea comes over me out of nowhere. Putting my hand over my mouth, I race to the pitcher of water on my dressing table and empty my stomach contents into it.*

*I'm just wiping my mouth when I hear, "Abigail!" A sharp voice coming from the door to my room.*

*I turn to see my mother standing in the doorway, her eyes bulging.*

*"Mother! What are you doing here?" I wasn't expecting her until later in the morning.*

*"I came over early; Mathilda wanted a knitting pattern..." she starts to explain and then realizes I've distracted her. "Never mind that...you're pregnant," she says, a smile spreading over her face.*

*"Shhhh!" I grab her hand and pull her into the room, closing the door. "I haven't told Will yet."*

*"Well, he mustn't be very observant then. How can he have missed it?"*

*"I've only started getting sick just today."*

*"Well, you better tell him right quick now or he'll be the last to know. Your maid will have told the whole household by breakfast." She gestures toward the water pitcher.*

*I laugh giddily. "You're right."*

*My mother folds me into an embrace. "Oh Abigail, I'm so happy for you."*

*Will must be downstairs taking his breakfast already. A thought strikes me...a clever way to let him know that he'll be a father soon. He's always loved charades and games like that. He'll get a kick out of this.*

*After my maid has wrangled me into my outfit for the day, I take a pillow off the bed and stuff it up under my dress. I look at my silhouette in the full-length mirror. The layers of petticoats, bustle and underskirt already transform my shape significantly, but now I also look outrageously pregnant. It looks like a baby might pop out at any moment. I chuckle to myself.*

*I flounce down the stairs and into the breakfast room.*

*"Good morning, sweet husband," I chirp in greeting, heading*

*past him to the food on the buffet table at the end of the room.*

*"Good morning, sweet wife," he parrots, not looking up from his newspaper. Darn the man!*

*A servant enters the room at that moment and, seeing me, she stops short. I put a finger to my lips to silence her. She stifles a giggle and leaves the room.*

*"I've had this new dress made. Do you like it?" I ask, twirling in front of Will.*

*He glances up at me briefly, then goes back to his newspaper. "It's fine indeed."*

*"You don't think it's too tight...across my stomach?" I ask pointedly.*

*Again, he glances up, ever so briefly. "Never, dear," he says.*

*I'm confounded. "Will!" I say sharply. "Don't you notice anything different?" I turn from side to side showing off my new shape.*

*He looks directly at me. "You look the same as you always have," he says, then his lips twist into a smile, and he laughs outright. "Sorry to spoil your fun, love, but I've been expecting this news for at least a week. I wondered when you would finally tell me."*

*I stare at him. "But how did you know?" I ask.*

*"Abby, you have been positively glowing, you profess to suddenly be unable to eat your favorite pickled herring, and you ate more than I did at dinner last night. What kind of husband would I be if I didn't notice?"*

*His ear-to-ear grin makes me laugh. "So, you're happy about it then?"*

*"Delighted!" he responds, getting up to put his hand on my pretend belly. "You know, you look the size of a train caboose, what with the bustle in the back and the pillow in the front..."*

*I laugh, only because I thought the same thing, looking in the mirror. "That may be true, but when I really do get to this size, I will gleefully throttle you if you dare to say so."*

*Will gives me a squeeze around my ample waistline. "Don't worry, I know better than to provoke a pregnant woman," he says. "Now why don't you go take that belly off while you still can, my love? Then come have breakfast with your adoring husband. I promise to wait on you hand and foot for the next nine months, and then to spoil the two of you for the rest of your lives." He smiles at me and kisses the top of my head fondly.*

The charming domestic memory has me feeling blissful when I wake up. A pregnancy. How lovely. Abby really did look huge with the pillow and the...My thoughts come to a screeching halt as I put the pieces together. A pillow mimicking a pregnancy. Could Sofia have faked her pregnancy? *Sure, she could have. But why would she? It doesn't make sense.* This must just be my subconscious wrestling with all possibilities. I can't see the motive.

Vaguely, I remember that the tarot cards had predicted I wouldn't put together the message of a dream but that it would come back again more clearly. Is this what the message referred to? Misinterpreting these dream-memories isn't uncommon for me. Often, I'm confused about what my subconscious is pulling up from my multi-life memory banks. The first dream with Abby had her dressing for her wedding in elaborate layers with material under her clothing creating the desired silhouette. But it also related to a wedding, and I had that on my mind what with Isabella's upcoming marriage. But now...this dream much more directly insinuates mimicking a pregnancy.

It's not until I'm getting dressed that a thought occurs to me. A thought that, if true, changes everything.

I race to the precinct as fast as possible to check.

# CHAPTER THIRTY-SIX

When Joe arrives, ready for another workday, I'm already waiting for him.

"You're here early, Kruse," he comments.

"Come over here, look at this," I say, excitement making my voice pitch high. "It changes everything."

He glances at me, taking in how serious I am. "You're freaking me out here, Kruse. What could be so earth shattering?"

"You'll see."

I've been running the surveillance video from above the entry door on the night the judge was killed, over and over. I start it one more time. "Tell me what you see," I say.

Joe plays along. "An intruder gaining access to the judge's home by breaking down the side door."

"Right. What are your thoughts about the intruder?"

"He's slight but strong. I can't tell height because of the camera angle. He carries a focused strength and confidence, his movements are deft and sure," he starts. "And he's meticulous. He's obviously been well trained; he gets in and out very quickly. This is clearly all planned out ahead of time. I suspect he's done this kind of thing before. He knows the layout of the home in advance. There's no wasted time. He's a pro."

"I agree. That's what I thought too. But just one question... why do you think it's a man?"

"Uh...I don't know," Joe says. Doing a double take, he looks back at the recording. "Play it through again." I restart the recording and he watches it again. "Well, the killer seems strong, but I suppose it's more of a 'strategic' strength than brute strength; they know where to kick the door to break it. Most assassins are males, so I guess I'm biased. It could be a female. Why? Do you think it is?"

"I think it's Sofia," I say.

Joe looks at me like I've lost my mind. "Kruse, she was four months pregnant, you noticed it yourself when we interviewed her. With the tight clothing the killer was wearing, there's no way we would miss a pregnancy bump."

"But what if she wasn't pregnant?"

"What do you mean?"

"What if she put on one of those fake pregnancy bellies for this very reason? To make it seem impossible that she could have been the intruder." I put my hands over my eyes. "Ahhh!" I groan. "We never even suspected her. Not for one minute. She had us fooled the whole time!"

"Now wait a minute," Joe says reasonably. "This is an interesting theory, but how could she pull off pretending to be pregnant for four months? Do you think she was planning it all that time? Surely the judge would've tried to feel the baby kick or at least put his hand on her belly...at least once in all that time. He would've known right away."

"No. I don't think she had to fool him for four months. Think about it. We have no proof that she was pretending she was pregnant *before* the judge was killed. *She says* he was thrilled, that he couldn't wait to have a daughter, that he bought little pink outfits. *She says*...but what proof do we have?" A thought occurs to me. "And," I say, excited, "*and* Anna didn't know about the pregnancy! She dismissed that fact because some women don't tell everyone during the first trimester, remember?"

"True...I guess," Joe says, still not convinced. "So, assuming that technically all that could be true, I still can't imagine Sofia as an *assassin*? Come on, Kruse, you really think she's this person on the footage? A cold-blooded killer? And the intruder leaves the house, and enters the house...where did she go? She was there when the emergency personnel got there. Did she come back?"

"No. I think she got in and out through the guest room window. It's just a few feet away from this door. And I think the dog lost her trail, not because of the citrus spray but because she climbed back in the window. She didn't leave the yard, so it had no trail to follow."

"This idea is so out there, it just might be true," Joe says.

"I know. I've been sitting here trying to poke holes in the theory, trying to prove it wrong, but you know what?"

"No holes?" Joe asks.

"No holes."

"What about Sofia being stabbed?" Joe asks. "Assuming she's the killer, did the cartel contract her to kill the judge or is she one of them? Would they do that to one of their own? Maybe as a warning to keep quiet?"

"I've been thinking about this." My dream about Dr.

Abrams and Tony, with the self-inflicted wound to cover his guilt, makes me think my subconscious was questioning the validity of the stabbing. "I think Sofia stabbed herself to make us think she was a victim, to steer us away from her involvement. And it worked."

"She stabbed herself? Wow, this theory is getting wilder." Joe is not convinced. "Who would do that? And to put her own health and the pregnancy at risk…"

"I know, it seems extreme. But remember…she probably wasn't pregnant. And the wound luckily avoided all major organs. Was that a coincidence or good planning?"

"She had me so convinced that she loved the judge and that she was excited to be carrying his child, I'm not sure what to believe anymore," Joe says.

"The way I see it, with the stabbing, she killed two birds with one stone. She threw us off her trail and she was able to explain away a lost pregnancy before we caught on that she wasn't actually pregnant."

"But wouldn't the surgeon have discovered she was never pregnant when he operated?"

"I bet she never told them she was supposedly pregnant. She just told Anna she lost the pregnancy. If she took off the belly before EMS responded to the stabbing…they never would've questioned it."

"Okay, maybe," Joe allows. "But, getting back to the original murder. Why would she want to do everything within the time frame of an EMS response? It's such a quick turnaround, she would've only had something like ten minutes to pretend to leave, get back in the window, hide her clothing and the gun and get the pregnancy belly and pajamas on. Instead, I'm sure she could have shot him before he called 911. Why involve EMS? She could have just killed him and then pretended to come upstairs much later and find him."

"It's so much more convincing. There's not much time; she has to time it perfectly. It seems impossible, but it's not. She changes and pretends to be sleeping. And I remember thinking that the killer went right past her asleep in the guest room. The timing is so tight that no one would suspect her. But if she says she woke up later, there's time to cover her tracks. We might have been more suspicious of her."

"What about the murder weapon? And the dark clothing? We didn't find anything like that at the house," Joe points out.

"True. She would've had to hide it. And we looked over every inch of that place on the night of the murder. She might've hidden it and then removed it later. Or it could still be there, hidden."

I think of the dream I had about George finding the note in the false bottom of the box. I thought I was dreaming that because of my anxiety that Blake might find someone else, but maybe there's something in the house that my subconscious picked up on. Some clever hiding place.

Joe nods. "Let's get a warrant for her place and go back and look around. See if we find anything supporting your theory," Joe says.

"Already done," I reply.

# CHAPTER THIRTY-SEVEN

Sofia is recovering from her wound at Anna's home, so it's the perfect time to execute the search without letting Sofia know we're suspicious of her.

We bring a locksmith and Simon, the IT specialist, with us. The locksmith gets us in the side door easily. Simon is already familiar with the alarm system so he disarms it remotely.

Simon is sent to look at the security feed and see if there's any footage from the stabbing. We set the locksmith up in the primary bedroom drilling a hole to access the interior of the safe.

Donning gloves, Joe and I start searching. The items we're most interested in finding are the gun and the dark clothing the assassin wore, but we look around for other things that might implicate Sofia in the crime. Things we might not have thought of.

We search every inch of the guest room, thinking it would've been the closest place to hide the clothing and gun. But there's no sign of either, even though we look in the dresser drawers, behind the dresser, in the bedding and mattress, and even the toilet tank.

Not finding anything incriminating in the guestroom, we start searching the rest of the main floor. When we enter the kitchen, I see the ultrasound with the image of a fetus that I'd spotted on the tack board beside the fridge on the night of the murder. I'd forgotten about that. Typed over the image is "it's a girl!" Sofia couldn't have faked an actual fetal ultrasound. So maybe she is pregnant.

I take the image off the board. Something about it is bothering me, but I can't put my finger on it. There's Sofia's name and birth date above the image. *Okay, I guess I'm going to have to admit that I was wrong about her.*

I start to pin the image back to the board but then stop. I know what's bothering me. Usually these are printed on shiny thermal paper. This one is on regular printer paper. Could Sofia have gotten this image off the internet and put her name on it? Theoretically, it's possible. I'm not sure if she placed the ultrasound here the night of the murder or if she'd shown it to the judge. Either way, I'm not convinced it's real.

Calling Joe over from the other side of the room, I tell him my thoughts. He nods. "Stick it in an evidence bag and let's file that away in our own minds as uncertain evidence. I'm not sure exactly what it means."

While we're discussing the ultrasound I notice a message Sofia wrote to her husband on a sticky note, stuck to the front of the fridge.

"Hi love. I'm getting my hair cut. See you at dinner. Love, Sof."

"Joe. Do you have images of any of the death threats we thought Greenworth wrote?" I ask.

Grabbing his phone, he logs in securely to the precinct evidence files and pulls up one of the threatening letters that Barry supposedly wrote to the judge. It reminds me of the dream I had of Sam where she was so worried about Devin getting into her lunch that she failed to see it was the janitor in league with Devin all along.

So why would Sofia, or anyone else for that matter, have made it look like Greenworth was threatening the judge, when he wasn't? Was it so that if something happened to the judge, law enforcement wouldn't look too closely at the person who actually wrote them? Only...the judge would surely recognize his own wife's handwriting if she'd written the death threats.

Sure enough, the note from the fridge doesn't match the threatening letter. "I guess even if Sofia did write the notes, she would've disguised her handwriting," I say.

Joe puts the note back, taking a photo of it on his phone so we'll have it if we need a sample of her handwriting later.

Joe zooms in on a part of the note, examining it. "Look at this though." He shows me a blown-up image of the "y" with an unusual backwards loop connecting the upper part with the tail. "It's the same as on the threat: 'Hang you up by your...'"

I look closely. "You're right! Let's have a handwriting analyst look at these two samples and see if they think both could be Sofia."

We move to the other areas of the house but have no luck finding anything else suspicious. We do find a few baby items, including the pink outfits Sofia said the judge ordered.

When we get to the primary bedroom, the locksmith has the safe open. We take out the items inside it, searching through them. They're the same valuables and jewelry we saw on the night of the murder, nothing more. We check behind paintings in the bedroom for another safe, but there's just the one. We look behind all the clothes in the closet, check all the couch cushions, bedding and mattress, and check all the floorboards. Nothing.

I plop down on the couch in the sitting room off the bedroom, feeling a little defeated. We haven't found anything that would definitively implicate Sofia. *Maybe I was just wrong.*

I try to think of hiding places we might've missed, but we've searched every nook and cranny of the home.

Joe sits down opposite me. "I liked your theory, Kruse, but without the gun and clothing, it's just that...a theory. Sofia probably got rid of them, if she's smart. Or we might have to consider that she's not the killer after all."

"Yeah, you're right," I sigh.

I close my eyes, thinking again of the dream of George and the box with the false bottom. What triggered that memory? Was it just my fears of Blake finding someone else? I look around the room for a similar box. There's nothing like it.

Determined to leave no stone unturned, I recheck the rest of the house, looking for a box or item that might have a false compartment.

I look high and low but there's nothing like it. I guess the dream really was just me having romantic insecurities.

Feeling guilty for suspecting Sofia, I walk around putting some of the items back, so she doesn't return home to a total disaster. I put the valuables back in the safe. As I lift a jewelry back in, I have a thought. The safe is lined with fabric. Feeling around, I notice the back wall has a bump in the lining at the left edge. I can't see it, but I can *feel* it. My heart skips a beat.

Did I feel this when I looked in the safe on the night of the murder, but not register it consciously? Or did the safe just remind me of the box George was exploring? *Could it really be this simple?* Is the hiding place the most obvious of hiding places? I pull at the lining, and a whole section of fabric, secured with Velcro, pulls away from the back wall. There's a tiny, recessed latch behind the fabric. When I pull on it, the left side of the back wall pops out toward me.

I'm excited now!

I remove all the items I placed back in the safe so I can pull the back open.

And as I look into the hidden space in the safe, I finally see them—the tools of a killer.

# CHAPTER THIRTY-EIGHT

I call out to Joe as I pull out the hidden items.

Joe hears my excitement and rushes over to have a look. He gives a low whistle. "It sure looks like you were right. Sofia banked on no one finding that compartment and sure enough, we missed it the first time and almost missed it again. She must've put these things in the safe just before EMS arrived on the night of the murder. What all is in there?"

We examine the items one by one.

"We have one murder weapon," I say, holding up the .22 caliber Ruger and silencer. I remove the ammunition and place everything in an evidence bag.

"Here's the dark clothing she wore." I pull out a roll of black clothing and unfold it. "And inside it: shoe covers, gloves, and a ski mask."

I hold up an aerosol can. "Orange spray to trick the dogs."

Joe pulls out the last item. A laptop. "Let's get Simon to look at this too." Joe looks at the empty space. "I thought we would find a fake pregnancy pillow in here too."

"She must have been wearing it up to the time she says she lost the baby, so yesterday. Let's check the garage. That's where she was when she called EMS to report the attack."

"What we have now is enough to arrest Sofia," Joe says. "I can't believe she was under our noses this whole time. But here it is, the proof that she was the murderer. We've got her now."

We descend the stairs with the evidence and head to the garage. Lifting the trash bin lid, I look in. Empty.

We search through the storage bins, in the cars, under the cars. Nothing.

I open up the deep freeze, moving aside frozen foods. And there it is. One fake pregnancy belly. She didn't have time to hide it very well. Clearly, she was confident we didn't suspect her and wouldn't search the house. If she'd disposed of the items we found in the safe then we would have no evidence against her. It seems her confidence might be her undoing.

As we reenter the house, Simon comes out of the judge's study. He waves at us to join him, and we follow him back in.

"The original computer that the judge used is still in evidence," he says. "But Sofia Clifton set up a new computer. She hadn't had a chance to improve the surveillance, but you can see the driveway from the camera by the front door."

Simon brings up the footage. "Here you see her going out to the road and collecting the trash bin. As she returns to the garage, she moves out of camera range."

"So, you can't see the alleged attack?" Joe asks.

"No, if the attack occurred in the garage as she reported, it would be outside of the camera's view."

"So, it might have happened like she said," I say.

"Yes, it's possible. However, the camera doesn't pick up

on anyone following her. If someone else entered the garage, it would have to be from the far side, outside the camera's reach."

"So, hypothetically possible, but no proof that it happened like she said."

"Correct."

We give Simon the laptop from the safe, and do some fishing of our own on Sofia's new desktop computer.

"One thing I've wanted to check…" I pull up Sofia's credit card account. Her password fills automatically. Sure enough, a purchase at BabiesRUs is listed two months before the attack. Harry didn't order the outfits. She bought them to support her story that the judge knew she was pregnant. A long time before the murder.

"Based on this, it seems like she was already prepared," I say to Joe. "So what changed? What made this the right time to kill him? Did the cartel order a hit? Was he cheating on her? Did he abuse her? Why kill him now?"

"I've been wondering that too. The murder looks like a hit, not the emotional revenge of a jilted spouse. Seeing her on the surveillance…she's a pro. She's had some sort of training. So, *who is she?* A spy? A cartel member?"

"Do you really think she could be involved in the cartel? Could Manteris have placed her with the judge?"

I google Manteris and a formal photo of him celebrating his birthday with friends and family comes up. It's recent. Too recent for Sofia to be in it. I scan the crowd, thinking I might recognize one of his henchmen. I zoom in on a person who looks familiar. A younger man. He has a scar on his face, so he stands out. *Where have I seen him before?* I'm sure I've seen him somewhere recently.

Suddenly I have it. I run back to the foyer. There's a photo on a table at the bottom of the stairs. I knocked it over the night the judge was murdered. I'd glanced at it as I put it back upright. It's Sofia and Harry's wedding day. They're in the center, surrounded by friends and family and there—in the background, posed like security, is the guy from the photo with Manteris. I snap a picture of it on my phone.

I rush back and show the photo to Joe, pointing out that the same man is in the photo with Manteris. "Sofia must be involved with the cartel. But why? What would they gain by placing someone in the judge's home?" I ask.

The IT tech looks up from the laptop. "I may have some answers for you."

"What did you find?" Joe asks as we position ourselves behind Simon.

"This laptop you found in the safe was used to hack in remotely to the judge's main computer—the one I took to the precinct the night of the murder. From his home screen, she would have access to anything he could access. She might have to know some passwords, but a lot of them autofill. Even two-factor authentication for the courthouse network would come to his email, which she could open from the home screen."

"That's a lot of access. Can you tell what she was doing?" Joe asks.

"Yes, I'll show you. She has screen shots of what she'd been up to, probably as proof for the cartel. They're deleted but I was able to retrieve them. There's trial information, lists of which judges were assigned to which trials, and it looks like she got into the police database from here also. By piggybacking on the judge's access, she managed to hack her way into information that even he couldn't see. So, for example, here... she had first-hand information about upcoming drug raids."

He lets this sink in for a moment and then pulls up two identical-looking screen shots. "I looked back to see if anything looked like it was tampered with. Here, look at this." The two screenshots are of the judicial assignments for the Apple-A-Day Orchards trial.

"I'm not sure what I'm looking at," I admit.

"See here. This is the clerk of the District Court's list of case assignments. There is the original assignment, then after she hacked into his roster...see...the assigned trial judge was changed. She put Judge Harry on this case."

"Wouldn't the clerk have noticed that?" I ask.

Joe looks thoughtful. "I know cases are assigned according to when courtrooms become available. The clerk likely wouldn't notice unless there was a time conflict. Or, if they did notice, they might've thought it was their mistake since they wouldn't have a reason to suspect that someone hacked in to such a secure system. It was Sofia's access through the judge that allowed her to get in."

Joe and I look at each other in alarm. The cartel had a lot of power through Sofia's access. They wouldn't have wanted to give that up easily.

"So, let's work this through," I say. "Sofia assigns Judge Harry to the case. He has a reputation for being sympathetic to the plight of the downtrodden so they gamble that he will side with the immigrants with the terrible working conditions. This will leave the Apple-A-Day Orchards vulnerable for takeover by the cartel."

Joe nods. "So, they planned this from the beginning. Mason didn't have a chance. And they targeted the judge. I wouldn't be surprised if the whole 'spilled drink at a bar' meet-up was orchestrated."

"I'm sure it was. He was in their crosshairs. Maybe the lawyer that took such an interest in helping the immigrants was on the cartel's payroll as well," I say.

"That would make sense."

"Just when I felt good that someone finally stood up for their rights, and it turns out to be all with the purpose of enslaving them anyway. Disgusting." I shake my head, feeling sick.

"One other thing I found, detectives," Simon says.

We turn our attention back to the screen.

"Here, there's a screen shot. It looks like Sofia had remote access to the judge's computer at the time. But she must not have been aware he was online. This is his desktop...and he discovered that someone was moving things remotely. He typed out a message on a word document. It says, 'I see you moving things around on my desktop. Sofia, is that you? What are you doing?' The screenshot was taken on the evening before the judge was murdered."

"So, that's the motive," I say. "He figured out she was accessing his computer remotely and suspected she was doing things she shouldn't. She knew that when he got his computer access evaluated, they would see what she'd been doing and then the cartel's underhanded dealings would all be revealed and the orchard operation would be compromised. So, she deletes all the evidence and takes him out before he can report her."

"Using a plan she already had in place for just such a possibility," Joe adds.

"True. Remember she said the judge had a cold and he

told her to sleep in the guest room so she wouldn't catch it. I thought it was sweet because she was pregnant and he was protecting her. She was probably there because they were fighting over what she did," I say.

"There's still something I don't understand," Joe says. "Why did she send the death threats from Greenworth, and for that matter, why make it look like the judge was taking a bribe by offering money to Anna? Why go to the trouble to set those things up?"

I think of Devin and the janitor. "She was trying to throw us off her trail. Make us look the wrong way. And it worked. All these things were in place to provide her a way to continue overseeing the orchard operation, even if the judge found out."

"But then her plan starts to go south," Joe says. "We find out about the cartel, so she panics and thinks to herself, what's the best way to make sure no one looks into her. So, she fakes her own injury. Win-win. We think the cartel is trying to get to her, and she loses her pretend pregnancy, gets some sympathy from her sister-in-law and makes sure we're looking the wrong way. Thank goodness you figured out she was faking the pregnancy, Kruse. That was the only thing that tipped us off."

"Speaking of being tipped off," I say, a chilling thought occurring to me. "We better hope she doesn't have remote access to the home security cameras, or she may already be getting away."

# CHAPTER THIRTY-NINE

We put the cruiser lights on as we speed the short distance to Anna's place. I contact the officer monitoring the house.

"Is Sofia still at the house?" I ask immediately when he responds.

"She hasn't left," he replies. "I'm watching the front of the house."

"Thank goodness." I sigh in relief, explaining that we need to talk with her.

As we pull up in front of Anna's home, the officer gets out of the unmarked cruiser parked across the street and joins us as we approach the front door.

Aslan sets to barking in response to our insistent knocking and ringing. "Detectives! What's the emergency?" Anna asks, opening the door. She takes in our grim expressions. "What's wrong?" she asks.

"We need to talk to Sofia."

"Of course. Come on in. I'll go get her. She's been having a nap." Anna heads to a bedroom at the back of the house.

Aslan runs back and forth between Anna and the kitchen, whining plaintively, set off by the charged atmosphere.

Anna returns a moment later, a worried look on her face. "She's not there."

"What do you mean?" I push past her, running down the hall and into the bedroom.

The sheets on the bed are messed up but there's no sign of Sofia. I check the window latch. It's unlocked. The overnight bag is gone. *Shit!*

I turn to Joe who's in the doorway. "She's gone. Belongings are gone too. Window is unlatched."

Going back to the kitchen, I find Anna. "When is the last time you talked to her?"

"I'm not sure. An hour ago maybe, when I brought her some water. She said she wanted to get some sleep," Anna says.

*Shit! Shit! Shit!* She must've been alerted that we entered her home and thought we were on to her.

"Is she in danger?" Anna asks tearfully.

"We need to find her," I reply.

"Where is your car parked?" I ask.

"In the garage." Anna points to a detached garage at the back of the yard. She grabs her purse and pulls out a Chevy key fob. Thank goodness. She didn't take the car. How far could she have gotten on foot?

"Keep Aslan inside," I tell Anna.

"I'll go and drive around the neighborhood to see if I spot her walking," the officer says. Joe nods.

Joe and I run outside and around to the bedroom window. He points to light footprints leading through the backyard. We follow them to the garage door. She must have exited through the back of the garage since the yard is fenced.

Joe draws his gun and tries the door handle. It's open. He flings the door open and points his gun into the space. Then he relaxes. "She's not here. But the vehicle is gone."

"What?" I gasp, looking inside. Sure enough. There's no vehicle in the garage.

Anna is heading towards us across the yard. "Do you have another key fob for your vehicle? And what's the color and model?" I ask.

"Yes. It's a silver Traverse," she says and runs toward the house. We follow. She goes down the same hallway as the bedroom Sofia was in. She opens a cabinet in the hallway. Several keys are on hooks inside. "It's gone," she says.

Sofia might've gotten quite a distance if she left an hour ago. She has an impressive head start.

I hand Anna my phone. "Can you put your car's license plate number in here?"

When she hands my phone back, I issue a BOLO alert.

"What are you doing?" she asks.

"Issuing an alert for Sofia's arrest. We have evidence she murdered Harry. She's very dangerous. If you hear from her, you need to let us know right away. She might put you at risk."

"You have to be joking, Detective." Anna looks at us sideways. "Sofia is a victim in all of this. She lost her baby. And now you're going to haul her in for questioning?"

"We don't have time to explain," Joe says. "Trust us, we found the murder weapon, she's the killer. Do you have any idea where she might have gone?"

Anna looks shocked, not knowing what to believe. She shakes her head numbly.

Joe and I head back to the cruiser.

"Where do you think she would go?" I ask.

"Somewhere she feels safe," Joe surmises.

"Could the guard we saw in the photo have a place near here?"

With that in mind, I call Bob and give him a brief update. "I'm going to send you a photo. Can you run it through facial recognition and see if the man with the scar is in the system? We need his location."

"Got it," Bob says. "I'll stay here at the precinct until the facial recognition gets done. Hey, I noticed something while I was leaving my shift at the safe house a few hours ago. I wanted to ask you about it,"

"Yeah, what is it?"

"I heard a drone....I'm pretty sure that's what it was. It was so far off, I couldn't really see it. But that sound they make ... it's pretty distinctive."

A chill runs down my spine. I hope to never encounter another drone for the foreseeable future. A drone outside of the Masons' safe house might not mean anything but then again, it could mean the cartel has found them. Could that drone that chased us have followed us all the way to the safe house? I kept thinking I was catching glimpses of it but I thought I was just being paranoid. Those drones that chased us had me pretty rattled.

Bob's voice breaks into my thoughts. "So Sofia's mixed up with the cartel, and now she probably knows you're on to her, and she has nothing to lose?"

"Probably." My gut clenches, knowing exactly what he's going to say next.

"Do you think she might have orders from the cartel to take out the Masons? And now she knows she's running out of time?"

"Yes! I bet you're right. We'll head over there now and check on them."

"I'll send backup," he says, hanging up.

I signal Joe to start driving. "Head to the Masons' safe-house," I tell him urgently.

"My God!" he exclaims, putting on the siren and lights and speeding down the road. "You think she went there?"

"Could be. We better check," I reply.

The officers currently at the safe house are Joan Wallace and Jimmy Chen. I attempt to contact them but neither answers my call. Damn!

"Hurry up!" I urge Joe.

He gives me a glance. *I know.* He's going as fast as possible.

When we arrive on the same block as the safe house, we slow down to get an idea what we're facing. From a few houses away, all looks quiet. We spot Anna's silver Traverse parked a ways down the block. *Shit! Sofia's definitely here!*

There is an imminent threat to the Masons' lives and we don't know the situation inside the house yet, but it doesn't look good. A crucial decision needs to be made: either try to sneak in close and see if we can determine the situation in the home, or secure the perimeter and wait for backup. This is a call our Chief needs to make.

We pull in behind Anna's SUV. It's large enough we can stay out of sight of the house. I call Garcia and inform her of the situation.

"Damn!" Comes Garcia's response when we tell her Anna's vehicle is here. "Secure the home the best you can until back-up arrives and attempt to contact Sofia—you need to stall her, do whatever you can to distract her and keep her from hurting the Masons. I'm on my way!"

"Here, you drive up and contact her," Joe says. "You have a better rapport with her. I'll go around and secure the back."

"Okay," I say, going around to the driver's side. "Be careful."

He nods, looking grave. "You too." Then he heads through the neighbor's yard toward the alley behind the home.

I pull the cruiser up in front of the house and bring Sofia's cell number up on my phone. I hit "call" and the line starts ringing.

Without warning, a gunshot crashes into the side of the cruiser. Shit!

I guess she doesn't want to talk.

I try texting her: "Sofia, we don't want anyone to get hurt. Can we discuss terms for you to release the hostages?"

My phone lights up with an alert. A text from Sofia: "Let me go and I'll let the Masons live."

My heartbeat picks up. *They could still be alive!*

I text back. "Can you send proof of life?"

Some time passes and then a photo comes back of the son, bound and tied, but alive. While I was waiting for her response, backup has begun to arrive. A few other vehicles join me, securing the perimeter. Other officers approach on foot, hiding behind trees on the side of the home. I see some heading around the back.

"How about the others?" I text.

"That's all you get," she responds. "I want to talk to someone in charge."

"Okay, the Deputy Chief of police, Elizabeth Garcia, is on her way now."

"Okay. I'll wait."

Garcia arrives a few minutes later. With her are officers in

SWAT gear, an ambulance, and snipers. The entire entourage assembles on the street in front of the house. Roadblocks are put up and a perimeter is now firmly established.

I brief Garcia, her face registering the gravity of the situation. She dispatches officers to evacuate the surrounding homes.

"We need to take this slow and make sure no one gets hurt," she says.

She takes my phone and scrolls through the texts, then types out her introduction. "Sofia, this is Deputy Chief Elizabeth Garcia. I can help you if you'll let me."

"I'll believe it when I see it," is the response.

"Help me understand what's going on in the house right now. What do you need?"

There's an ominous pause. I feel the tension between my shoulder blades.

Then, finally, a reply. "The Masons are all here and restrained."

"How about the officers?"

A longer pause.

"They're incapacitated but still alive."

"Can you send the officers out so we can attend to any injuries?"

"I'm not giving up my bargaining chips that easily. I'll send them out when you confirm you've arranged safe passage out of here and transportation."

"I understand that getting out safely matters to you. How can I help?"

"I want a helicopter and pilot."

"That will take me some time," Garcia responds. It's a big ask.

"Okay. I can wait."

*But the officers might not be able to, depending on their injuries.*

"While I do that, tell me what you need right now. Food? Water? First aid supplies?"

"All of the above."

"If I can get you these things, can you release the hostages?"

"I can release the officers, not the Masons."

We'll take what we can get. Garcia gets on the phone, looking for possible transportation options. There's no way Garcia will allow Sofia access to a helicopter and pilot. She needs another option that Sofia will consider safe. I'm certain Sofia knows this; that she asked for something impossible with the hope she'll at least get something workable.

Joe and the officers behind the house inform us that the blinds are drawn in the back of the house. They'll continue to monitor the exit.

We gather food, water, and a first aid kit. It takes what seems an excruciatingly long time. Garcia continues to communicate with Sofia, asking for regular status updates. Sofia continues to reply that everyone inside is restrained but doing well.

Bob calls back. "I have interesting news," he says cryptically.

"What is it?" I ask, forcing my mind back to his task. Our discussion seems like such a long time ago. He was running facial recognition on the cartel security guard with the scar on his face.

"Well, the man with the scar is a cousin of Manteris, but that's not the interesting part."

"Really? What did you find?"

"I sent the photo to a police precinct in Mexico where the cartel is located and they were the ones who identified the man with the scar, but they also recognized Sofia."

"Who is she?"

"One of Manteris' daughters."

The implications hit me. Sofia is an important member of the Manteris family. She's trained as a skilled assassin and who knows what else. Her presence marks the orchard takeover as an important operation. Likely she was sent here to make it happen and to oversee it, which is why she protected it so fiercely by taking out the judge when he discovered her part in it. She's also bound to be skilled at negotiation. We better not underestimate her.

I bring the information to Garcia. Her eyebrows knit together in concern. The chances this ends peacefully have plummeted. As someone so high up in the cartel hierarchy, Sofia is not going to allow herself to be interrogated. She'll insist on safe passage. The alternative is shooting her way out. The chances she leaves Greg Mason to testify against the cartel is similarly unlikely. *Is he really still alive in there?*

The next step in the negotiation will be crucial in determining Sofia's willingness to let the hostages go free. We now have the supplies, so Garcia texts Sofia. "We have the provisions you asked for. An officer will place them near the front door. Once you have the supplies, send out the officers, as you agreed." *Will she do it?*

"Okay," is the response.

An officer with SWAT protection gear brings the supplies up to the home. The surrounding officers raise their weapons. Sweat breaks out on my brow. Everyone holds their breath.

Mason's son appears at the door. We can see a gun trained

on him from inside the house, a person hidden behind the door. Sofia is taking no chances with the snipers.

The son looks around nervously, collects the provisions, and brings them back inside. The door closes.

We wait for a few minutes for the officers to appear. Nothing happens.

"Shit," Garcia swears under her breath. She grabs the phone and texts: "It's time to release the officers so we can tend to their injuries, as you agreed."

"I've changed my mind," she responds.

Garcia paces. *Are the officers still alive?* "Is there something I can do to facilitate the officers' release?" she tries.

"Get me that helicopter."

"I was able to obtain an armored car for transport," Garcia replies.

"I'm waiting for the helicopter."

"I'll see what I can do."

Garcia gets back on the phone. Sofia holds all the cards and we know it. Providing a helicopter and her unconditional safe transport isn't feasible. She's gone for the biggest ask. Why? She must know it's too big a request. Is she hopeful Garcia will come through or is she just stalling for time? *Why would she be stalling? How are we going to get past this stalemate?*

My thoughts slip back to Sam in the break room with the janitor and Dr. Abrams negotiating with Al Capone. *What am I missing?*

My thoughts are interrupted by the sound of an incoming text.

Garcia reads it, looking puzzled. I take a look over her shoulder. "As a show of good faith, I will send out my guard.

If you shoot him, I will shoot the hostages one by one."

"We won't shoot," Garcia responds.

After a pause, the front door opens. The man with the scarred face is standing there, hands raised. He walks out slowly and stands in the yard. Officers with SWAT protection gear apprehend him, getting him to lie on the ground, placing him in cuffs, and patting him down.

He's brought over to Garcia.

"You need to tell us the condition of the hostages or this negotiation is over," she says.

The man looks her boldly in the eye. "You have no idea who you're dealing with. You've been outplayed." He sneers. "Sofia left the house in my car before you even arrived. She got on a private jet while you were negotiating with me on her phone. I just received word five minutes ago that she is safely out of U.S. airspace." The smug look on his face says he enjoyed delivering the grim news. Sofia has put one over on us yet again.

Garcia's face pales. "Take the house," she commands the SWAT team. My heart rate spikes. *Is he telling the truth?* The SWAT officers swarm the house, brandishing their protective shields. They enter, one after another. The house is silent. *What is happening?*

Then the SWAT team starts to reappear. First are two SWAT officers supporting the officers that were in the home protecting the Masons. *Thank goodness, they're alive!* Both are rubbing their wrists, chafed from zip ties. They have gags pulled down around their mouths and look a little bruised and battered. EMS personnel bring them to the ambulance backed in beside us.

Next comes Mason's son and wife, looking much the same,

with gags and bindings, frightened but alive. Garcia breathes a sigh of relief.

Then nothing.

We wait. A SWAT leader comes out finally and heads over to Garcia.

"Greg Mason is in the home, but he's dead," he says. "We've searched the house and no one else is there."

"Damn!" Garcia smacks her hand on the side of our cruiser. "So it's true. She left before we got here."

Garcia turns to the officers. "How did she get into the house?"

"She turned over the trash bins in the back yard. Made a lot of noise. When I went out to check, they'd strung something like fishing line low across the backdoor. It tripped me up and I fell down those three stairs at the back. Her guard got the jump on me," Joan says. "Jimmy heard the noise and managed to step over the fishing line but the guard hid by the house and while Jimmy was focused on Sofia, they got him too. She shot Mason, tied up his family, then left."

Garcia looks at the officer, her expression one of someone who took a bite of something that didn't taste good at all.

# CHAPTER FORTY

Pinning Blake's boutonnière in place, I straighten it, stepping back to admire my handiwork. *Okay. Maybe I'm admiring more than that.*

"You look so handsome in a tux," I say, smiling.

"And you look beautiful," he says, pulling me closer.

"None of that," I say, swatting at him playfully. "You'll undo my hair."

"I can undo other things instead..." he suggests.

I laugh. Making up with Blake has been...*diverting*, let just say.

We're barefoot. The floor is sand, the room a fancy tent at the beachside. Several of these tents have been set up for the wedding party to get ready. A full-length mirror is hung on one wall of the tent, a table and chairs are placed in the middle. I glance at our image in the mirror. Blake's tux is rolled up at the ankles, no tie, shirt unbuttoned at the neck. So sexy. I'm in my blue maid-of-honor dress, hair in loose waves, corsage on my wrist. The wedding attire is a tasteful mix of formal and casual. It perfectly reflects Isabella herself.

"Do you remember our reading that we had at the Tarot Room?" Blake asks. The mirror has made me think of that moment as well. The mirror we stepped through into the speakeasy.

"How can I forget? She told you that you had a *dangerous love,*" I say.

"Well, that part turned out to be true, didn't it?" He smiles. "I remember she said there would be a confrontation, a flash of truth that burned away the illusion, and that it would change everything, leaving only what was real."

"Sounds right," I murmur.

"She said we had to overcome the hidden threat. I feel like we've done that. You stopped putting paper in the door and wearing your gun out to dinner..." He stops and pulls up the hem of my dress. "You're not wearing one now, are you?"

I slap his hand away. "Of course not!" *Okay, so I did think about it, but the important thing is—I left the gun at home.*

"For what it's worth, I feel less worried the more I manage to let go. I have you to thank for that. Not that you could protect me...look at these flabby muscles," I joke, poking his rock-hard biceps. "I just mean that you helped me to see the error of my ways."

"That's all I can ask," he says. "Now, how about your tarot card reading? Did you ever have any dreams that needed reinterpretation?" He raises an eyebrow.

"Hmmmm, maybe. There was that one on the beach that I told you about..."

He looks down at the sand between our toes. "Right, let's reinterpret that one later tonight..."

The truth—the one I still don't feel comfortable sharing

with Blake—is that I did have several dreams that I misinterpreted. Or, as I prefer to think of it, that needed time for the true meaning to be revealed. The dream I had about Abby's wedding hinted at clothing being used to create a desired impression, but I didn't see it until the dream I had about her using a pillow to imitate a pregnancy. That dream led me to rethink everything. *If I'd never had it, would we have ever suspected Sofia?* She might have gotten away with everything.

*Or maybe not.* Other dreams might have eventually led me to suspect Sofia. Dr. Abram's run-ins with the mob were leading me to the cartel and the self-inflicted wound. And Sam's dreams of Devin and the adulterated lunches were leading me to think of someone hiding in plain sight.

So, my dreams really did help me tease out what my subconscious was beginning to suspect. They helped solve the murder. *Again.*

And now I'm aware of a new past life. Sarah, the woman that witnessed the witch trials. Her memories led me to understand the motivation behind a false confession. For Bethany, it was her own safety. For Barry Greenworth, it was the safety of his family. Joe and I have been back to visit Barry and Sean to see how they were faring. Barry has stepped begrudgingly into the role of grandfather, but I think he likes it better than he thought he would. At any rate he appears to be thriving under his son's care and Sean, for his part, is thrilled to be able to repay the kindness of his father. It's a heartwarming thing to witness.

As for Barry's relative that we suspect was Speck's true killer, Barry isn't talking. I suspect he never will.

I'm jolted out of my reverie by the beat of native drums coming from the beach. Isabella has chosen to include a few

Haida traditions to honor her native heritage. Handheld drums will accent the ceremony. And I helped to place native carvings amid the centerpieces on the tables in the dining tent. Even the natural setting was chosen to honor her ancestors.

"Come on," I say to Blake. "It's nearly time."

We emerge from the tent onto the beach. The flower arch and assembled chairs are lit with the colors of the setting sun. The beach is beautiful tonight with the air still warm and scented with salt.

We head toward our designated chairs, and I pick up the blanket on my seat. When it's time, I'll pass the blanket to Isabella's mother, and she and Darius's mother will wrap the couple in it to represent the love and care of family and the joining of two families.

Darius is already in front of the arch, along with a friend who will perform the union. I take my place with the other bridesmaids and groomsmen beside the arch.

Once everyone is in their places, the drums start up again. The drumbeats feel like a slow and steady pulse.

My breath catches when I spot Isabella making her way down the aisle with her father. She's magnificent in her beautiful dress, white eagle feathers in her hair.

She smiles at me, and I know that, at least for that moment, all is right with the world.

# EPILOGUE

My dearest Harry,

Now that I am safely returned to the arms of my family, I find that I am compelled to reach out to you—though, of course, this letter can never truly find you. But I find myself in need of your forgiveness and so I ask for it just the same, hoping to find some small measure of comfort in the asking.

It may seem as if I never loved you, when in fact quite the opposite is true. Knowing you as I do, I'm sure you would point out that my initial contact with you was carefully calculated, for it put me in a position to oversee a very important operation for my father. This is certainly true. I did, in fact, practice tripping and spilling a drink for the better part of two weeks before I got up the nerve to perform it in person in the pub.

I was quite drawn to your position and power before we had our first encounter, yet in meeting you, I found that it was your kind smile and eyes that took my breath away. I did not expect you to reveal yourself as the generous man I came to know. And it was with some reluctance that I found I was beginning to develop true feelings for you. Reluctance because my love for you put me in a very dangerous position.

You see, I trained all my life for the purpose of inserting myself so seamlessly into American life. From my earliest memories, my lessons taught me of your culture and how to become a part of it. As a female from a foreign nation, I was perfectly positioned to take advantage of your biases—to fade into the background. Your culture's failing was my strength. I'd been trained to nudge and guide from the shadows. But, even more importantly, I'd been taught to never grow attached—to shield my heart so that it might not betray me when the time came to make an impossible choice.

But then I met you, and I came to understand what love could be. The protective shell I had painstakingly created over so many years when I was being shaped and molded by the cartel into a lethal pawn—it began to crumble.

That night when you discovered what I was doing on your computer and knew me for what I was—a spy and an imposter. When you flung open the door and found me in the guest room on my laptop—I saw such betrayal in your eyes that it nearly broke my heart. But what truly weighs on my soul is the look of disappointment. Like you truly saw me for the first time and found me wanting. This is the frayed string of my tightly held self-worth that will surely continue to unravel. It will be my undoing.

I know you will not see it as a kindness, but I took your life that night, swiftly and kindly. If left to the cartel, your death would not have come so easily, I assure you. And it would have come. As inevitably as the sun rises. Now I sit in my father's home, my every need provided for, but it is you I think of—my one true love—and I wonder what could have been if love had won out over fear and darkness.

Forgive me my trespass on your life. My eternal love,

Sofia

Sofia lets the tears come now. Just this once. Only this one moment will she allow herself to feel the sorrow for all that has been lost, all that could've been. Then she will push it back down once more. And she will try to forget.

At a noise from the hallway, Sofia crumples the letter and throws it into the brightly burning fireplace. The letter twists as it's consumed by the flame. Soon it is no more than a whisper of ash.

# ACKNOWLEDGMENTS

Thank you to all those who helped bring this book to life.

Thank you, as always, to my family—Dan, Ashdyn, and Jordan—for your infinite patience. If it wasn't for your encouragement my books wouldn't see the light of day.

Dan, my husband, continues to be my most dedicated fan, for which I am forever grateful.

The work of art on the cover is once again conjured by my talented daughter, Jordan. As well, she is a gifted proofreader, providing both grammatical and narrative improvements.

To my daughter Ashdyn, it's been amazing planning your wedding together this year. I love the time we manage to borrow from our busy lives to spend with each other.

Thank you to all of you who provided advice and feedback. To Judge William (Bill) Connolly, thank you for your helpful insight into the life of a judge and your help with the legal aspects of the book. Any legal mistakes remaining are mine alone. To Andrea Beck, Heidi Lierz, and Jordan Anderson who generously gave plot and editing advice. To Jolene Zetterman, and Mary Dek for test driving the final storyline.

To the Shady Book Club, and the ladies of the Bluewater Book Club, thank you again for your support and encouragement of all my books and for the shared enjoyment of all things book related. You continue to make reading the fun it should be.

Thank you to my mom for her unconditional support in everything.

And to my dad, who passed this year and is dearly missed, this book is dedicated to you for a lifetime of the kind of unspoken and constant support that is provided by the very best of parents.

Thank you to Lydia Kang, Andrea Beck, and Polly Kronenberger for your invaluable support as fellow authors.

And once again, to the families in my pediatric practice, thank you for sharing your amazing children with me, it means the world.

To my wonderful editor and publisher Jessica Powers, who supported the Kaitlyn Kruse series from its inception, thank you for your plot advice, which is always on the mark, and your promotion of the book. And as always, thank you for your friendship and mentorship.

Thank you to the team at Flare Books, Kathy McInnis, Matt Powers, Britain Powers, Lora Parker, and Henry Trotter for your support of the book in so many ways.

Finally, to all of you who found your way to these pages as readers, listeners or supporters, thank you.

Please find me at my website karolineanderson.com to sign up for email notices and to write to me. I love to hear from readers, and I'll respond whenever I can.

*Author Karoline Anderson*

Karoline Anderson is a pediatrician with a love for books. Born in Vancouver, Canada, she currently lives with her family and cat Smoky on a lake in Nebraska. She runs whenever she can and has completed several triathlons and one marathon. This is the third book in the Kaitlyn Kruse series. Her debut novel *Killer Insight* was a finalist for Thriller of the Year, and her second novel *Dangerous Insight* was a finalist for the National Indie Excellence Award.

www.ingramcontent.com/pod-product-compliance
Lightning Source LLC
LaVergne TN
LVHW100912220826
846271LV00024B/129
* 9 7 8 1 9 6 3 5 1 1 7 2 7 *